AN OCEAN BETWEEN THEM

AN OCEAN BETWEEN THEM

CHERYL ESPINOSA-JONES

SAPPHIRE BOOKS

SALINAS, CALIFORNIA

Editor - Kaycee Hawn
Book Design - LJ Reynolds
Cover Design - Treehouse Studio

Sapphire Books Publishing, LLC
P.O. Box 8142
Salinas, CA 93912
www.sapphirebooks.com

Printed in the United States of America
First Edition – September 2018

This and other Sapphire Books titles can be found at
www.sapphirebooks.com

Early praise for An Ocean Between Them

"Cheryl Espinosa-Jones writes of grief and reconciliation and their subtle interplay with much understanding and love." ~ **Sheila Kohler,** award winning author of *Once We Were Sisters*

"Cheryl Espinosa-Jones' compelling book An Ocean Between Them is a pleasure from beginning to end. A page-turner filled with strong and memorable characters, this story helps us transform life's challenges into wise and loving action.

Espinosa-Jones introduces a diverse family of mixed races, beliefs, ages, and sexual orientations struggling with old and seemingly irreparable wounds.... The main characters know they may have limited time to learn to love and trust again. As a therapist and host of a radio show about grief, Espinosa-Jones gently weaves in the power of honest communication, community, heart-felt apology, and hospice support.

Throughout the book, I was deeply moved by the courage of the strong women characters. I wept with them over their losses and celebrated their second chances and achievements. After reading An Ocean Between Them, I know for sure that human hearts heal when they are loved rather than judged."

Elaine Mansfield, IPPY award-winning author of, *Leaning into Love: A Spiritual Journey through Grief*

"In An Ocean Between Them, Cheryl Espinosa-Jones reminds us there are gifts in even our deepest pains, and that if we're open and courageous enough to acknowledge them, we can change our lives in transcendent ways. This heartwarming, beautiful novel is a love story on many fronts — between adoring spouses, between a community of friends, and perhaps most poignantly, between a mother and daughter who find a way to reconnect and forgive one another when it matters the most. This book is a testament to the power of acceptance, commitment, and love."

Scott Stabile, Author of *Big Love: The Power of Living with a Wide-Open Heart.*

"Cheryl Espinosa-Jones displays the full range of her great, universe-wide heart through the most intimate exploration of what it means to love, to lose and to grieve the very specific things that fill our worlds with color, and in so doing, lets us know that as she has done, our own lives may be richly transformed and burnished into diamonds of clarity, seeing and even greater living."

Marie Matsuki Mockett, author of *Where the Dead Pause and the Japanese Say Goodbye*

"Cheryl Espinosa-Jones tackles the complex dynamic of mother-daughter relationships with aplomb and searing compassion. An Ocean Between Them is a moving tale full of rich characters that will leave readers both deeply satisfied and ultimately more heart-wise than ever before." —

Claire Bidwell Smith, author of *The Rules of Inheritance*

Dedication

For my wife, Deb

My life

My love

My heart

Chapter One

Sally

The house was still dark as Sally wolfed down her morning ritual, a cinnamon roll and coffee. There was a silence through the bones of the house, as if conversation had faded into the wallpaper and become monastery hushed. When the phone rang, it pierced the air, seeming out of place and inappropriate. Recovering her senses, Sally glanced at the call monitor and, seeing it was her sister Adele, did nothing. She wasn't in the mood for Del's disapproving manner. She imagined her sister's face as she made the call, half frame glasses part way down her nose, looking like a button-down schoolmarm, as she found the number – she wouldn't know it by heart and it wouldn't be on speed dial – and pressed the buttons. She'd be regretting whatever made her feel she had to make that call. Just to stop the picture in Sal's head, she turned on the TV, but really didn't watch it. Instead, she stared out the window, barely registering the one puny tree she could see out in front of the house. Its under-watered leaves hung like loose clothes from the limbs, visibly withering away.

"Hey, Sal, give me a call. Wanna tell you something. Should be home around five."

What was wrong with Adele's voice? She had a choked sound, very soft, her "something is wrong" voice. Sal's sister, usually determined and certain, sounded lost. This was so unusual when it came to Del that the irritation brought a flush to Sal's face. Why didn't she just spit it out? Did she have to add drama to the intrusion? Sal huffed to the bathroom, deliberately avoiding the message, which blinked insistently from across the living room. Her first response to nearly anything her sister did or said was a resounding "no." And today would be no exception.

Del and Sal had been dancing their sister dance ever since Sal was born. Del was three at the time and considered this little wrinkled thing an imposition. Mary, their mother, had had very little to offer in the first place, and adding another child to the mix did not improve things. Del ignored and occasionally taunted the little thing, and, as Sal began to realize that the object of her fondest hope, her big sister, had no wish to know her, she learned to act as if she didn't care and learned how to needle Del to blow up in front of their mother. One time, the needling led to a punch in the nose, bleeding down Sal's clean little pink t-shirt, ruining it. Their mother, not geared towards creative solutions, said the same thing every time, "Del, you're the older one and I expect you to act better." She would then promptly leave the room.

So, as anyone might expect, Sal took her time returning that call. That day, a Sunday, she cleaned the whole house top to bottom, all two bedrooms, living room, bath, and kitchen. Top to bottom was just a figure of speech, since it was a tiny one-story bungalow. She even cleaned the windows, though she couldn't remember the last time she had, and it showed in the dirty, greasy streaks across them. She had avoided shame about those windows, and every other dirty corner of the house, by gradually reducing the number of visitors she invited in.

ᨆᨆᨆᨆ

Sal hadn't opened her eyes to really look at that house in much longer than she could remember. As she scoured the sink and toilet, she noticed that the whole place, not just the windows, had taken on a kind of grey tinge. Nothing had been painted since she and her ex first got the house, a few years into her marriage to Stan. They had big plans back then, but after the first kids came and the arguments amped up, none of those hopes and dreams ever moved forward. Half the time she was thinking, "Why would I fix up a house I'm going to have to get rid of when he leaves me?" Then, after he did leave, and all the kids finally grew up, she didn't care anymore. Looking back, criticizing each other about what the other wasn't doing had quickly become their favorite hobby.

The tiny North Oakland Craftsman was remodeled in the sixties, before their time, popcorn ceilings and white paint, when the goal of a remodel was to make a house look like it would if it was recently built. If Sal ever thought about the great price they'd gotten on the house, she imagined no one wanted to fuss with the potential mess that might come with trying to fix what had been done to it, or the asbestos that could, very possibly, be involved. People around their neck of the woods liked the houses better if they were "original." Sal and Stan, later Sal alone, didn't really care about that; they were too busy with kids, arguments, and bad jobs. Then, after Stan left, Sal resented the house, as if he had left because of it. Even though she got the house in the divorce, she still had to get a job at the nearest coffee shop, Daily Grind, to make ends meet and keep health insurance. It was really the only one she could get since she had little to no work experience. Anyway, why clean up when she was the only one there? What did it matter?

But that Sunday, Sal got everything spic and span, and it felt pretty good, after all, to look around at the clean formica counter and the dusted table and the clean sheets on the bed, rose colored like she liked. Even with the uncorrectable dingy paint, it did look better after a little elbow grease. And besides, in the background of her mind was the sense that she had won the latest round with Del by not returning her call.

༄ ༄ ༄ ༄

The next day, Sal woke up tired and glum. All the pep of the day before, along with an unusual sense of accomplishment, had vanished like a dream. She pulled herself out of bed and picked clothes that felt as much like pajamas as she thought she could get away with. She went to work in the morning and tried her best to blur through the day, barely conscious. She never once looked out the window to see that it was a bright, crisp day, blue as the sea and smelling like spring. By the time she got home at three, she had pretty much given up on the day. She turned the TV on and watched Real Housewives shows for the rest of the night. Didn't really matter which town. Was it New Jersey or Orange County? It didn't once cross her mind to call Adele. Or, to be more truthful, she was thinking about it but did not consider actually doing it.

What Sal was loath to admit was her jealousy of her sister. Del had a great husband who made plenty of money, two kids who adored her – unlike Sal's three who actively avoided her, and the fourth, Chloe, whom she actively avoided – and a good group of friends. Plus she had always been the pretty one, by everyone's estimation. Their parents didn't try to protect her feelings by keeping that opinion to themselves. So to think about her sister was to feel bad about herself, one and the same, which she needed no help in doing. They might talk at most four times a year, even though they lived a couple miles apart.

≈≈≈≈

It was getting late and Adele's message was still lighting up the machine, but Sal wasn't looking. The little red indicator cast a faint shadow on the still grey wall behind it, the glow nearly ominous. Sal had just begun to drift off, the TV blaring loud enough for the neighbors to hear, most likely, when the phone rang again, and again Sal jumped, startled out of her reverie. But this time, before she had time to think about it, she'd picked it up.

"Sally, I'm glad I got you."

"I was just falling asleep, Del. What's up?" Sal hoped Del would take the hint that she really wasn't in the mood for a talk, as if she ever was. Del seemed to ignore that.

"You talked with Chloe lately?"

"Del, you *know* we don't talk." Sal heard the bitter edge to her voice, as if this was Del's fault and she should be embarrassed to bring it up. Would she never leave Sal alone about that girl? Would she never understand why Sal just couldn't have Chloe in her life?

"Well, Sal, I don't know if I should be telling you this, if she'd want me to, I mean, but she had a doctor's appointment the other day, and they found something. It's not good, Sally."

At that moment, it was as if the room collapsed and all Sal saw was the phone book, sitting across from her, with all her mostly out of date numbers in it. The gold writing on the cover and the brown, worn out leather, sitting on the little old table that belonged to their grandmother. Sal insisted she should have it when she died, along with the chair Grandma had needle pointed and the little toothpick cup. Sal just stared at first and didn't say a damned thing.

Finally, she said, "What are you telling me? I don't get it."

"Damn, Sally, I'm telling you Chloe is really sick. She has breast cancer and it's not the easy kind, whatever that is." Sal took a breath, stunned into silence again, but minus the resentful, obstinate feeling of a few moments ago.

"Are you still there? Should I have told you?"

How was Sal going to answer that? Should she have told her? Would Sal ever have known if she hadn't? Would one of the kids have called, or Chloe, or that woman she tried to call her wife? Would Sal have answered the phone?

"I have to get off the phone now, Del," Sal said quickly and slammed the phone on the hook, way harder than she'd intended. Her antiquated phone, still requiring a dial to use, could actually slam. She stunned herself with the noise. *My first born has cancer,* Sal heard in her head, *my first born has cancer.* Repeating, over and over, until she recognized that she hadn't called her that for years, since that day she invited Sal to lunch to tell her she was with a woman. "My first born…" It hit her like a tank. "Chloe is my first born." The air went out of her and she stood there for a minute, watching the landscape of her life shift, like the tectonic plates they talked about after an earthquake.

❧❧❧❧❧

Just because Sal was going to go crazy if she stood there anymore, she started to clean again, going over the same spots she'd covered just a day ago, but with added fury, rubbing the wood, running the vacuum over the floor three, four times. Anybody watching would have thought she thoroughly liked to clean. She couldn't stop.

Then her fury hit her, boiling her blood and bringing a fierce tension to every muscle! *She's ruined her life and now she's gonna go and die,* Sal thought. *She's gonna run out of time to make this right! She robbed me of my child and now I can't get her back! It's not fair!*

Later, Sal would be embarrassed to admit that's how she'd felt, but in that moment, the rage consumed her, leaving no room inside for anything else. She had been thinking that Chloe's life was designed to hurt her for so long that, even at a moment like this, she couldn't give it up. She was going to go down believing that Chloe had destroyed her life by going in the wrong direction. She didn't even question why she thought so. It just seemed obvious.

If Sal were being honest with herself, she'd say that none of her kids had lived exactly as she wanted. Chase, number two, lived in a little basement studio and did odd jobs. Candice got pregnant very young and stayed married to the guy until the previous year, when she finally admitted to herself what a loser he was. So now she had two little kids, Josie and Ralphy, and a pile of bills and a boring job. Then there was Grant. He started off good, going to college on scholarship and even graduate school but he just couldn't finish it. Adele called him a perpetual student and Sal had to admit Del was right about that.

That night, when she ran down her list of the offenses her children had committed against her, there was only one item on Chloe's list. She was a homosexual. She had told Sal lesbian was the word she preferred, but Sal could never bring herself to say that. It always sounded so nasty. Now Sal noticed that she knew so little about Chloe, other than that one fact. She hadn't allowed anyone to talk about her and she didn't do her own research, even though she had a Facebook account and could have looked; Chloe wouldn't have known. But Sal had created a vacuum where Chloe used to be. Now a crushing pain suddenly filled that cavern inside. Sal's baby was sick.

⁂

Sal wasn't sure how many times Adele called that week, but when she looked back on it later, she had to admit that was nice of her. Sal didn't go near the phone or call her back. In fact, she didn't go anywhere, just called in sick and stayed in bed, feeling sorry for herself. She never once thought that maybe she had made a bad choice or that she should try to make things right with Chloe. She was still blaming Chloe for the mess she believed Chloe had made between them and, out of habit or stubbornness, was sticking to her guns. She was sure not going to call her and lower herself. Though she ached for Chloe now with every cell in her body, she was not going to make the first move.

How long did Sal stay like that, suspended between a terrible past and a worse future? There was a trip to the store for cat food about a week in. She might have ignored that little calico if she hadn't been yowling in a thoroughly unacceptable tone. Otherwise, it was just an endless stream of reality shows and every bit of ice cream she had in the freezer, which was not a little bit. A few glasses of wine, too, and once all the glasses were dirty, Sal swigged out of the bottle. It was the lowest she'd been since Stan walked out.

It would be hard to say, in retrospect, how she began to inch back towards living. First, she looked at her checkbook and acknowledged that she was close to the bottom of the barrel. She dragged herself to Daily Grind and stood at the counter, usually taking orders, sometimes making drinks. At first, it felt like a big imposition when someone ordered their skinny extra strong triple pump latte with whipped cream, but after a few days, it began to comfort her to do familiar things. She knew how to make a drink. She knew how to say good morning, four dollars and fifteen cents please, have a good day. She knew how to wipe the counter, count the tips. Life resembled an ordinary pattern. She didn't have to drag herself around as she had when Del first told her about Chloe.

At that point, the nights became unbearable. Sal added extra shifts just to stay occupied. A few nights she drank herself to sleep, even though she'd never been much of a drinker. She finished off the pain pills left over from a sprained ankle and was lucky there were not more. She might have tried to end it if there had been enough. She had never been good at reaching out when something was wrong and avoided it even more now. In fact, right then, she truly believed that she was entirely alone in the world, that no one cared if she lived or died.

What preyed on her mind was that no one would really notice if she never came out of this. Adele continued to call now and then and leave a message like everything was normal. If she'd been dead, there would have been no way for Del to know it. Sal didn't call back, just the same as always. After that one time, she kept her guard up, prepared for Del to call, so that without much effort, she didn't pick up the phone. She even wondered if she should have it disconnected. *Waste of money*, she thought. But she never did. It would be quite a while before she admitted to herself that she kept it for only one reason. Chloe had that number.

✣✣✣✣

As the weather changed, Sal began to perk up just a little. In what might have seemed an odd thing to an outsider, as winter came to her neighborhood, with its California rain and cloudy days, she started to cheer up. The weather matched her state of mind and that was oddly reassuring. Life took on a pattern, however vacant, of home and work. Work and home. Grocery store. Drugstore. Home and work.

Sal hardly noticed when the thought began to plague her mind, *you've got to talk to someone.* Such an unusual thought for her, the loner chick, the "needs nobody" lady. But there it was. *You've got to talk to someone.* At first, it would pop into her mind occasionally, at odd moments, unbidden. She shooed it away as if it was nothing. Sal just wasn't the type to need stuff from other folks. Her ex, Stan, used to say he felt a little useless, just standing there while Sal dominated everything. The way he said it was mean, but he wasn't wrong. That made it a real shocker when once, while Sal was working, she had the most overpowering urge to say to a regular customer, "I haven't seen my oldest child in ten years and she has cancer." It was as if the force of the universe wanted to come through her mouth and it took a tremendous act of will not to say it. Was it the softness of her eyes, or the way she said, "thank you," as if this simple cup of coffee and the person who delivered it made a real difference in her life? Whatever it was, Sal couldn't shake the voice, *you've got to talk to someone,* and it started seeming like that had something to do with this woman she didn't even know.

After that first time, Sal took extra effort to chat with her in the mornings about little nothings, really. Did she live in the neighborhood? Did she want a muffin or a breakfast sandwich? When she ordered her coffee, Sal would take the effort to smile though she was usually all business. She knew her name, Kim, since she wrote it on her latte cup every morning, and found herself reaching out.

"How are you this morning, Kim? I know I'm weird, but I'm enjoying the rain."

Responding to this new warmth, Kim asked about Sal. "Do you have children?"

"Yes, four." There was a shock through Sal's body when that number erupted from her lips. After she'd told Chloe she was dead to her, she always told anyone who asked she had three children. Yes, two boys and a girl. She'd been telling that lie so long it seemed like the truth. But somehow, she couldn't pretend with this stranger.

She was working up to ask Kim what she did for a living. By the time she did ask, she'd told Kim more about herself than she told her friends. About loneliness, and old friends who were gone, and not seeing much of her children or grandchildren. Nothing about Chloe, of course.

When it happened, it seemed so natural. "What do you do for a living?" How did Sal know it was an important question? But she'd been afraid to ask, knowing that it was.

"Do you work near here?"

"Right around the corner."

"Oh. What do you do?"

How had she managed to sound so casual?

"I'm a counselor."

"Oh, that sounds like interesting work."

That's all she could manage right then. Kim smiled and moved to a one-person high table, pulled out a computer, and began to do something on it. In Sal's imagination, Kim was solving someone's problem, completely and forever, right there in Daily Grind. She imagined the person on the other end, grateful to receive the warmth and care this kind woman offered.

That was a Friday and Kim didn't come in when Sal worked the next day. No surprise, since Sal had found out she didn't live near the shop. Sal was building up her courage, for what, she couldn't say. She just knew that she'd need it for what came next.

࿘࿘࿘࿘

Monday was sunny, incongruous with Sal's state of mind. Her insides were swirling and her knees felt weak. For no reason that was clear to her, Sal still felt like something big was about to happen. She walked to work instead of taking the car, putting off getting there. The line was out the door by the time she arrived. They'd be charging up the Monday morning hordes heading to work. All those long lines of folks tanking up on their caffeine. Daily Grind addiction, they'd joke in the back room.

Sal almost thought Kim wasn't going to show up. Why did she care? Sal couldn't understand herself because she didn't believe in therapy, counseling, whatever you want to call it. She had been quick to offer the opinion, whenever the subject came up, that people who went to therapy were a bunch of navel gazing into themselves entitled bitches. But she was imagining herself asking, *how much does it cost? Can I come talk to you? I need to talk to someone.* The persistent ring of her own voice in her ears was louder every day.

Finally, Sal saw Kim walking towards the door. She took a deep breath and got ready. There she was.

Chapter Two

Chloe

It had taken a long time for Chloe to let go of her mother. As a child, her mother had told her they were two of a kind, that no other child of hers could ever be as close to her. Two peas in a pod, she used to say. Same red hair, fierce temperament, energy. Then when Sally cut her off, she wondered whom her mother had been close to. Not the real Chloe, for sure. The real Chloe was her own person, with likes, dislikes, beliefs, and truths of her own. She was not just a reflection of her mother. Acknowledging that she was a lesbian was just the tip of the iceberg on their differences. But it was also the one fact about her she couldn't hide or get around. So, when her mother refused to have anything to do with her, she had to face the fact that Sally, who had adored her, had never loved her.

She knew some people didn't make it through these things, but that just wasn't her. There was an optimistic streak in her that simply couldn't be killed. She didn't know where she'd gotten that, since both her parents were glass half-empty people. So, since she wasn't a quitter, she set to work trying to get over her mother.

The first thing she did, even though she couldn't see the connection at first, was break up with Daz, the woman she'd been seeing. She just couldn't keep it up, dealing with all the shit they had between them and getting over her mother's rejection. She knew she wasn't making a mistake when Daz said, "You are such a load of crap!"

The next thing she did was email all the people she trusted in the world to ask whether they knew a good therapist. She'd gone a few times when she was trying to figure out why she felt nothing when she dated men and it had been okay. The therapist hadn't even been that great, but she could see the potential.

This time when she stepped into the therapist's office, she was nervous, but less than she expected. Her friend, Claire, had told her to go to Angie, a woman who had been helping people deal with coming out for twenty years. Chloe tried to reserve judgement, to play it close to the vest, not risk too much, but by the end of the first hour, she was telling Angie things she hadn't told anyone ever.

Such as, her childhood best friend had cut her off after asking her to play naked house with her – "You be the boy and I'll be the girl" – and then, the very next day, telling her she was a lezzie and they couldn't be friends anymore.

Or the times when her classmates whispered behind her back and, when she came close enough to hear, laughed and shut up.

Or hearing, when her mother took her to church, a rousing sermon about all the ways a person could go wrong, touching yourself, touching someone else you're not married to or, God forbid, someone of your own sex. She never told Sally why, but she refused to go to church from then on.

So those were the kinds of things she suddenly

told Angie, this person she had never even laid eyes on, about herself. Angie was not one of those silent, nodding therapists. They had a two-way conversation, but it was clear that Chloe was the center of it. She tried not to look at Angie, but the intensity of her deep blue eyes was hard to avoid. She had to stare hard at the pillow she had grabbed off the couch when looking at Angie became too much. Angie asked her questions, suggested ways she might look at all this, asked her if she knew anyone else that had been through anything similar. "What you're feeling is so familiar to me," she said. "It is such a tremendous loss when just being yourself sends people packing." Chloe left that office shocked and not a little worried, but also strangely comforted.

At home later, when she tried to figure out why she had said so much, she just wasn't sure. She did know that it had been a long, long time, if ever, since anyone had paid that much attention to her.

That had been three years ago now, and she had gone to see Angie for two, walking through each painful part of losing her family. Because it didn't take long to see that, even though other people in the family still kept in touch, now and then, they were in and she was out. When she did see them, it was so uncomfortable she just wanted to go home. She always wanted to ask them, "Why do you let her get away with it? Why do you keep seeing her when you know it's at my expense?" But she never said anything.

Somehow, magically, working with Angie helped her to accept all that. She even imagined that maybe she came to love herself a little better. When she told Angie that she was ready to go it alone, Angie said something she thought of each and every day from then on. "You have had struggles, and you have faced them. Now you are going to have a beautiful life, because you know struggles don't have the power to take your own amazing life away from you."

And she said to Angie, when Angie asked what was next, "I'm setting out to find a kind of love that doesn't hurt me."

She thought that might be impossible, and she prepared herself to live a good life without a special someone. She had finished college in literature a few years back and never used it, so now she began a search for a career that would get her back to her great love of words. Almost by magic, she got a job editing books. A friend had a friend with a small press and they gave her a try. She loved it! All day reading and working to improve the beautiful books her boss had chosen to publish. Suddenly, life was something to treasure.

She even put the love thing on the back burner; she was having so much fun with this new life. All the pain had been worth it. She could almost call herself happy!

≈≈≈≈≈

The day Rhonda walked into the office, Chloe found herself suddenly shy. She was at the front desk, which was unusual, but she'd been filling in for the receptionist, who had a terrible flu. She knew there was a new writer coming in. It wasn't decided yet who was going to edit the book, but there was lots of excitement about this one. Sometimes the books just seemed like business as usual, but Chloe's boss had said, when she told her about it, that this book could "put us on the map." She was a very subdued type, so that was saying a lot.

Reception faced the entrance, fully blocking access into the rest of the offices. Every visitor had to stop there, no choice. When Rhonda bolted through the door, Chloe almost imagined she felt a wind whooshing through too. The first thing she noticed about Rhonda was not a detail of her looks, but that Chloe herself suddenly felt alert. Something in her whispered, *I know you.* Rhonda was oddly familiar while also seeming absolutely new. And Chloe found her more beautiful than any woman she'd ever seen.

Rhonda couldn't have looked more different from Chloe herself. Chloe's red hair fell long down her back, while Rhonda's was jet black, short, and in soft dreadlocks. Chloe had moon cheeks, as if she'd never lost all her baby fat, while Rhonda was lean and just a little muscly.

Chloe imagined standing in front of her, looking eye to eye. In her mind, they were exactly the same height. She stood up to see if she was right. With her four-inch boots, Chloe was a little taller. Chloe worried that she looked foolish standing for no reason and fiddled with the filing cabinet behind her as if there was something very important to attend to.

Rhonda walked over to the desk and asked for April, the boss. Caught off guard that Rhonda spoke first, Chloe turned quickly to face her and had a little trouble forming the words when she said, "Sure, just a minute." She was suddenly terrified that her telltale blush, bright red, had risen up her cheeks. There was a good chance it had, because she suddenly felt feverish. If she could have put off the moment when Rhonda headed back to April and the meeting room, she would have.

Chloe had never before plotted for assignment to a particular project. She loved the adventure of knowing almost nothing about a book before she opened the first page. She loved knowing that she and the author, no matter who it was, were embarking on a journey to put words between two covers or, in the case of their growing e-book business, onto the internet. She would never have chosen many of the books she ended up editing, but she always learned something of value, from the book or its author. A few times, what she learned was how to work with difficult people, but that was valuable in its own way; it made her appreciate the many other writers who made her work a sheer pleasure.

None of that came into play one way or the other when Rhonda came through the door. All she could imagine were endless hours in her office, on the phone, heads bent over the page, maybe even getting a drink afterwards, intimate in their discovery of what Rhonda's book could be. Just the idea of reading what this creature had to say seemed beyond any fantasy she'd ever had about the possibilities of being an editor. She was certain that Rhonda was an amazing writer with important things to say. And this was before she even knew whether Rhonda had written a novel or a book of essays.

She wasn't sure how to work the angle. April didn't like her staff to have strong opinions about their assignments. She liked to be the leader. She believed she had the best line on who was good for what book. In all fairness, she was usually right. As Rhonda passed the front desk on her way out, Chloe looked up just in time to say a quick, "Nice to meet you." Without turning around, Rhonda raised her hand in the air, an almost wave the only clue she had heard.

∿∿∿∿

Chloe didn't have to wait long, or waste too much strategic energy. April called her in within the hour.

"Did you meet Rhonda Flax out there?"

"Yes, I did." *Don't give away your secret, Chloe. Stay cool.*

"She's an interesting author. It's a novel. She's a lesbian, but the only lesbian character in it is pretty minor. When I asked her about that, she said she doesn't want to get pigeonholed. Doesn't want to be the 'lesbian writer.'"

Chloe thought it was best to look interested and say nothing.

"Anyway, I hope you won't take this the wrong way, like I only want you to work with her because you're gay, but I think you might be good for the project. What do you say?"

Chloe was not sure she could say anything. She swallowed hard, then "sure, why not?" came from her throat. It seemed as if someone else was speaking. Did she sound casual enough? Too blasé? But April didn't seem to notice.

"I know I usually wait for the editor's meeting, but I already know I want you to do it, and we don't have another meeting for a while. How close are you to being done with Mick? I want you to have plenty of time."

She'd been editing Mick Patterson's book about Stonewall for what seemed like forever. April didn't want Chloe to think she gave her all the gay projects, but she couldn't remember the last one she didn't give to Chloe. Chloe's best friend at work, Emily, said she had a corner on the market. "When can a straight girl catch a break?" she said when Chloe got the Stonewall book, because it was Mick's tenth book and he sold well, and there was going to be her name in the acknowledgements, "Thanks to my amazing editor, Chloe Bess, without whom this book would be in the toilet."

She paced around the office, which was conveniently laid out in a circle around the building, until she found Emily. Before they met, Chloe never thought she'd be able to dish with a straight girl, but Emily had just the right blend of academic interest and bald humor. Once when Chloe told her Daz' parting shot, after recapping the worst relationship she'd ever been in, Emily said, "Wow, she's such a guy," and Chloe couldn't stop laughing, to the point where she lost her breath.

Emily told her all about her dates with men, and appreciated Chloe's critiques. Some of the guys Chloe truly seemed to like better than Emily did. She'd tell Emily, "Why don't you straight women like men as much as me? It's weird!"

So, with all of that going on, this latest Rhonda adventure must be shared. Emily was hanging out in the coffee room, steeping an endless cup of tea, or, as she'd call it, "meditating on her next chapter."

"Emily, I've just been introduced to my new life."

"What are you talking about?" Chloe always had to earn it with her.

"There's this new author. Rhonda Flax. Oh my God, Emily. I think I'm in love."

"Chloe, I thought you weren't gonna go nuts on me anymore."

"Wrong, apparently. I am gone!"

"Oh, God, I can't wait to talk you down off the ceiling when she turns out to be a loser."

~~~~~

Chloe couldn't sleep the night before their first meeting. They had arranged everything by exchanging what seemed like an endless string of voicemail messages.

"Hello, this is Chloe Bess, an editor at Pace Books. You can reach me by phone at...or email..." The communications were so mundane that Chloe bored herself.

Then she'd get one back. "Hi, this is Rhonda Flax. I can meet anytime Tuesday."

"Tuesday isn't good, how about...?"

It was almost an anticlimax by the time they sat down in Chloe's office to try each other out. Meeting in person did not dilute Chloe's enthusiasm, even though Rhonda seemed a bit guarded. Half way in, Chloe realized Rhonda might not know Chloe was a lesbian. Many people didn't, since there was no giveaway in her style. She liked her dresses, skirts, long hair, and makeup. She'd tried the shorn, tough style when she first came out, but it never fit. So now the only problem was somehow letting people know when she wanted them to know.

Rhonda was all business. She brought the manuscript, "in case," she said. April had given Chloe a copy the day before, and she'd read a few chapters. She was relieved not to be disappointed. It was good, maybe even excellent. The characters moved through the story, jumping off the page and demanding that you like them. Even the villains were nuanced and complete – real human beings. There was insight into their motivations and windows into their deepest selves. And, even so, there was room for a serious edit. They would have to meet many times to get this done. Chloe would be able to help make this great book better, if Rhonda could trust her.

"I love the book," she said.

"Great! I guess we can call it done and get the thing published!" Rhonda replied, only half joking. Chloe was glad that she responded to Rhonda's joke by laughing, but only a little bit. She was suddenly afraid that if she spoke, she was going to make a mess of it.

"I'd like to know what you think could improve it," Chloe said. She was falling back on her usual tactics with writers, let them think all the ideas were theirs, approach gently, support, then stubbornly insist on the changes she knew the book needed if they couldn't get there on their own.

"Well, I wouldn't touch chapter three; it works just the way I want it to. That's the only one I really don't want much of an edit on, unless you see any typos. The first two chapters work in general, but they feel a little too much like I'm trying to get the background over with, which I was, and I want them to catch the reader up in the story a little more. Chapter four and seven need major editing. I want you to say what sections you think need more, maybe a little about what's missing, then I want to work on it, then check back, your usual high intensity edit. The rest are mostly right; we need to tweak them. The last sentence I refuse to change for any reason."

"Wow, I haven't quite finished the book – I got it yesterday – but everything I've read I had the same hit as you. That sure doesn't happen often. Let's start with the first two chapters, since I've read them, and then call it a day."

Once Chloe was engaged in her work, she forgot to be nervous, tongue-tied, or crushed out. She was in her element, making suggestions, giving Rhonda her best, and they worked together well. For the next two hours, it was all about the book. But right as they were finishing up, she remembered that, with most of her writers, she only had the one face to face. This had already gone on longer than most. From here, she usually did everything by email and phone. Her heart dropped. What to do.

"You know," Chloe said, "I usually don't do this but, since you're local and today worked so well, I wonder if maybe we should do a lot of the editing across a table like this."

Rhonda looked at her for what seemed like a long time, her face betraying nothing of what she might be thinking. Chloe couldn't remember a time she had been looked at so thoroughly.

"I'd like that," said Rhonda. And at that moment, as if this had always been coming, Chloe's life turned on its axis.

☙☙☙☙

It wasn't until their fourth meeting that things took a turn. Chloe thought Rhonda was maybe the most interesting person she'd ever met, and her crush did not diminish, but at the same time, she was a little hesitant to mess with a work connection. If she offended Rhonda or made her jittery, it could hurt the book. Chloe was pretty ethical when it came to work; she didn't mess around. Emily would have said she was a morality freak. That made it hard to imagine turning this work connection personal, especially before they finished the work. The other thing Chloe hated to admit about herself was that she was never forward when it came to potential romantic interests. So, it came as no surprise that the first move was Rhonda's. When it happened, it seemed a little bit strange that it hadn't happened before.

They were sitting in the trendy little coffee shop down the street from the office. Brick walls and rough metal table, lights that looked like they should hang over a typewriter table in an old-fashioned newspaper office. They had figured out this was the best place; away from distraction, from phones, from anyone paying any attention to what they were talking about. They always sat at a corner table that was blocked off, but right by a window. If it wasn't free, they waited. It seemed almost superstitious, but they were really productive here. They had gotten to the fourth chapter in just three meetings.

"Are you not asking me out because you're not gay or because you're not interested?" Rhonda said, looking straight at her with her intense green eyes.

"I'm not asking you out because I'm afraid of rejection," she said before thinking, and then registered it was the exact truth. She didn't hesitate because she was meek, or shy, or didn't know what she wanted. She hesitated because she didn't want to hear no!

"Well, you sure won't hear 'yes' if you never ask!" Rhonda said, and stood up, ready to go.

"If I ask, what will you say?" Chloe heard her own timid voice.

As Chloe could have predicted, Rhonda came back in a hurry. "You'll have to ask and find out," she said over her shoulder, already at the door.

Chapter Three

Sally

Sal didn't know what she expected when she walked into the office of the counselor Kim had referred her to, after she disappointed Sal by saying she thought they knew each other too well to work together, but it wasn't what she saw. The room where she sat waiting was more like a living room than any office she'd ever seen. Couch and chairs, a few recent magazines, unlike her dentist's office, where they were always at least a year old.

In the corner, there was a water cooler and some cups. Just because she didn't know what to do with herself, she poured herself a glass of water and sat down to drink it. She was early, which really wasn't like her at all. She was usually dashing to wherever she was going at the last possible minute. But at a certain point, running herself around in her head, wondering what she was doing and how it would be and whether there was anyone anywhere that could help her, was exhausting and she just had to go ahead and leave the house. She had to stop thinking about how expensive it was, or whether she'd get anything out of it, or whether she had picked the right one, or what bullshit she thought it all was. Just had to go find out.

Even though she was early, Lonnie Shaw came out to let Sal know she had heard the bell and she'd be ready in a few minutes. Sal had only talked to her on the phone, and she was different in person. For one thing, she was black, and Sal hadn't picked up on that; it was a shock. She imagined she could always tell, but apparently not. The next thing that was pretty weird was how tall she was, around six feet. And warm. And well dressed, but not in that snobby way. She enjoyed colors and fitting her form – which was a bit ample – into the clothes. Her smile was disarming and Sal noticed, with some suspicion, that she wasn't feeling nervous. Was Lonnie Shaw doing something to catch Sal off her guard? Was Lonnie Shaw messing with her mind?

True to what she said, Lonnie came back out in a few minutes and asked Sal into the office. It was even nicer in there, all cozy and inviting. It crossed Sal's mind that if she didn't think it was trite to lay on a couch at a therapist's office, she could just curl up in that comfy couch and take a better nap than she had in about three years. Sal sat up straighter and got ready to be questioned. What was she going to ask, and how was Sal going to get around to telling her stuff she didn't want anyone to know?

"Sally, I'll tell you how I usually like to start out, and see if it agrees with you, okay?"

"Sure." *That* sounded dumb.

"We're just getting to know each other here so I can go in the direction you want to go. I always imagine people think about coming to therapy long before they come, and I'd really appreciate hearing what finally got you here. Also, what would you like to be different? If our work together was a great success, what would have happened?"

Sal sat still for a minute. She wanted to keep most

of it to herself. She wanted to tell her only what she could tell her easily.

"Well, I don't get along very well with my sister, Adele, and that bothers me. I think we should be close and instead I just think she's trying to show me up. She's always more together, like, a better parent, she didn't get a divorce, and she doesn't work in a lousy coffee shop. You know, just all around better life. It's annoying, really."

Sal looked over to see if Lonnie could tell she hadn't really told her what she was there for, but if she knew, she didn't let on. And then Sal had the weirdest, most uncharacteristic thought. *I'm paying a hundred dollars to sit here with this woman, and that's a discount on her ridiculous fee of $150! If I don't tell her why I'm really here, I'm wasting my money!* Sal took a deep breath.

"You know, that's not why I'm here, really."

"No?" Lonnie said.

"No. Here's the deal. I've got four grown kids. None of them would win a prize but there's one, Chloe, who I don't talk to. We haven't talked in, like, ten years. And a month ago my sister calls me up out of the blue to tell me that Chloe's got cancer, the bad kind, and then the weirdest thing happened. Even though she's not in my life and I decided that a long time ago, I got down-on-the-couch-can't-get-up-hardly-able-to-get-to-work depressed. Does that make sense? I should be saying, 'what difference does that make to me?' But I really can't get over it." And Sal burst into tears.

Lonnie Shaw didn't interrupt. She let Sal cry it out, all the time looking at her with something Sal rarely saw and even more rarely took notice of – kind eyes. She hung on every word but she didn't intrude. She just made room for the tears. Sal couldn't remember crying like that since she lost her first baby to a miscarriage. She cried a lot harder than she ever had over Stan. That cry seemed to last forever, and Lonnie Shaw wasn't doing anything, but she wasn't doing nothing. She was just there. She was paying attention to Sal maybe more deeply than anyone ever had.

Finally, the crying ran its course. Sal's breathing went back to normal and she wasn't hiccupping anymore. She was just sitting, emptied out, calm, on Lonnie Shaw's wonderful couch.

"Would you be okay with a question?" Lonnie asked, ever so tentative, as if to say, 'I don't need you to say yes. Just asking.'

"I don't know until you ask!" Sal said, with a little bit of a punk attitude.

"Why did you kick your daughter out of your life?"

"Why is *that* important?"

"Never know, you might want to reconsider the decision some day and I want to know if that's a good idea."

Then Lonnie waited. Sal didn't say a word right away. For one, she thought she might start bawling again. For another, she really had to decide if she wanted to embarrass herself by telling Lonnie the most shameful thing she could think of about her children. What had Sal done wrong that Chloe turned out like *that*?

Then there was that voice again. *Why waste your money by not saying anything?* And so, Sal told her everything.

꠴ ꠴ ꠵ ꠵

Every week, Sal could hardly wait to see Lonnie Shaw. Lonnie didn't bring up the stuff with Chloe right away. She just started helping Sal feel better. She "prescribed" Sal a walk three times a week and started focusing on what Sal liked, what comforted her. Sal went back to making little pictures because she had always liked that and Lonnie helped her discover that she felt better after she painted. Lonnie emphasized that the subject didn't really matter, that the act of painting would soothe but, more and more, Sal found herself making little colored drawings, then painting them, of Chloe when she was little, before they were broken. She had to go through the cupboard in the front hall and find the pictures she had hidden back when she didn't want to look at them. Sal was relieved she hadn't tossed them. Chloe had been such a beautiful, kind, and funny kid. Sal was having a memory a minute, and it all came out in the pictures.

Sal couldn't admit it mattered *what* she was painting until one day, about the fourth time she brought a few to therapy, Lonnie Shaw said, "Did you ever think you would kick this child out of your life?"

By that time, Sal knew Lonnie wasn't judging, just super curious.

"I never did," Sal said, and in that moment, knew that it was true.

♪♫♪♫

Sal didn't realize when things started to turn, but somehow, she really began not to be able to remember why she had refused to talk to Chloe. She knew it didn't happen immediately after Chloe told Sal she was attracted to women. At that point, Sal was intent on giving her a hard time. Sal thought she could change Chloe into a straight girl if she tried hard enough. About six months in, Chloe said, "Mom, we have to stop talking about this. I'm not going to change, and neither are you."

It was only remembering that day when Sal really saw, for the first time, how sad she'd made her daughter. She had thought Chloe was defiant but now, really looking at it, remembering the look of defeat in her eyes, Sal could see that Chloe couldn't change and that, if she could have, she would have to please her mother. Sal even imagined that maybe the worst thing that happened to Chloe before cancer was the thing with her. As she gathered her strength to face the truth, she felt bad in a way she never had before. Instead of feeling bad about how everyone treated her, she felt remorse for what she had done. Without Lonnie's continual support and caring, she would have turned and run the other way.

She still didn't feel any different about the gay thing. It was wrong! But what kind of a mother never speaks to her child again, even if she *is* wrong? A kind of guilt or maybe shame she had never gotten close to acknowledging before consumed Sal.

Lonnie Shaw didn't really want to support the guilt. She said feeling bad about yourself never ever made you a better person, that mistakes were to learn from, to give you a chance to grow. And that self-criticism only led to more self-criticism, not to any improvement.

"Okay," she said, "so you acted human! How are you going to make it right?"

She said a lot of other things too, and some

stuck like rubber cement, coming back to Sal at odd moments. Sal almost didn't come back to see her when things were hard to hear, but by this point, those weekly hours were like the rope leading from the life raft to the ship in the middle of the sea. Without her, Sal would be *really* lost.

Sal began to consider that at the center of her life, not just her relationship with Chloe, was a huge helping of false pride. Even as she slowly neared being ready to have Chloe back in her life, she couldn't admit she was wrong and that made it impossible to call her. When Sal said she was stuck, Lonnie said, "Stuck is just the place where your old way of doing things doesn't work anymore and you're not ready for the new way." That relaxed Sal a little, as if being stuck was sort of normal, but she still couldn't take any action.

Every week, she went to see Lonnie Shaw and repeated all the reasons why she could never make it any better. Lonnie listened patiently, suggesting small changes in how she was looking at it, never requiring her to do one thing different, the most supportive person you'd ever want to know. And then one day, it was the first day of spring that year, she said, "You know, Sally, you can take as long as you want to get ready to jump that fence, but I think we have to be honest that if you wait long enough, she might not be on the other side."

Chapter Four

Chloe

The next time Chloe was set to meet with Rhonda, she almost didn't make it. She suddenly had to take a long bath. She was hungry; certainly lunch must be eaten before she left the house. It was a rainy day; maybe she shouldn't go out at all. Maybe she should postpone the meeting. Her house was a mess. Maybe she needed to clean.

She had to admit sooner or later that she was scared. Scared of a "no," of course, but scared of a "yes" too. She couldn't remember ever feeling so exhilarated and at the same time so paralyzed. *What are you afraid of,* she kept asking herself. It was as if she had walked out in the winter in the cold. Exposed. Risking life and limb.

They had agreed to meet for another editing session at three p.m., usual spot. At 2:55, she knew she wouldn't make it in time, even if she ran. She called Rhonda's cell phone, which she had gotten with the initial demographics from work and never, ever, used. First time for everything!

"Hey Rhonda, I'm running a little late. Don't leave; I'll be right there!"

Before she could think about it, she grabbed her warmest coat against the chill and ran out the door.

≈ ≈ ≈ ≈

The cafe was mostly empty that day, which was strange in the late afternoon. Chloe found her way to the table, aware that Rhonda was watching every step. She felt like every move was slow motion, as if she'd never make it to the table at all. But, no, progress was slowly being made. At the last few steps, she almost turned around. Inside her head, she heard an insistent, *Show some courage, Chloe.*

The first few moments after she sat down were some of the longest in her life. She literally couldn't speak, and Rhonda wasn't going to help her out any. She just looked at her, in a way she'd never been looked at before. Penetrating, unnerving, but somehow soft at the same time. Chloe wondered to herself if Rhonda was enjoying her tongue-tied silence and the red that was creeping up her neck, without her permission. A blush is a white girl betrayal, she'd always said.

Finally, it was just less terrifying to speak than to continue to be looked at like that.

"Here's the thing," she said, surprised that she sounded almost normal, "I never date anyone I meet at work, and especially not before we finish the book, but I seem to be willing to make an exception in your case."

Did she really say that? It sounded so pretend smooth, presumptuous, high and mighty, maybe even crazy.

"How very generous of you."

And then they both broke up laughing. And they couldn't stop.

When Rhonda laughed, it was as if tiny bits of light danced over her cheeks. Chloe didn't think anyone she had ever met looked happier when they laughed. Including her little brother Grant who, at one year old, laughed literally all the time. Rhonda's laugh so captivated her that she kept laughing just so Rhonda wouldn't stop. At first, they didn't notice it, but after a while, they both looked out into the cafe and saw that everyone in the whole place was staring at them. They were making a scene.

More abruptly than she meant, Chloe blurted, "Be right back," and headed for the bathroom. She covered her face with water from the high tech stainless steel sink and turned on the hand drier, straining and stooping to put her face in the way of the air. Not succeeding completely, she took the bottom of her shirt and dried the rest of the water off, doing her best to use a part of the magenta shirt that wouldn't show once she let her jacket drop back into place. She took a deep breath, doing her best to pull it together. And then, before she could get to the door, it opened. Rhonda stepped in and locked it, then walked towards her, pulled her into a breathtaking, swoon worthy embrace, and kissed her.

❧❧❦❦

Waking up next to Rhonda a few weeks later, it took Chloe a moment to register where she was. Her eyes opened to a sheer curtain over a nine-light window, which looked out over the back yard. Rhonda lived in a cottage behind an old Craftsman bungalow. The owner, Dani, who lived in the front, had built the place to work in, but now was retired and, in exchange for keeping an eye on things and doing a little gardening, rented it cheap. Rhonda had been in a writing group Dani still occasionally led and had been the first to see the "cottage for rent" sign go up. She moved in within the week and, three years later, was still here. She hadn't just done a little yard work; she had turned the yard into a magic, secret garden, with blooming flowers and bending trees, seats tucked away where you could hardly see them, paving stones ready to invite you to walk through. And behind it all, a large cottage. Dani had built it as one huge room at first, but now, Rhonda had slowly evolved it into a snug three bedroom. Dani paid for the materials; Rhonda put in the labor. Chloe was entranced.

༄ ༄ ༅ ༅

The night before was, in name at least, their first date. Later, they would count all the editing sessions as dates too, because that is where their relationship really started. But last night, a Tuesday, was the first time they went out, book left at home.

Rhonda picked Chloe up in a rundown Toyota, circa who knows. The paint, which had been red at some point in its life, was now a kind of cherry color, with patches of white where even the cherry had muted out. The inside still looked decent, and Rhonda let her in with a quick, "It still works."

Chloe was used to writers who had very little money and, even if they had some, didn't know if they would ever have any again. The car did not put her off. In a way, she found it a little romantic, going on a date with a starving artist. It would be a lot later when she would take it in that Rhonda was an artist, but not starving. Her parents had a ton of money, and they were generous. They bankrolled Rhonda's artist life. She had the car because she didn't see the reason to get rid of a car that still worked. But that first night, Rhonda also didn't see the need to say all that.

Once she had won the fight to have Chloe say aloud that she wanted to date, Rhonda took over. They flirted over the next few editing sessions then, one unseasonably warm day, at the end of the meeting, she said, "I want to take you out Tuesday." When Chloe said, "What're we doing?" Rhonda said, "It's a surprise."

༄ ༄ ༄ ༄

The air was cold again by Tuesday, January in the Bay Area changing seasons every few days and sometimes several times in the same day. Chloe had given Rhonda her address and then regretted it. Her studio apartment was one big room and she never kept it as tidy as she thought she should. She spent the weekend cleaning, partly to make a good impression and partly from nerves. She tried to tell herself it was no big deal, just a date, she'd been on them before, but it didn't work. She was still shaking in her shoes.

When Tuesday came, she realized she didn't know what to dress for. The opera? McDonald's? A hike in the Berkeley hills? She even felt a little irritated that Rhonda wasn't sharing the info. She finally chose a pair of black pants, a colorful shirt and some ballet shoes, red of course. Middle of the road. Non-offensive.

When she looked in the mirror, she took it all off and started over. Trendy skirt, vee cut shirt, low heels. No. Nice jeans, shape-hugging sweater, boots. Then back to the first thing she had put on. That would do.

By the time Rhonda came to pick her up, she was exhausted from getting ready. Being flagged was nearly helpful. She was almost too tired to be nervous. Almost.

ᘓ.ᘓᘓᘓᘓ

They drove to the pier at Jack London Square and parked. Rhonda took her hand and pulled her along to the ferry, pulling out tickets she already had in her pocket. They were only a little early and found seats in the cabin. Too cold for the outside, for sure! Out the window, the water was choppy and deep green, the sky a blustery grey. They sat close on the bench, the place where their sleeves touched electric with attraction and nerves. They talked with their heads close together, pretending it was because there was noise on the boat.

Chloe felt as if time was standing still, or that it was moving incredibly fast. She thought that it was so unusual to know that something important was happening when it was actually happening. But she *knew*, with a certainty that had her staring at Rhonda's shoes instead of her face. Her face was just too close.

Within that first hour on the boat, they had talked about her split from her mother, and Rhonda being beat up as a teen, being called a queer. They had talked about their favorite books and their favorite music. They had talked about their dreams for life. Wanting children, a special someone, home and family. They had examined every seam of each other's shoes, avoiding eye contact. The ride was almost over.

When they pulled up to the pier, Chloe looked up for what seemed like the first time since they had set out. To her left, she could see the bridge, lit up in the early night darkness. The city rose like Oz, out of the water, office buildings glittering, lights on even at night. She could not imagine how this night would turn out, but she felt the momentum of that sharp turn in her life again. Her body felt the impact.

When Rhonda took her hand, it didn't seem like it was the first time. Chloe let Rhonda pull her to her feet.

"We're gonna have a good night," Rhonda said and smiled in a way that shook Chloe to her shoes.

⚞⚞⚟⚟

The club was a short cable car ride from the boat. Rhonda yanked her onto the car as if she rode it every day. They hung to the outside, in the midst of the crowd, unable to avoid looking at each other, unless they wanted to fall off. Time seemed to speed up yet again. Up the hill, Rhonda said, "Time to jump off," and they jumped, laughing as they skipped to the sidewalk, following a neon sign advertising *Comedy Club.*

"Are we going to see comedy?" Chloe asked, finding it hard to believe that this woman, so close to being a stranger, could know her so well.

"What else?" Rhonda answered, as if she had an inside line on Chloe's every wish and desire. The marquee said, "Mary Graves." Chloe had never seen her but had almost seen her several times. This was an added bonus; Rhonda had chosen a date so right for her that she felt a little exposed.

They walked into the club and, when they reached the check-in table, the woman behind it said, "Hey Rhonda, haven't seen you in a while!" Chloe's ears perked up. Did she come here often?

"You know I can't come out when I'm finishing a book. But now it's just editing, and I need comic relief! And distraction; that's where my editor seems to come in." She glanced over at Chloe, making it clear that she was the editor in question, and that this was definitely a date. The woman, whom Rhonda introduced as Meg, developed a charming twinkle and said, "Glad to see you back."

They laughed so hard that night Chloe's stomach hurt when they walked out the front door. It was late; and the streets were wet from a rain that came, unexpected, while they watched the show. They walked slowly, and Rhonda slipped her hand into Chloe's. They held hands lightly, tentatively, and walked down Mission Street towards the BART train. It was too late to take the ferry back.

"She's a riot!" Chloe started, bubbling over with enjoyment, remembering the show.

"What was your favorite?" Rhonda asked, ready to laugh again.

"Hmm. The lesbian parent jokes, I think," Chloe started, "What does the kid with lesbian parents call them? Stereo moms! 'Pick pick up up your your room room! Do do your your home home work work!'" Chloe did a pretty good imitation of the comic, whipping her face from side to side.

Still laughing, Rhonda said, "I liked the date jokes the best. 'I don't see how lesbians ever get to the point of having sex! Do you want me to make love to you? Oh, no, you first! No, how about you? Oh, let me make love to you, then maybe.' Remember how she rolled her eyes and said, 'It's *tiring*'?" Chloe didn't feel as if she and Rhonda were going to have that problem any time soon, but just remembering some other times, with other people, she laughed, and they were still laughing as they arrived at the BART station.

Boarding the last train over to Oakland, they sat close on the bench, facing backwards, and spoke in hushed voices.

"I feel just a little scared," Chloe started.

Rhonda said, "Yeah, me too. More than a little."

"I don't think I've ever felt so sure..."

They looked each other in the eye and held their gaze all the way home. When the stop came, they almost missed it. Finally, the message came over the loud speaker, "Rockridge," and they ran off quickly, laughing and nearly tripping over the escalator stairs.

"Are you coming home with me?" Rhonda asked, and Chloe couldn't speak, but she smiled until her cheeks hurt.

Chapter Five

Sally

A few months into the therapy thing, Sal started to consider that rejecting her first-born child was not the best decision she had ever made. She still didn't want to consider that maybe she was all wrong about the lesbian thing. Lonnie Shaw suggested that maybe it was worth trying on the word that Chloe had preferred, and it didn't feel as bad to say it as she'd always thought it would. But was it really the worst thing she could ever have done to Sal? And had Chloe done it to *her*?

When she got home from work at night, she sat at her kitchen table and stared at the wall, especially the crumbly part, thinking, s*he could be dying right now. I could never see her again. And I'd only have my own damn self to blame.* At the same time, she knew she wasn't ready to do anything about it, but she had begun to consider that she should do something, even though her therapist said, "You've been should on long enough."

Then one day she woke up super early, because she knew Del did. She still wasn't ready to call Chloe, but maybe she could work up to it by calling the other person she had been avoiding.

"Hello?" Del said, in that, 'do you really need to be calling me' way she had.

"It's me, sis," Sal started, trying to keep it light.

"Oh, hey." She was noncommittal, bracing for the attack, ready to hang up at a moment's notice.

"I know I don't deserve it, but can you tell me how Chloe is?"

There was a pause on the other end. Sal figured she was trying to sort out whether she was breaking any code in telling her anything. Or maybe she was just shocked Sal asked. Lonnie said, often, Sal should "consider other possibilities" when she thought she knew what someone was thinking. So Sal just sat quiet, waiting for Del to say something. No matter what Del was thinking, Sal needed to prove she wasn't that bitch she'd been when Del called Sal about Chloe in the first place. The wait seemed endless.

"I'm surprised you want to know, Sal. What changed?" She wasn't going to let Sal off easy.

"I've been seeing a shrink, Del, and I think that I can't live with it if I never make things right with her. I'm not saying I approve or anything, but I need to accept that she is what she is. I don't want to lose her, Del."

"Well, I think you already did that. Not sure what it's going to take to get her back. But I guess that's not my part of the story. She's had two chemos. She is supposed to have ten all together, if her body will do it. I have her kids sometimes so Rhonda, her wife, can focus on her. Sometimes it's one of your other kids or one of their friends. They have some kind of unbelievable bunch of friends. Chloe tells me LGBT people have to make family out of their friends because so many of them don't have family. Honestly they do a better job of being family than a lot of family."

Sal vaguely knew what LGBT stood for, but

she didn't want to embarrass herself and ask for clarification. And she chose to overlook the potential hidden message about people being bad at being family. If she was thinking that, Sal guessed she'd have to admit it was true.

When Del said "Rhonda" and "wife," Sal almost had to break in. It had never really occurred to Sal that Chloe would have a real person to love, with a name, that she would have children and friends, a real life. It took Sal's breath away.

"Del, what's the best way for me to try to get back in with her?"

"Write her a letter and apologize. Don't make anything her fault. Take all the responsibility. Let her control how it's going to go. Don't write her again unless you hear from her."

☙ ☙ ☙ ☙

Sal's next session was difficult. She came to the office door late, scared of what she knew she needed to do. She wasn't very good at apologizing and was even beginning to realize that she never really thought anything was her fault. She always laid it on the doorstep of someone else, her kids, her ex, her sister, anyone but Sal. And when she thought back on it, Chloe had really tried, for a very long time, to keep her relationship with Sal. She had to face the truth; Sal, herself, had failed.

And so, in that painful hour, Sal started trying to tell Chloe she knew it.

"What's your first sentence, Sally?" Lonnie asked.

Sal said, "How can I ever make up for what I've done? Maybe there is no way, but I'd like to try."

Once Sal had gone that far, it was almost easy to write the rest. She described how she felt when Del called and told her Chloe was sick. She told her she was seeing a therapist, trying to change herself so that maybe they could start again. She congratulated her on finding someone to love and having children and she told her how sorry she was that she didn't know her kids. She asked her to please consider letting her back in her life. She sent it the same day, before she had a chance to change her mind.

❧ ❧ ❧ ❧

In some hidden corner of her mind, Sal expected to hear from Chloe the moment she got the letter, like Chloe was busy aching to hear from her. The first few days, she honestly thought the mail was slow and cursed the post office. The next few days, when she knew the letter had been delivered, Sal began to consider that the answer might be no. It was torture not writing her again, insisting that they talk. But Sal knew that was the opposite of what she needed to do. Lonnie gently encouraged her to let Chloe take her own time, told her that if she pushed her, it might be a push away. At this point, Sal had accepted that Lonnie knew more about these things. But she still struggled with letting things be and almost forced things many times over the next week. At her next appointment, she told Lonnie that she knew absolutely nothing about letting someone else take charge. Lonnie just smiled, letting the insight take up all the space in the room. Then she got the letter.

"Dear Mom,

"I hope you know I love you and I appreciate that you have done a ton of work to say the things to me that you said. I have to say that I didn't ever expect to hear from you again, and I also need to tell you that I am really afraid to let you back into my life. I went back to my own therapist to talk about this, because it's really bad timing for me, with feeling so sick and spending the better part of every day lying in bed.

"On the other hand, I don't want to punish you. You are a person with your own struggles and I know you hurt me out of ignorance more than anything. I want to forgive you, but it will take time.

"I need a safe way to come together, and this is what I've come up with. You can come over in two weeks on Friday. Not before because this week is my good week and I need to be there for our kids, and not next because I have chemo. I will have a few of my best friends there, and my wife, Rhonda, because I feel pretty scared and I need the support. We'll eat dinner and not talk about any of this that night. The kids will not be there, because I need to get used to the whole thing before I involve them.

"I know this may be uncomfortable for you since everyone knows what happened between us and they are very protective of me, so if you need to, you can bring someone with you, but please be careful about who. Make sure they don't have big judgements about my life, because no one stays at my home for long if they are openly homophobic, or even just biased against a person on any other basis than how they treat others.

"If all this is acceptable to you, I'll see you then. Only let me know if you're not coming."

Sal was reading the letter in her most comfortable

overstuffed green chair and she sank in a little deeper and didn't move for a long time. She thought about how hard it was going to be to wait. She thought about her fear that Chloe was never going to answer and realized like a bolt of lightning that that would not have been like her. Because unlike Sal, she was a kind, compassionate, and accepting person who wanted the best for everyone. Without Sal's permission, she heard the voice in her own head, the quiet friend who was becoming a frequent companion, *Chloe may be the best thing you've ever done.*

Chapter Six

Chloe

The first few months of Chloe and Rhonda's love passed in a fog of passion. Not just the physical passion, which was there, but also the passion of absolutely appreciating another human being. They talked for hours, sharing every aspect of each other's lives, and ignored their wonderful friends. They had time only for each other.

They continued to edit the book and Chloe knew it was going to go places. Rhonda had the uncanny ability to capture people with words and created a background so vivid that Chloe started to dream scenes from the book. Rhonda was never defensive when Chloe suggested a change, but would fight to reject a change she didn't believe in. In that haze of new love, they were always honest but never argumentative. The magic threw a blanket over everything and, as they got close to the end of the work, they both felt sad they wouldn't be working together anymore.

"I'm going to miss this table," Rhonda said, as they sat for one of the last times in their "office."

"We can still come here," Chloe said, suddenly afraid the relationship would end when the book was done.

"Yes, we can. Do you want to?" Rhonda was always straightforward.

"I would sit at this table with you for the rest of my life. Happily," Chloe answered. It was true.

"I don't want to be without you, Chloe. Wanna move in with me?"

Chloe caught her breath and tears sprang to her eyes. "Of course I do," she managed to say.

◁▷◁▷◁▷

The ceremony was the best day of both their lives. It was in the garden at their house. Dani asked if she could host the thing and got decorators to outfit the garden. It didn't need any planting since Rhonda kept it looking gorgeous, but Dani brought a tent in, and small, beautiful, multi-colored lanterns strung from tree to tree. They made a plant arbor and laid out chairs on the small patch of lawn. Rhonda and Chloe made a little altar covered with everything important to them, a picture of their dog, a copy of the book they had made together, a poem from Rumi, a bowl of water, and a beautiful fabric underneath. They asked each person to bring something, a wish, a prayer, or a symbol of the relationship they hoped for the two women. Rami, a friend who was into all kinds of Buddhist stuff, was their sort of minister, although she didn't really resemble any minister either of them had ever known.

After Chloe and Rhonda walked in, she asked them to sit on two gorgeous pillows she had made for them out of rich, brocaded Indian print. She had each person in attendance walk by and touch each of their two heads at the same time, as a symbol of the joining between them. Then she lit incense and looked up to the sky with her eyes closed, asking for blessings for their union. Finally, after a very long time, she asked them to speak their vows to each other.

"I promise to honor you in every corner of my life, to be loyal, true. I promise to claim you and defend you and try, in every way I can, to support your life, your heart's desires, and greatest wishes. I promise to be your beloved regardless of what challenges us in this life. I am yours and you are mine."

When they had made their promises, she asked the group sprawled across the grass to promise too, to support them and the family they would create. Rami told the crowd that they must now be family for Rhonda and Chloe, filling in for Chloe's mother, who refused to acknowledge the beauty of her daughter's love. She said that no one knew the value of love like those who had to fight for the right to it, and so theirs was a love truer, stronger, purer, for the sacrifices they had made for it. Even Rhonda's family cried.

Then they partied! The food was delicious, the music was inspiring, and the champagne was plentiful. But what was more important was all the smiling, laughter, and pure joy they all felt.

When everyone had left, Chloe and Rhonda fell into their bed, exhausted and overjoyed. Rhonda turned to Chloe. "It was perfect," she said, her face open and full of love.

"Yes, almost," said Chloe. "Except my mother wasn't there." She looked at Rhonda then, with the same love in her eyes, but sad tears filled those eyes, too.

❧ ❧ ❧ ❧

Chloe and Rhonda were the first of their many friends to have a kid. As they were deciding they wanted to be parents, they spent endless hours talking about how to do it. Insemination, of course, but anonymous? Friend of a friend? What?

One day, Rhonda came home ready to bring something up. "Is now a good time?" she asked, a great habit she had of never assuming Chloe was free to talk. "Sure," Chloe replied, strangely nervous.

"I've been thinking about this biological father thing," she said, the words falling from her lips just a little slower than usual. "I have an idea I'm not sure you're gonna like." Long pause. "I want to know if you would consider asking my brother, Graham."

Chloe almost interrupted, freaked out by the whole idea. Rhonda had been so careful to respect her in the conversation, and Chloe decided she deserved a full hearing.

"I know it might seem a little weird, but the idea of our child being related to me physically too really means something. I know what you're going to say, why does biology matter at all, but you're the one who wants to be pregnant, to carry the baby. I know we'd love a kid we adopted exactly as much. Or a kid by an unknown father, that wouldn't matter either. But I don't know, Chloe, I trust my brother. He's already gonna be a great uncle. Why would I prefer someone I don't even know?"

Chloe could tell that she had thought about this a lot. Chloe was at a disadvantage, because Rhonda's idea had never once occurred to her. She wanted to be open-minded but she was finding it hard to imagine how she would feel, hanging out with Graham at every family event, every holiday, their child knowing him as both uncle and biological father. They had already decided they wanted someone they could identify, at least when their baby grew up. That conversation had been long too, and they had slowly evolved to the place where they were willing to take the chance. This was going a lot further.

"I'm a little worried it would feel like incest, Rhonda. He's my brother-in-law."

"That's ridiculous, Chloe, he'd be a donor, not really a father." Rhonda had broken in, unable to maintain her measured and reasonable approach to the conversation.

"Are you planning to force me into it?" Chloe's voice was tense, and she recognized they were closer to a fight than they usually went.

Rhonda made a quick exit, closing her lips to trap the words she knew she wouldn't be able to take back.

"So you're dropping a bomb and then leaving?" Chloe yelled, even though she knew that Rhonda had saved them both.

It was almost an hour later when Rhonda opened the door, walking quietly back into the house. She sat down next to Chloe, who wouldn't look at her at first. She sat a little too close, if Chloe was the judge, and then did the unthinkable and grabbed her hand. Chloe found she wasn't able to pull away.

"Damn you, I can't even stay mad at you!" she said, dropping her resolve to stay away the rest of the day in an instant.

"Chloe, I'm not going to force you into anything. I don't do that and when you act as if I do, it really pisses me off. But I can't let it go unless you really consider it. It feels right to me, but I've thought about it for a whole lot longer than you have, so take your own time. I'll do my best just to listen to what you're thinking unless you ask me for my opinion. I'm really only going to be satisfied if I know you've really thought about it."

It wasn't an easy thing to consider, but Chloe knew that Rhonda was asking for something fair. She scheduled a few sessions to talk with someone other than Rhonda and Emily absolutely got an earful. Slowly, over the next few months, she warmed to the idea. She wasn't going to sleep with Graham, so it wasn't really incest. What won her over in the end was the idea of a baby who looked like both of them. It was a little bit irresistible, once she tried it on.

☙❧❧❧

They asked Graham, who lived in Los Angeles, if they could come down and visit. They cooked him a great meal, brought a good bottle of wine, committing the unpardonable sin for Californians of making it French. Over dessert, Rhonda started in.

"Graham, we have something kind of big to ask. You ready, kid?"

He looked a little apprehensive. He poured another glass and settled into his couch. He fit some stereotypes that folks had about gay men, including his great sense of decor. He looked almost like a king in the beautiful chair, and Chloe wondered if their child would also look like royalty, assuming he said yes. "Yeah? What's that?"

"Well, you know we want to start a family, right?" He nodded. "We wondered if you would consider helping us to have the child."

"Help you how?" he said, looking sideways like he always did when he thought Rhonda was acting a little crazy.

"Like, be the bio dad," Rhonda continued.

Chloe wished there had been a way to capture the changes on Graham's face between that moment and the next time he spoke. Shock, turning to incredulity, to curiosity, and finally, an almost smile.

He said, "Let me think about it." He looked as close to pale as he was capable of. He made it very clear the conversation was over for now. He didn't get back in touch for a solid week.

He and Rhonda usually talked nearly every day – it always amazed Chloe how close Rhonda's family was – so they felt sure he was pissed or terrified. When he finally called back, he said, "I had to think it through. How will it be to be the uncle of my own child? Would I need him or her to know? Would it affect us as brother, sister, and sister-in-law? Well, I haven't figured all that out yet, but I do know that the answer is yes. I called as soon as I got clear. What's next?"

ล.ม.ม.ม.

It wasn't an easy thing to get Chloe pregnant long distance. Even though Oakland to LA was drivable or flyable, it was not always easy to pick up and go at the right moment. They went to a class to learn how to figure out when to try and how to insert the needleless syringe in the most pregnancy friendly way. Usually Rhonda and Chloe took time off and drove to LA. A few times, they flew. That last time, Graham came up. From then on, they always wondered if being more relaxed, not having to travel, made the difference.

Those many months, Chloe felt like she might be going crazy. She had to wait for something she just couldn't wait for. Minutes seemed like hours, hours days. Through it all, they helped each other, consoled each other when it didn't work, reassured each other. "Average time to get pregnant, six months." After six months had passed, it changed to, "that's *only* an average."

Rhonda told her parents eventually, just to explain why there was so much travel back and forth. Clarence and Fay walked around, from then on, in a state of perpetual anticipation, unable to contain their excitement.

They checked in a little too often, suddenly began calling Chloe out of the blue. "How are you feeling, dear?"

Rhonda felt a little claustrophobic. "Back off you guys." But Chloe loved it. She had been tentative in this family at first, finding every reason to expect them all to reject her.

About a year in, Fay called her one day and said, "Chloe, I think I've got to say something to you, and I just want you to listen, honey. I love you. I love you because Rhonda loves you but that happened when she told me you were it. What I want to tell you today is that I love you for you. You are my daughter, sure as Rhonda is, and if she were trying to hurt you, I'd be on *your* side. I don't want you to ever forget that. I wanted to tell you before you guys have kids together, so you won't think it's just about the kids. Well, that's it. Gotta go to my hair appointment now." And she promptly hung up. Chloe sat there for a very long time, smiling as the tears fell down her face, her neck, and into the collar of her shirt.

❧ ❧ ❧ ❧

The day Quinten was born, Chloe stayed in bed. Past her due date, the effort to cart herself around was getting to be a lot. She stayed in her silky robe, propped up on the twenty pillows that had slowly accumulated in the bed, and watched show after crummy show on

TV.

Now that she had lived with Rhonda for a few years, she could see why Rhonda was a success at writing. Nothing stopped her. She got up in the morning, drank coffee, chatted with Chloe for a few minutes if Chloe didn't have to leave early, then closed the door to the writing room and didn't open it again until the morning was over. She was serious.

Just this one day, Chloe wished she had made an exception. She wanted Rhonda right by her, and she didn't know why. She imagined the comfort of hearing the low noise of the TV and drifting into a short nap, waking to the smell of Rhonda around her. Although she still loved to make love to her wife, she sometimes thought she liked the casual way they wrapped themselves around each other in an everyday embrace better. Even when they fought, which wasn't often, Chloe was unable to imagine herself with anyone else. She felt solid and complete with Rhonda, although she would never say Rhonda completed her. They were just able to be whole with each other, to encourage each to be themselves.

Around ten, Rhonda made an unexpected appearance in the doorway of their room.

"Can't do it anymore!" she announced, bounding for the bed and nearly colliding with Chloe's enormous belly. When Chloe said, "don't leave me," she felt the first pang and took a deep breath, remembering all the practice she'd had getting ready for labor. It was time.

❧❧❧❧

Chloe had prepared for a long labor so when Quinten came fast, she found it startling. They had driven to the hospital a few hours after the labor started, expecting to be sent home. The contractions were only three to four minutes apart, which seemed awfully frequent, and the hospital was just a few miles down the road, so they took the chance.

Chloe found the glaring hallways a sharp contrast to their dimly lit, cozy house. The room, which they got her to fast, was decorated with baby prints and cheery paintings, but behind that, it was just a plain hospital room, filled with medical equipment and surgical supplies. "Can you turn the light down?" she asked, in a voice that could barely be heard. They put a towel over the lamp, and that was the last she thought about the environment.

She and Rhonda made a good team, breathing when the contractions came and resting in between. Rhonda had the whole room laughing with her baby jokes. "If the kid has eleven toes, just let us discover it ourselves!" "Hey, when the baby comes out, instead of saying whether it's a boy or girl, could you just say 'it's a human?'" The only one not enjoying herself completely was Chloe, and even she managed a weak laugh.

The longest part was pushing him out; a full hour that felt like a day! Chloe felt his head moving down through her, as if the world were, for once, all moving in the same direction. Rhonda's face was her focus point and, when it broke into a luminous smile, she finally heard the words. "Chloe! I can see the little head!"

The nurse handed her a mirror, which she almost refused. She was suddenly terribly afraid to see this little life coming out of her body. It seemed some sort of bizarre invention, suddenly not natural. Kindly but firmly, the nurse insisted, and she looked, with wonder, on the head, covered with curly dark hair, of her child.

Chapter Seven

Sally

Sal read the letter at least one hundred times. Could she read hatred, resentment, between the lines? Had she intruded, broken rules, made a bad situation worse? Because suddenly, Sal cared a whole lot about making things easier for her, for *them*, even. This nemesis, the nasty lesbian who had Sal's daughter, had gradually become someone Sal cared about, almost loved. She was there taking care of Chloe, when Sal had failed her.

Lonnie's office was bathed in light the day she arrived to share the letter with her. By this point, she always came in happy to be there, any shred of old objections gone. She'd sink into the sofa, and no longer pulled threads out of the embroidered pillow to avoid looking at her. She was more than comfortable; she felt at home.

"I got a letter!" she exclaimed, a little like a child who had suddenly discovered she's on her way to Disneyland.

"Can I read it?" Lonnie said, with nearly as much excitement in her voice.

That was the thing about her. Sal could tell she genuinely cared. A few months in, she realized that Lonnie was maybe the only person ever in her life who didn't have an agenda for her. Wherever she was at, there was Lonnie. Sometimes it made her think about how little of that her kids had gotten from her. But Lonnie had helped her learn to resist the urge to guilt herself about that. "Observe and learn," was her favorite expression.

She read the letter carefully, seeming to absorb every word with special attention. It took her a long time, and Sal thought she saw her start at the beginning again at least a couple times.

When she finished, she looked up and smiled at Sal in that knowing way. "Your daughter has done her work. She is something else."

Not that long ago, Sal might have felt criticized in some fuzzy, not quite definable way. There was none of that. There was almost a kind of pride. This woman, who Sal respected so much, admired her child, found her wise and "emotionally capable," another expression she loved. Although Sal knew she had not fostered this in Chloe, still, she felt a strange and personal sense of accomplishment. This amazing person had come through her.

༄ ༄ ༄ ༄

Sal was jumping out of her skin the night of the dinner party. In those two weeks, it was a physical torture to wait, knowing she'd see her. Still, she knew she had some preparing to do. She knew she was eager, but not ready. The feeling reminded her, in reverse, of the two years it took to get the divorce done. Stan was a constant pain in her side, every time they had to communicate an agony of anticipation, fury, and recovery. Even though this time she was waiting for something she hoped would be a good thing, she still felt as if each moment could have been a year.

Sal made extra appointments with Lonnie, putting it on her credit card. She told Lonnie she needed help to figure out how to handle it, but really, it was because the hours with her were the only relief from the endless wait. On her couch, Sal felt as if everything would be all right, even good, and the grip in the pit of her stomach eased for the moment.

The second appointment, she asked Sal, "So, going it alone or taking someone?" As usual, she betrayed no opinion on the matter, but Lonnie was letting her know she thought Sal ought to think about it.

"Lonnie, I don't know who in the hell I would take except maybe you."

She smiled, accepting the compliment while letting Sal know they were going to keep it in the office. They had already talked about her maybe having a couple times with the two of them if they needed it, and she wasn't going to complicate that by coming and meeting everyone in Chloe's life.

"What about your sister?" she asked, even though she knew how complicated all that was. If it had been when Sal first met her, that would have made her mad, but now Sal knew she only suggested it because she wanted her to have someone to support her.

"I feel like it's going to be worse if someone's there with their opinions. Maybe I'll just go it alone. I just plain don't feel close enough to anyone to ask them."

Lonnie left a space in the conversation then. She did that sometimes, to allow things to settle in or because she was considering what she wanted to say. It seemed a little longer than usual this time.

"Okay, let's talk about how you want to be when you go. Open and friendly, protected, however you feel at the time?"

Sal hadn't thought at all about what it would be like to actually be there, at Chloe's house. She'd been all about going, getting there, seeing her. The terror of really having to talk to people, eat food, smile, shake hands started to sink in. She imagined it would feel more comfortable to face a firing squad! She started feeling a little tremor that rose up through her body, settling in her hands. Sal had a moment of regret. Lonnie had helped her learn to pay attention to what happened in her body.

"Well, I guess I just don't know." This time it was Sal's turn to take a long pause.

"What's it usually like for you when you meet new people?"

❧❧❧❧

What a question! The only time Sal could remember meeting new people in the past few decades was when she started the Daily Grind job. That had been rough. She only managed to get through the interview because she was desperate. The manager was about half her age, and Sal just pretended she was one of her misbehaving kids when they were about twelve. Sal kept picturing herself telling her maybe boss to go to her room and it kind of took the edge off. She hoped the manager read it as confident.

When her first day of work came, terror rose up through her body. She learned the job with no trouble but talking to the customers didn't come easy. Randy, the friendliest counter person there, took her aside in the first week.

"Want some pointers?" he said, and she almost refused, even though she could tell he was just being nice. He made his gayness so obvious to everyone in the place and, of course, Sal had a problem with that at the time. On the other hand, she knew she wasn't going to keep the job if she kept barking at people.

"You are in the business of giving tons of people their first pleasure of the day. They want to be happy, but they are in a rush and they haven't had that wonderful cup of coffee yet. All you have to do is smile and be more awake than they are. In half a second, they are going to be grateful."

He put a hand on Sal's shoulder then, very comforting, and in spite of herself, Sal started to like him. When she found out about Chloe, she told him a little, that one of her kids was sick. Never about the other stuff. He was sympathetic. He told her he had an older friend, closest thing to a father in his life, who was really sick with AIDS and he went after work every day to cheer him up.

It occurred to Sal that if she didn't need to tell him why she had to reunite with her child, why they had lost each other, he probably would have gone to dinner with her. Then she busted out laughing as she said to Lonnie, "That would be kinda like 'Guess Who's Coming to Dinner' in reverse!"

Chapter Eight

Chloe

Chloe and Rhonda spooned on the hospital bed, trying to rest while the baby slept. Rhonda went out like a light, exhausted from the intensity. Chloe was wide awake, so happy and at the same time aware that her mother would miss this too.

It would have been the most natural thing in the world to share the baby with her mom. Back before the divorce, Mom had been great with kids, before she became bitter and lonely. Chloe remembered a time when she was about ten. Sal offered to take her neighbor's kid for the weekend. They piled in the car and took the winding road to Santa Cruz. This was before Chloe's dad left, when she paid very little attention to her parent's marriage. Her world was her mother, with her dad weaving in and out without changing things much unless he and her mom had a fight. So it wasn't any big deal to go down without him. What was different was that all her siblings were busy with other things, sleepovers and parties, so it was just her and Anna, the neighbor kid.

Her mom got them singing in the car, "Mares Eat Oats" and "Does Your Chewing Gum Lose Its Flavor on the Bedpost Overnight." Neither of them knew the songs were from a long ago time. They sang happily mile after mile, repeating the songs at least fifty times.

Sal showed no signs of impatience, listening as if she was hearing the music for the first time, occasionally joining in.

When they got to the pier, it was packed. Sal took them straight to the ticket window, buying them each an all-day pass. Chloe was used to the hawk eye mom right next to her, making her hold hands way past the point when she knew not to run into the street. She got herself ready to argue, to say they could go off on their own, they were old enough, *c'mon* Mom!

"Okay. Here's how it's gonna go. I'm going to go lay on that beach right there. You're going to watch me go so you know where I am. You are not going to leave each other, under any circumstances. Every hour, you are going to come down and let me know you're fine. If you can catch my attention from up here, fine. Otherwise, walk on down. If you miss a check-in, I will follow you the rest of the day."

Chloe and Anna ran off the moment Sal planted herself on the beach, putting up the umbrella and pulling her book out of the bag. They didn't want to give her any time to change her mind. Even though the pier was packed, they could work in at least two rides an hour. They rode the water roller coaster at least ten times, coming off and getting in line again over and over. When they had a choice, they chose the car that splashed into the water at the bottom of the roll, leaving them soaked and overjoyed. They were not going to mess with Mom, so they checked in, as demanded, every hour. The delicious taste of first-time freedom made them more responsible, determined to prove that freedom had been offered way past the time they could have handled it.

As the evening came, they piled down to the

beach and ate sandwiches Sal had brought, tasting so delicious to them after all that excitement and exercise. After a short swim in the bitter cold ocean, she sent them back up with money for a treat, and they chose cotton candy, sticky and sweeter than sweet, pink for Chloe and blue for Anna.

When they got into the car, they slumped to the middle of the back seat and slept that way, leaned into each other with their mouths open. Chloe remembered opening her eyes once and saying, "That was fun, Mommy," and then sliding back into a delicious dream, waking the next day magically in her bed.

Chloe wondered why that memory attacked her now, lying in bed with the woman she loved and her beautiful little boy. Why was she even thinking of her mother, whom she had learned to live without, claiming her life for herself? Someone looking in from the outside might have been able to say that every major life event pours gasoline on grief, painting in vivid color the picture of what is missing. Chloe wasn't able to see that for herself. In that moment, she cried quiet tears for the mother who had chosen to miss all of this.

❧ ❧ ❧ ❧

Rhonda took a maternity leave of her own making, languishing day after day in the love of Quinten, their son. They gazed for hours, whether he was eating, or sleeping, or staring at them, a head on top of a body he could not control. She had given herself a month of no writing, the longest break she had taken since childhood, and she stuck to it, now disciplined in the opposite direction. Chloe began to wonder if she would go back to writing but laughed at herself not one moment after she had the thought. Imagining Rhonda giving up writing was impossible. She would never give it up. It was essential to her, almost as much as Chloe was.

A week before she had planned to, Rhonda quietly headed for her office during naptime. Chloe and Quinten had fallen asleep after feeding, Chloe in the bed and Quinten in the little sleeper they had attached to the bed. Rhonda looked at her family, satisfied with life, and then went and put an hour in. It was bliss. When she came back, and Chloe was awake, she read her the result. A blog about their new baby, about being a couple and all the things she was thinking and feeling. It was the most personal piece of writing Chloe could remember ever coming out of her.

"All of a sudden, I want to write about my own life," she said, rewarded with a kiss Chloe leaned forward to offer.

※ ※ ※ ※

They didn't want Quinten in childcare, so they rearranged their schedules and took care of him themselves. Rhonda wrote from seven to ten a.m., pulling herself away from his delightful smiles and coos, and when he was a little older, hugs and kisses. Chloe set up an office in the living room, able to do most of her work from home. When Chloe couldn't get it all done at home, she went into the office in the afternoon. April didn't see any harm in being flexible, since Chloe was one of her best editors, as well as being the most popular with her writers. She knew what happy employees produced for her, so she let Chloe do it her own way. They set up a portable crib in Chloe's office, for the times she needed to come for a meeting and bring Quinten.

The only problem was whether the other editors, including April herself, were likely to get anything done with that baby around. As soon as he came through the door, a riot of excited adults congregated, waiting for turns at holding him. He did not disappoint, offering smiles, coos, and little giggles to one and all. They took to calling the office Disneyland, because if a child was this delighted from the moment he came through the door, this must be an amusement park.

⁂

Every first Friday of the month, Emily came over and watched Quinten so Rhonda and Chloe could have a night out. She had started the practice about three months in, over the protests of his parents, who insisted they weren't ready to leave him, only half implying that he wasn't old enough.

"No," she said, in that emphatic way she had, "I know a lot of parents and they all get really unhappy together a few years in unless they get to remember what they like about each other."

The first few times, they sat quietly after saying everything they could think to say about Quinten. They insisted Emily send pictures; Quinten eating dinner, Quinten in the tub, Quinten reading his night night book, Quinten tucked into bed. They watched their cell phones, running home when they figured the time was long enough to seem like they'd really gone out. That was less than two hours the first time, and Emily looked at them as if they were lame, but she packed her stuff up and left anyway.

Six months in, they settled into a keen enjoyment of this oasis of time together in the sea of baby time. They began to remember what it was like to talk for endless hours and hear everything each of them had to say about life. On the blackboard calendar up on the kitchen wall, they listed upcoming events and their date night was all caps. They began to occasionally go out on other nights, asking Rhonda's parents or their other friends to come over. A time or two, they even dropped him off at Emily's, letting go of the reins they held so tight at the start.

They were ready to plan a night out of town about six months in. Emily knew how to put Quinten to bed, feed him, and make him laugh. Rhonda's parents were great too, but living all the way out in Palo Alto, they thought Emily would be a good first choice. They weren't going to tell anyone else; why inspire jealousy?

They rented a cabin in Inverness, a place where they had spent many happy weekends looking out over the inlet, taking rides to the lighthouse and the beach. They packed two small overnight bags, the lightest they had travelled since the baby, and jumped in the car, Indigo Girls on the player, Power of Two.

✢✢✢✢

"Wow, what a dinner," Rhonda exclaimed as they came back to their little cabin. They had been ready for this. No lack of things to talk about and plenty of flirting across the table. They had eaten more than usual, fish, greens, and crème brûlée for dessert, savoring the food and the Pinot Noir their waiter had recommended. Chloe thought she could get used to this, having Rhonda to herself. She had forgotten that look in her beloved's eyes, as if she were a gift greater than gold. She knew she was looking back with the same fierce love. They were barely back in their cottage before their clothes came off and they fell on top of the bed, enjoying the touch of skin to skin, savoring the luxury of knowing they wouldn't be interrupted.

☙☙☙☙

Before the baby, they had shared a fear that parenthood would end sex. Although they were close in many ways other than physical, they loved that part of their relationship and they hadn't wanted to lose it. Of course, things had changed. First, there was the end of the pregnancy, when Chloe felt like a manatee stretched across their bed and could hardly imagine exerting the energy it would require to make love. Then, as they should have expected, the healing process. That was so much harder than they'd both anticipated.

After that, though, the only difference was a severe lack of spontaneity. They got used to planning their rendezvous, leaving notes for each other. "Tonight? After he goes down?" Sometimes, it felt as if they were having a secret love affair. Other times it was a necessary plan. They knew, always, that it was important.

They woke up the next day curled around each other after a sound sleep. They kissed, waking each other up the way they always had in the years before their first thought in the morning was, "He's awake. You or me?"

They had enough time to be lazy and cook the

food that the cottage manager left at the door – the
fresh brown eggs, homemade bread, pungent berries,
tea, and coffee. They planned to stop on the way back
for lunch, so they took the slow road, exploring, not for
the first time, the coastline on the way to San Francisco.
They stopped for lunch near Half Moon Bay, happy to
find a place with a view of the ocean.

Halfway through the meal, Chloe began to look
contorted. Rhonda kept an eye on her, waiting to see
what was up, but when Chloe didn't bring it up herself,
Rhonda had to ask.

"What's up, Petunia?" Chloe would never
understand how she had gotten that name, but she had
grown to love it.

"Oh, nothing…" she started, trailing off instead
of continuing.

"You are the worst liar I have ever known,"
Rhonda said, almost laughing but a little too worried
to go for it.

"I'm really *really* liking being alone with you, so
it seems weird I'm thinking what I'm thinking but I'm
thinking it…"

The look on Rhonda's face reminded Chloe of
those unreadable, penetrating looks she got when they
first met. The silence was long, and Chloe knew very
well Rhonda wasn't going to break it.

"How would you feel about another baby
sometime soon?"

Rhonda's broad smile said it all.

Chapter Nine

Sally

At the start of the two longest weeks of Sal's life, time felt empty and crowded all at once. She knew she wasn't ready for what was about to happen, but she didn't know if she could *get* ready either. She was less and less comfortable with her hermit life, wishing she had stayed in touch with friends, gotten out more. It was sort of weird that she felt the loneliest at work, when she was around hundreds of people. She had long since learned how to seem like she was okay whether she was or not, but that didn't help the empty space in the pit of her stomach.

She kept it up that way for the first week, but then it fell apart. She'd gone outside for her break and was sitting there with a coffee when racking sobs that she couldn't control overtook her. They moved through her body like a wildfire, burning her up.

Her own wracking sobs were so loud that she didn't hear Randy coming up behind her. Before she knew it, he had wrapped her in his very long arms from behind, something she would usually pull away from, but at that moment, she sunk into the embrace, surrendering to someone, anyone, offering a physical balm for this terrible emergency.

"What's up, girl?" he said, real concern showing in his voice. How could she tell this man, who had been nothing but kind to her, what the problem was? He would be sure to take it personally, feel rejected by her bad opinion of people like him. Still, she didn't really know how to get out of explaining in some way. She cried it out and then took a stab at it.

"I'm going to apologize in advance, Randy. This isn't gonna make me look good. I haven't seen my daughter for ten years, my choice, because she's a lesbian. And now, as you know, she's sick. Cancer! And I'm trying to make it right with her and I'm invited to dinner and I'm not even close enough to anyone to tell them all this and I'm afraid to go alone and I feel like such a terrible person for being like I was. Not to mention everything I've missed; her wedding, her kids being born, knowing what's going on in her life. I just don't know how I'm going to face all that alone. Really..."

"How about if I go?" Randy said, casual, but warm.

"You'd do that for someone as evil as me?" she said.

He answered, "It's not how long you think wrongly, it's how hard you work to change. I admire you more now, Sal."

Before Sal knew it, she was bawling again, hardly seeing the surprised pedestrians walking past the crazy lady in front of the Daily Grind, losing it.

ৰ৶৶৶৶৶

Sal thought long and hard before she said yes to Randy. Would it seem like she was bringing the only gay person in her life to look cooler? Would she end up embarrassed in front of him when she wasn't able to be the person she should be, when she was awkward and inept? She started to wish she had kept the whole thing to herself and not shared it.

Lonnie spent almost a whole hour playing it out with her. She said Sal didn't have to close her eyes, but it might be easier to imagine if she did.

"Okay. You're walking up to the door, just you, climbing the steps. You ring the bell, and Rhonda answers. You're not sure at first if it's her but she tells you who she is. You can't tell how she feels about you being there. You come in and meet a dozen people you've never met before and you are seated at the table, across from Chloe. After dinner, you all sit around the living room together, thinking of things to talk about. Okay, now take as long as you like to register how your body reacts. What's it like for you to go alone?"

Sal took her time, really trying to imagine that she was at Chloe's house, with her friends, having dinner. Her belly was tight, her throat closed, with a tingling in her fingers. She was not able to get comfortable in her body.

"All right, Sal, now let's try it this way. You're coming up to the door, Randy is right behind you, you're knocking, and Rhonda opens it…"

It was so remarkably clear how much better that felt. There was a warm sense of comfort rising up through her, and all her objections seemed silly and irrelevant. She was amazed that this thing really worked. The decision was easy. After the session, she stopped in at the Daily Grind and took Randy aside. "I want to take you up on your offer."

❧❧❧❧

Sal had come to love the walks that Lonnie

suggested she take. At first, they had been a terrible burden, something she had to force herself to endure. Over time, they became such a pleasure that it was hard to remember a time she hadn't loved them.

Her favorite walk was down by the Emeryville Marina, past the docks to the path by the Bay, where San Francisco stretched out across the water like a magical glistening quilt of buildings. She'd trek from one end to the other and think her thoughts, walking at a good clip and greeting the other walkers.

Sometimes the walkers seemed to be part of a secret society. She called them The Walkers in her mind, as if they had all been especially invited to be a part of this exclusive club. She still got surprised that the thoughts in her head had slowly turned from sour and resentful to optimistic and supportive. She was long past the point where she fought with the negative ideas her mind could produce, but even when she heard the same old stern condemnation, she didn't believe it any more. They came, they went, and she smiled. She had invented a new friend inside of herself, who encouraged her and lifted her up, who reliably produced an alternative to dire predictions.

The morning after she asked Randy to come with her, though, she had a relapse. *This is going to be hell,* she thought, *they're all going to hate me. Why shouldn't they? I'm a bitch. A freak mother who rejected her child. I'm a loser.*

The acid tongue of that voice in her head shocked her, even though it had gone on unnoticed for so many years before that. The tyrannical voice went on and on, expressing every nasty thought about Sal she had refrained from thinking these past few months. Then, out of the blue, when she didn't know how she would bear it any more, she remembered something Lonnie had said a while back. "Take tea with the enemy, Sal. Invite them in, find out what makes them so mean. Make cartoon characters out of them. Why should *they* have all the fun? If the voices in your head sat behind you at dinner, you wouldn't be able to eat! You gotta learn to face up to them."

Just bringing Lonnie to mind helped a little. Sal got curious. "Why are they raking me over the coals right now?" The answer came, clear as a bell. "Don't worry, Sally, you're just scared."

By the end of the walk, calm had returned to her troubled mind and, still a little scared, she headed home.

❧❧❧❧

Del had been on Sal's mind ever since she got the letter, but she had lacked the courage to call her. When she called the Monday after the self-criticism crisis, Sal made herself pick it up. It was sinking in that avoiding a thing didn't make it go away, just made the pain go on longer.

"Del. Hi," she said, noncommittally.

"Hi, Sal, good to hear your voice!" Del sounded so chipper Sal wondered if she was high.

"A little bird told me you have something rather big coming up," she said, and Sal could see the smile through the phone wires.

"What little bird?" Sal asked, not putting it together right away what she was talking about.

"I was over at Chloe and Rhonda's last night for dinner," she said, almost beaming through the wires.

"She told you. Wow, I'm surprised. What did she

say?"

"Well, she said that she was scared and excited and glad her friends would be there."

"That's about how I feel, without the friend part."

"You're not going *alone,* are you?" she said, sounding sincerely shocked.

"I'm taking my friend from work. He offered." Even if it was a little true, Sal didn't want Del thinking she had rejected her as an option. These days, she didn't want to hurt her feelings.

"I can understand why you didn't ask me, but I really wish you'd consider me coming."

Adele had never asked Sal to consider *anything* with such a considerate tone of voice.

"Del, why would you want to come?"

In Sal's old life, she would have added something on the end, if only in her mind, like, "just to show me up, witness my humiliation?" but she didn't add that, and she felt embarrassed by her old self. Sal really wanted to know why Del wanted to come. It came as no small wonder that she didn't assume she knew why or even that it was a bad reason.

"Well, Sal, believe it or not, I love you, you old crusty thing, and I keep thinking how hard it must be to walk through that door. You must be really nervous, and I'm proud of you for doing it anyway. I'd like to be there to support you, sis."

Of all the possible reasons her sister would want to come with her to Chloe's house, this one would never have occurred to her. She wanted to come because she loved her? That would not have crossed her mind. Maybe even a bigger surprise, Sal believed her. She had no ulterior motive, no hidden agenda, just a loving thought.

"I really appreciate that. Wow, that's really great. Can I think about it?"

"Sal, you can think about it up to and including the day of. I'll leave the night open."

"Oh, I'll let you know before that."

When she got off the phone, she sat in her favorite chair, yes, the green one, drinking a cup of peppermint tea, savoring the quiet. Somehow hearing that her sister loved her brought a peaceful and relaxed attitude to her day, even in the midst of the endless preparation taking her towards Chloe. Maybe more remarkably, she began to bring to mind all the people she loved, some of whom she had yet to meet. Rhonda, the kids, their friends, all began to occupy an empty corner of her mind. For that one moment, all her judgements of her children, her sister, the people she worked with, the friends she used to know, each and every person in her life, fell away and, just for now, she was drenched in love. Lonnie was going to be shocked to hear *this*.

Chapter Ten

Chloe

Chloe and Rhonda thought they should start trying for another baby as quickly as they could. It had taken over a year to get pregnant with Quinten, and if it took that long again, the kids would be further apart than they wanted. They called Graham right away.

"We're ready for number two!" Rhonda cried, no prep, no nerves.

"Not this month, you're not! I just booked a part in a play I even like. I can't afford the nerves. Next month works. Guess I can't ask you to come for the play if you're gonna be up and down the coast for the next year. Damn!"

Graham lived at Manhattan Beach, walking distance to the pier, in a small but comfortable apartment. From the window, if he craned his neck a little, he could even see the water. He made most of his money posing for print ads, being the beautiful man that he was, but his true love was theater. He had to take every part that came his way, since they were few and far between. He wrote plays for small theaters just to act now and then, but he was beginning to build a reputation for his poetic words and lovable characters. He and Rhonda shared a gift for words that Chloe hoped was genetic.

"We'll talk about it; maybe we can come down," Rhonda said, without thinking. It made Chloe tired to think about it, but she knew it was important for Rhonda that they keep the relationship she had always had with her brother. Rhonda didn't want to lose that because of the children and, when it came down to it, Chloe didn't either.

∿∿∿∿

They went down for the last weekend of the show, arriving a few days before so they could enjoy the beach, eat good meals, vacation a little. The night they got in, with Graham at the theater, they walked the pier, holding hands as the rosy sun dipped below the glistening water. An excited child pedaled his bike down the pier, almost running them over.

"It's a whale. A *whale!*" He whisked by them, on his way to the end. Before long, everyone on the pier was running down, catching sight of the whale and her baby, dipping and spouting in the water.

Chloe had forgotten how much she loved this place, associating it instead with the strained affair of inviting pregnancy. Down here just to visit, and without Quinten – Emily deserved a prize for best aunt – reawakened all the times she and Rhonda had come here to take advantage of Graham's LA life, meeting interesting people, and laying out on the beach for hours at a time, with nothing else to do and nowhere to be.

When Graham came back around nine, he met them at the best wine bar in town, Viti Culture, and they ordered a bottle, talking on and on about Quinten's huge smiles and attempts at crawling, and the sales of Rhonda's book, making the big splash they had all expected it to.

After a few hours, Graham said, "So what's the schedule like these days?" and they both knew he was talking about ovulation. Neither of them had ever come close to having a man be this aware of their cycles, and it was a little weird. On the other hand, it was so amazing that he thought of it on his own.

"Well, it's happening in a few days, so next month around the same time?"

Chloe had made a deal with herself not to mention her fertility this weekend, even if she was eager to get started.

Graham took a long pause, a nod the only sign he had heard.

"I guess we should just go ahead and try then. Shit, you're here."

ᴥᴥᴥᴥ

Even though Chloe and Rhonda were thrilled by the turn of events, they didn't expect anything to come of it. It had taken so long with Quin that instantaneous conception was out of the question in their minds. So when Chloe's period never arrived, they didn't register right away that it meant anything, getting frustrated they couldn't try again. Chloe was almost two months pregnant before they pulled out the pregnancy test and confirmed what they later thought should have been obvious.

When they called Graham, he said, "Wow, that's as close as I'll ever get to knocking someone up!"

And Chloe chimed in, "And that's as close as I'll ever get to *being* knocked up!"

That first week after the baby was confirmed, they walked through their lives, dazed. They had prepared for a long wait, protecting themselves in advance from the disappointment that had almost sunk them with Quinten. Chloe found herself lying in bed, just as exhausted this time around, staring at the Mary Cassat print on their wall, Mother and Child, an hour going by before she noticed the time passing. She couldn't have described where her mind went during these times, just that a kind of dazed joy overcame her.

Of course, that was during the hours when Quinten slept. When he was awake, he slowed down not at all to accommodate his mothers' levels of energy. At only a little older than one, he was running more than walking, exploring the small world of their cozy house with relish.

His little hands picked things up if they were left out. Their phones were his favorite, and they often had to conduct a search before they left the house. They tried never to turn the bells off, so they could call each other to find the phones in a hurry. More than once, they found a phone in the toy box, almost as if he had buried it for later. Then they made jokes about having brought a puppy into the world. They found his fascination so delightful that it was hard to unearth a stern look to send his way. They acknowledged they might be sending the wrong message, but could hardly hold back their desire to make him happy.

For those delightful hours with him, they were almost distracted from the inspiring actuality of another baby. Then all at once, Chloe would think, *two?* It was so hard to picture loving another baby as much as she loved him. Still, she never doubted that she would.

❧❧❧❧

They nearly didn't make it to the hospital when Arisa was born. Chloe had spent the day lounging, the first day after her maternity leave began. She slept late and made herself a good breakfast, while Rhonda played with Quinten. This time, Rhonda had started her maternity leave at the same time as Chloe, so writing was not on the table today.

In Chloe's dreamy, half-asleep world, their laughter broke through, a happy chaos of blocks tumbling and that push button doggie guitar, playing Quinten's favorite song over and over. "How much is that doggy in the window arf arf."

As Rhonda and Quin headed off to the kitchen for Quin's cereal and Rhonda's eggs, Chloe's sleep deepened, and she dreamed she was in a canoe, sailing down the Russian River, sun on her back and water lapping up on her legs. She passed sunbathers along the shores, basking in the late summer warmth, playing rock music on their little mp3 players. She looked down and saw that a miniature baby, just a few inches long, lay in a basket at the bottom of the boat. Perfectly formed, she looked up at Chloe, smiled a cheeky baby smile, and spoke!

"I can't wait, Mommy."

❧❧❧❧

Chloe awoke to a contraction, hitting hard and taking her breath away. She didn't move at first, riding it out in the cocoon of her pillows, breathing the same way she had for Quinten. When another came just a few minutes later, she picked up her phone and sent a message to Rhonda. This was something she made fun of her friends for doing, texting someone in the same house, but she made allowances in her current situation.

Rhonda came fast, as fast as she could without alarming their little man. He was absorbed with climbing on and off his little red fire truck and hardly noticed she left the room.

They rarely left him alone in a room, but Rhonda wasn't going to wait to check in with Chloe. When she saw her wife's face, she knew they were headed for the hospital. She sat down on the only available corner of the bed, the rest covered with pillows, and found Emily's number on her phone. "Hi, Emily, Rhonda here. How quick can you get here?"

Emily tore out of work, but then hit traffic. By the time she arrived, Quinten was down for a morning nap and Rhonda and Chloe were sitting on the sofa, breathing together through a long contraction. Emily glanced at the clock and was terrified to notice that the next one came just two minutes later.

"Get out of here, you guys!" she said, a little louder than she intended. There was no moving fast, since Chloe stopped progress every few minutes to stand and breathe. By the time they arrived at the hospital, Chloe had that look that Rhonda remembered from the first birth; she was ready!

"This baby is coming *now*," she told the nurse, hoping they would not take their time, that they would believe her.

"Come on in, honey, we'll check you out right away."

The nurse reminded Rhonda of her mother, solid

and enveloping with her "honeys" and "sweethearts." She led them to a birthing room and got Chloe up on the table, checking her progress.

"Ooh, this one was almost a bungee baby!" she said, somehow comforting them with the alarming words.

"What's that?" Rhonda said cautiously, not sure she wanted to know.

"Well, it's the kind that comes out so fast it almost bounces on the floor because Mom hasn't made it to the bed." They managed weak laughter, and then it was all business. Arisa was born in under an hour, beautiful and alert, staring at her mommies, and taking her first drink of milk. Now Chloe knew exactly what it was to love another child as much as she loved Quinten.

༄ ༄ ༄ ༄

With Arisa, Chloe took six months off. She and Rhonda wanted to guide their children into a close relationship. Maybe it was a little more important to Chloe, since Rhonda took her love for her brother somewhat for granted. Chloe always felt at odds with her own siblings, finding it hard to believe they'd all grown up in the same family.

When they were small, Chloe shepherded her siblings almost like a mother. They adored her and wanted to follow her everywhere and she let them, sometimes encouraged them. She played endless board games, even though they needed help. "What's a railroad again?" "Why do I have to go to jail?" "Do I have enough money for a hotel?" and she let them win to build their confidence.

Even in her teens and early twenties, they

continued to come to her for advice and stayed with her when they fought with her parents, since she left home at eighteen and they were all younger. Her favorite advice was, "Come in under the radar. Then you can do what you want without a fight."

It wasn't exactly that they disappeared from her life when she came out, but things were never the same. When she saw them, they shifted from foot to foot, uncomfortable and awkward. When she asked them about their lives, girlfriends, boyfriends, they stepped to the side of the questions. She couldn't get much out of them, even though in earlier days they had run to her to figure out what they should do next.

Once she said to Chase, after she had asked him whether he was seeing anyone, and his reply was dodgy, "Chase, being attracted to women hasn't really changed my ability to give advice; hell, I might have *better* advice for you. You know, been there, done that." He just snorted and then shut off, exposing nothing of whatever was, or wasn't, going on in his head.

They'd come around a little bit more when Quinten was born, almost as if they were going to become involved aunts and uncles, but it had trailed off quick. She imagined her mother resenting them for continuing to see her and said to Sal, in her head, "nothing to resent here." Her own disappointment had made Quinten and Arisa's life as brother and sister almost as important to her as her own parenting. So, she kept an eye on them, helped them to help each other.

Quinten took to his new role as big brother naturally. Even in his little two-year-old body, he found ways to include this new human curiosity. If Arisa was laying in Chloe's lap, he toddled over and patted her head, softly and rhythmically, making little cooing noises in her ear. Other times he rubbed her arm through her pajamas, waking her up to crow and murmur at her.

Quinten was the first one Arisa smiled at, just a day after she turned four weeks. He was bobbing his head back and forth, making noises from deep in his throat, dancing to a song on Disney Radio. She looked right at him and smiled, her lips seeming to expand to cover her whole face. He was delighted, dancing even harder to please her.

◄◄◄◄

As each new day added itself to the last, Chloe and Quinten, Arisa and Rhonda found new ways to love each other. Rhonda began devoting the last half hour of her writing time to little children's stories, written to amuse her own children. Chloe, who had always loved drawing tiny humans with colored marker, drew pictures to go along and they made miniature books out of the stories. Even at a few months, Arisa loved the stories, reaching out to touch the bright drawings and laughing when her parents reached her favorite words.

The house filled to the brim as they added toddler toys to baby toys, blankets on the floor for Arisa to have tummy time on, boxes that contained endless items their friends and Rhonda's family could not resist bringing every time they visited.

Graham had been busy with a movie when Quinten was born, barely able to get time to come meet him. With Arisa, he was between projects and came up often, having spent some real energy imagining what made someone a perfect uncle. He got down on the floor with the kids, let Quin climb on him – Chloe and Rhonda called him Jungle Graham instead of Jungle Gym – and fell asleep down there with Arisa splayed across his muscled chest. Sometimes Rhonda and Chloe would go take a little nap, sleeping or not, and they knew the kids were in good hands.

When Ari was about six months, Graham was up for a few days and they took advantage of the moment to lock their door. They made love sweetly and slowly, knowing he would watch the kids as long as they liked, kissing and smiling, Chloe petting Rhonda's face as she liked to do.

They didn't rush up, but lay together under the covers, happy for this moment. Rhonda stroked the top of Chloe's breast, enjoying the feel of the soft skin under her fingers. Without warning, she sat straight up and looked Chloe full in the eye. "Have you felt that lump in your breast?" she asked, alarm in her voice.

"What are you talking about?" Chloe said, still drifting on a cloud of satisfaction. Rhonda took her hand and led it to the hard, little bump, right near the nipple, unmistakable. "Wow, I never felt that! I'm sure it's nothing."

"Make an appointment, Chloe, it's nothing to mess around with!" Rhonda urged, and Chloe promised she would.

❧ ❧ ❧ ❧

The doctor's office was not like the one Chloe had visited when she was getting ready to have her kids. She hadn't gone to her internist for quite a while, feeling as if the pregnancy visits and then the well-baby visits were all she could manage. So, when she walked into Dr. Drew's office, she was unprepared for how stark it was. The furniture was the kind of garden variety Naugahyde that matched her picture of the fifties.

The wait seemed abnormally long, even though she wasn't feeling concerned. She was irritated that she was wasting all this time. She had become intent on conserving her time; as little work as possible, full on, and the rest for her family. Even paying the bills had become an imposition.

Waiting to hear that everything was fine got under her skin. She knew that she would have pushed just as hard if she had felt a lump in Rhonda's breast, but it still got on her nerves. Sometimes having someone this concerned about your being well was a pain in the ass.

She had insisted on coming alone. At least she could insist on that. Rhonda had been unhappy about it. She was a believer in support at health appointments. They had gone to all appointments together since the early days of being a couple.

"They take better care of you when you have someone there," she always said. "Besides, an extra pair of ears never hurts."

Chloe had never minded. She did remember things better when Rhonda was along, and she had frequently depended on Rhonda's memory, especially for the kids' ultrasounds.

"Did they say she was the right size? How many weeks did they say I am?" and Rhonda always had a crystal-clear memory.

If she had stopped to ask herself why she didn't want Rhonda to come to this appointment, she might have discovered that she was scared, already knowing somewhere deep within her that there was something wrong. Contrary to her own instincts, when Rhonda complained about her wanting to go it alone, she just said, "I know it's nothing and I don't want to make a big deal. Just stay home with the kids. I'll feel better." She knew that Rhonda couldn't go against her feeling better.

The nurse, who seemed disinterested and a little bored, led her into the exam room.

"Strip from the waist up and put this on. You can leave everything on from the waist down."

Then she was gone in a flash.

Chloe took off her shirt and her bra and put on the blue paper shirt that was laying on the cold leather exam table. It crossed her mind that this was no way to treat people who might be sick, and she thought she should do something about the terrible state of health care, since she wasn't sick herself.

Dr. Drew came in, warm but a little removed.

"Hello, Chloe. I haven't seen you in quite a while, have I?"

"No, doctor, I've been busy having babies."

"Congratulations! How old are they? I missed that chapter!"

They spent a few moments catching up, mostly about Chloe, everything that had happened in her life. Even in this impersonal room, waiting for good or bad news, the beauty of her life inspired her. Her wife, her kids, her friends. Still, always, her missing mother. Would she have wanted to come on this visit? Would Chloe have let her?

"Okay, Chloe. Let's see what's going on." Dr. Drew began the exam.

When Chloe pulled up to the house, she wasn't ready to go inside. Dr. Drew had been gentle when she delivered the news. "We need to check this out, Chloe."

Chloe wasn't ready to consider that this might really be something. She sat in the car, preparing to be positive. Rhonda knew her inside and out. If she were showing any worry, Rhonda would know. She wasn't ready for that.

She walked quietly into the living room, hoping for a moment of seeing them before they saw her. A view of them, Rhonda and the kids, on the floor rolling around together, rewarded her. She stood in the doorway, afraid to move and let them hear she was there. They were playing a pretend game, Rhonda in their crawl tunnel, peeking at them on the other side. Quinten was old enough to crawl through, screaming for his mother, excited because he could crawl at a good clip towards her. Arisa sat on the other side, chortling until they came through to her.

"I'm going to get you," Rhonda cooed, inviting Quin to get her instead.

Part of him ran towards her through the tunnel, and at the same time part of him hung back. Finally, he crawled towards her, ready to be caught up in the arms of love. They tumbled together, just outside the tunnel, a pile of pleasure with Ari crawling on top of them.

Arisa finally caught sight of Chloe, standing at the edge of their moment. "Ma ma ma ma," she sang, raising her arms towards her mother. She seemed about ready to cry, but close to laughter at the same time. Chloe ran to them and fell into the pile of delight her family made there on the floor. "I love you guys," she said, covering them with kisses.

☙☙☙☙

As hard as Chloe tried to hide it, Rhonda knew there was cause for worry. When the kids went down for nap, blessedly at the same time today, she sat close to Chloe on the sofa and asked what the doctor had said.

"It's probably nothing but just to be on the safe side, she wants me to have a biopsy."

Rhonda was sure that was not what Dr. Drew had said. She could tell by the pinched lines around Chloe's mouth and the stoop to her shoulders that the doctor was worried. She considered insisting that Chloe tell her the whole story but thought better of it. She already knew this was trouble, and it seemed like Chloe needed to imagine it wasn't for a little while longer. She was going to fight for one thing, though.

"Petunia, I can't let you go alone any more. It's too hard on me." She waited for an objection from Chloe, assuming she would have a fight on her hands, and willing to keep fighting until Chloe relented. She was not going to let Chloe go it alone.

"Good, because now that I'm scared, I don't want to do it without you." Chloe answered, and they sat on the sofa holding hands for the rest of their children's napping. Chloe heard her own heartbeat, loud in her chest, punctuating the quiet space. Rhonda took deep breaths, trying not to disturb the stillness that would soon be replaced with children's noises.

☙☙☙☙

Rhonda and Chloe's friend, Evita, was the best internet researcher they knew. The next day, Rhonda called her.

"Evita, we need some health research and you can't tell anyone else. Okay?" She let Evita know what was going on and that they wanted to go to the surgeon's office with plenty of information about the possible options.

When it came to pregnancy, Chloe had been a sponge for information. She read everything she could get her hands on, sometimes more than once, hungry for knowledge about what was happening in her body, what size her children were at any given moment, what she could expect during labor, how to prepare. She was the same now with their development. She already knew what she should be looking for before their pediatrician visits. Sometimes she was better informed than their Nurse Practitioner, asking questions the NP couldn't answer on the spot, but had to go research.

When it came to cancer, though, she could not get herself to find the answers herself. In the first few days after the visit to her internist, she tried to read up on what she was facing, but the feeling was too close to burning herself with a hot coal. She could barely get through a paragraph. She was usually so oriented to reading about everything that this came as a shock. Rhonda reminded her that when Dani had had cancer a few years back, she had a similar surprising reaction and wasn't able to read anything. They had done all the research for her and then shared the results. Chloe found herself wishing Dani had had breast cancer instead of cervical so that she would already have known everything Chloe needed to. Uncharacteristically, she was relieved when Rhonda took it out of her hands and asked Evita to help. She spent her time playing with the kids when they were awake and watching endless television when they slept. She didn't want even a moment to think.

Even listening to all the information Evita found exhausted her. It seemed like she was learning a new language. There was a fine needle aspiration biopsy (FNAB), a core needle biopsy (CNB), a stereotactic core needle biopsy, a vacuum-assisted biopsy done with systems like the Mammotome® or ATEC® (Automated Tissue Excision and Collection). At that point, she spaced out and didn't hear the rest. She could depend on Rhonda to hear the rest, take notes, and have an opinion. Chloe felt almost like she was drunk or on drugs, an experience she hadn't had often in her life. She looked at their familiar living room, the one maroon wall, the linen drapes, the familiar furniture, their art, mostly done by friends, all the awards Rhonda had received for her writing. It was as if all of that became more vivid but the sound of Evita's voice became dim, barely audible.

"Are you listening, Chloe?" Rhonda asked, looking concerned and tight.

"As much as I can right now," she replied. "Listen for me, honey," she added and Rhonda knew she was going to have to stay on top of things. Her super capable, take no prisoners, always take-charge wife had vanished into the haze of possible cancer.

❧❧❧❧

When the diagnosis came, Chloe was stunned to notice that dying was not her biggest concern. Her children not having their mother was what she could not face.

"They're too young, Rhonda. If I die on them, it will ruin their lives!" As she spoke, she shook from a place inside her she had never felt before. She imagined what it would be like to be a quivering aspen tree, shaking in the breeze, unable to be still. The loss of her own mother seemed so dim compared with the tragedy of her children being faced with losing her. Her friends wondered why she wasn't crying, but she told them some things were just beyond tears.

Rhonda held up well for the first week, then called her friend Deirdre, the one who could listen no matter what. They met at the same coffee shop where Rhonda and Chloe had edited the book, avoiding the table they had shared.

"I'm so terrified of losing her," Rhonda began, and then was unable to continue. Paradoxically, not much of a crier, she was overtaken by racking sobs that would not let her go. Unaware of the other people in the cafe, she gave herself up to the deepest sadness she had ever in her life felt. Deirdre, true to Rhonda's expectation, sat quietly and waited for her to finish. When the crying stopped, she took Rhonda's hand.

"You two are not in this alone," she said, quiet but sure. "I want you to remember each and every single person who promised on your wedding day to hold up your family in good times and bad. We didn't take that lightly. We meant it." Deirdre named off a string of at least twenty people who had been there, touched their heads, made a promise. That didn't change anything about the cancer or where they would end up. Mysteriously, though, Rhonda began to feel as if they could walk through this. Maybe they would be okay.

Deidre continued, clear and sure. "Rhonda, you need not to be in charge of getting the support together. I'm going to take that over, you hear? Your job is to be there for Chloe and the kids. I've been through this, you know."

Rhonda had failed to put two and two together. Of course, Deidre was the only friend she had who had lost a partner to cancer. Rhonda had been wiser than she knew in choosing Deidre to come out with her today.

Rosie and Deidre had been together for fifteen years when Rosie was diagnosed with pancreatic cancer. She lived for a year after that, much longer than anyone expected, but still such a short time for all of them. Rhonda had brought dinners, relieved Deidre when she needed a break, been part of their support community, but she hadn't thought about those times much in years. Deidre, though, had not forgotten.

"Here's what I want you to do. Go home and make a list of all the people you think might be able to help. Phone numbers and e-mails please. Put a star by everyone you two want to tell yourselves. I'll call everyone else. Then make some lists. In the end, we will have three: people Chloe would let wipe her butt if she couldn't do it herself, people you wouldn't mind having in the house, but no butt wiping, and people who could leave something on the doorstep but not much closer. My lists changed over time, but give me something to start with. When you need something, you're going to call me, and I'll get someone appropriate."

"I had thought I'd do all the taking care of her," Rhonda said, unsure about Deidre's all-out plan, grasping to be the one that would do everything for Chloe.

"Rhonda, your job is to be her wife. None of us can do that; you're the only one." And with that, Rhonda put their lives in Deidre's hands.

❧❧❧❧

HER2-positive, infiltrating breast cancer. The words had hung on the air, sounding almost harmless. HER2-positive. Chloe's mind played with the words, a favorite pastime since childhood. Her too positive, he too negative. An infiltration of anise or lavender. Smelly stuff. Her too? Not just me? She woke up to the fact that she hadn't heard the last few minutes of what this new, highly recommended, not warm doc was saying. She tried to come back into her body, to open her ears, to get there. Her eye caught the record feature on her phone, laying on the desk, the record button pressed, saving her from her own inability to hear the words or absorb their meaning.

Hoping to ground herself, she turned her head towards Rhonda, who was holding her hand and taking notes at the same time. Chloe hadn't understood why she needed to record and take notes, but now it became clear. Rhonda needed a way to stay focused, not to space out the way Chloe was, and writing always grounded her. Chloe didn't know why, but she hadn't expected to hear really bad news. The most she had let herself imagine was a little dot of cancer, that hadn't spread and was easily removed. Done. The idea that it had gone anywhere else in her body, that this might not be simple, that she might be at high risk, had simply been unimaginable. Now, here it was.

"Sometimes pregnancy hormones can trigger tumor growth, so it's plausible that this has grown since you had your kids, the last two years or so. If so, it's very aggressive. It doesn't appear to be contained so you have to look at some awfully big options. It may or may not be useful to remove the tumor or the breast. We'll look at this a little more carefully, but for the moment, you just need to prepare yourself to move fast. I'm hoping to get you started on whatever we decide in the next few weeks. I'm sending you down right now for lab work."

After he said his piece, he promptly left the room. They sat there without talking, looking at each other. It was a moment very like the moment they met, but in a completely different direction. Their lives had been changed. Life would never again look or feel the same. Now, though, they had each other to travel, side by side with.

ᘔᘔᘔᘔ

After two years of limited time away from their babies, Rhonda and Chloe began planning for a whole bunch of absence. There would be the medical appointments, the treatments, the sleeping that Chloe would, without a doubt, need, especially after chemo. Aside from the practical aspects, there was how they would talk to Quinten about what was happening. His sister was a little too young. They'd just have to keep things going for her, keep her schedule up, and leave her with people she knew, as much as they could.

At first, Chloe had no idea how they were going to make the decisions about treatment. Their friends sent her emails from folks who had been through it, and it was helpful to hear how they had decided, what their choices had been, but they all told her it was an individual thing. She would have to feel it out for herself, taking Rhonda and their children into account. Rhonda wanted to be considered. She wanted veto power, but thought Chloe should be the one to come up with the options.

Two things became clear right away. She was going to do everything she could to live. She was a mother, and, even if she didn't make it, she wanted Rhonda to be able to tell the kids she had done everything she could to be there for them. The second was closely tied to the first. Unless they could promise her it wouldn't make any difference, she was going to let go of her breast, maybe both. Her cancer had a tendency to migrate and, if the treatment worked, she didn't want the four of them ever to have to go through this again.

Rhonda agreed one hundred percent. Her priority was having Chloe with her for as long as possible. If she had thought about it theoretically, she might have expected to feel sad letting go of Chloe's breasts. Now, when Chloe's cancer was a painful truth, she didn't care about that. She would let go of anything if she could keep Chloe. They decided together against reconstructive surgery, because recovery would be harder and longer, separating Chloe from the kids even more.

They also decided together that even if that cold hard surgeon was good, he wasn't for them. They did their research, found someone for a second opinion, and changed surgeons. Dr. Levy was renowned and warm, making her the perfect one for them. At their first meeting, she asked about their family and acknowledged what a difficult time they must be in. Then she got down to business.

"Okay, Chloe and Rhonda," she said, including them both, to Chloe's liking, "here's what I recommend. I'd like to try to shrink that tumor with some radiation, so it will be easier to remove and removing a safe circumference won't be as invasive. There is a slightly higher risk with a lumpectomy for your kind of cancer, and treating just one breast, but I leave that decision up to you. Then chemotherapy, probably fairly aggressive, but we can decide that after we get the reports back post-surgery. What do you think?"

Chloe spoke first. "I think they should both go. First of all, we want to do everything we can, right, sweetie?" Rhonda nodded. "I don't want to worry that we should have done more. It's hard to wait while we do the radiation, but I have to trust you that it's worth it. Rhonda, any other thoughts?" For the first time since the cancer had been confirmed, Rhonda saw the wife she had had before all this, strong and sure. Chloe was ready.

"I agree completely," Rhonda said, trying not to think ahead to how it was going to be watching the person she loved most in the world going through all that.

They held hands in the car and sat out front for a long time before they came into the house, smiles and happy voices in tow, to greet their children.

❧ ❧ ❧ ❧

When Chloe's friend, Liz, found the breast cancer support group, Chloe was relieved. She'd read how much better women did with a group, but she was still not tackling the research part of this whole thing. She left Rhonda and the kids at home, doing bath time, and drove the car across town to the Cancer Support Center. She suddenly noticed she hadn't driven herself anywhere since all of this had started, and she took extra care. Just because she had cancer didn't mean she couldn't die in a car crash.

The Center was easy to find, with plenty of parking, which was good because she was at the end of her radiation and feeling really tired. No one had mentioned that exhaustion was going to come along with the rays of radioactive isotopes and she had tried to pretend for as long as she could that it wasn't really happening. Going from no symptoms to lying in bed for hours every day was a big shock, and one she resisted. The kids would sometimes come lay in bed with her, watching Sesame Street, Go Yabadaba. Before cancer, otherwise known as BC, Rhonda and Chloe hadn't let the kids watch TV, but now they figured it was a small evil compared with the possibility of not seeing much of their mom.

The door to the Center was open, and she walked in, heading to the back as the woman on the phone had directed her. There was art on the walls. She later learned that each person who used the Center made a picture of their healthy cells, visualizing a rise into wellness. She would have made fun of that idea in a former time, but now it touched her that the walls were covered with beautiful, healthy cells, crafted of colorful felt.

When she found the meeting room, she was surprised to hear laughter and music coming from the doorway. She walked in expecting a somber atmosphere, but that was nothing like the scene she saw. The eight or ten women who were gathered on sofas and comfortable chairs all looked up when they saw her, pulling out their friendliest smiles. One of them got up to give her a hug and said, loudly, "new blood, y'all!" It had been awhile since Chloe heard a southern accent and it made her feel right at home, remembering the relatives who sounded just like that. She settled into her seat, an old overstuffed chair, taking a pass when the check-in came to her.

"Just want to listen for a while."

The loud woman started in. "Chloe, my name is Samantha, even though I don't look like one. Y'all, this week was a loser, big time. My boyfriend has decided he doesn't want a woman with no tits, and he's packing up. Can you *believe* it?"

Chloe could not. She suddenly felt lucky, which was the first time in some time she had felt that way. "So I told him, just hurry up and get out of my house so I can use the spare bedroom. How did I miss that he was such a creep?"

Most of the other women in the room, Zelda, Ann, Mary, Louise, chimed in. Even though most had not struggled with their partners like Samantha had, they were happy to join her in some men bashing. "Men are so tit obsessed." "What am I, just a body?" On and on, with Chloe getting more and more uncomfortable. She was relieved when the last woman to share, Louise, said that she'd been dating and not one man had had a problem with her misshapen breast; they all just wanted sex with anything. The room erupted in hearty, deep down laughter.

It dawned on her then that it had been forever since she had to come out alone. Rhonda and she had gone to all the doctor's appointments, the kid's playmate's parents, the neighbors' parties, together. She suddenly felt lonely and out of place. Around the circle, everyone else seemed to have everything in common, beyond just breast cancer. She had a profound desire to go home and get in bed, only partly because she was suddenly so tired.

"What about you, Chloe? What have you got to say for yourself? And you can call me Sam, come to think of it."

Chloe took a deep breath and launched in. Because she needed this, and she wasn't going to let a bunch of straight women scare her off.

"I can't really relate to what you guys are talking about. I'm married to a woman, and she doesn't seem to care about me losing my tits, as long as she doesn't lose me," Chloe began, "My attention is totally on my kids, two years and six months, and what it will be like for them if I don't make it. And is anyone else more tired than they have ever been? I'm not even doing the chemo yet and I am so tired I can hardly get out of bed. I've had to go on a partial leave from work; I just can't think straight. Of course, I was never all that good at thinking *straight* from the get go." After she made the bad gay joke, she caught herself. How would they react? The whole room broke into laughter, and then Samantha, again, spoke for the group.

"Maybe I should try women," she said, and more than a few heads nodded in agreement.

꙾꙾꙾꙾

Surgery day came and with it a visceral, physical fear. Chloe would be put out, then wake up in pain and without the two breasts that had been with her since middle school. She would have tubes coming out of her and she would be sick, maybe very sick, from the anesthesia. Rhonda saw the panic and suddenly got very calm. "I'll be here; I'll make sure they keep you medicated. We're going to get through this." Chloe looked around at the stark, antiseptic hospital prep room and wondered why this great big system paid so little attention to how it actually felt to be waiting for surgery, trying not to fall off a narrow cot when the drugs started to kick in. She closed her eyes and tried to bring a picture of the ocean to mind, as she'd learned to do when she was in the worst of it with the loss of her mother. It was hard to reach.

In the end, Chloe had to accept that she couldn't bargain with this fear; she was just going to have to do it anyway. Looking back, she would say, "How was I so afraid of something I can hardly remember now?" The room where she was prepped, although "room" was hardly the right term, came back to her mind often. She was put on a gurney in a curtained off portion of a huge holding tank for twenty people about to have surgery. The curtains were dingy and old, even though they were bleached and clean. The surgeon and the anesthesiologist paraded through, hardly making an impression, but the nurse they would remember for a long time. In her mid-forties, Ann had been a prep nurse for twenty years and she knew the drill. That was comforting in itself, but what was even better was her confident tone.

"Hey, you two are new to the cancer adventure, huh? Well, I've seen lots of people go through this. It doesn't seem like it, but it's doable. I promise."

And in the end, it was.

❧❧❧❧❧

Their friends threw Chloe a hat party before she started chemo. They came with beautifully wrapped packages, mostly hatboxes, and spread them out on a blanket in the back yard. The kids toddled around, happy to see all their favorite people. Rhonda's parents had practically been living with them, trying to take the pressure off them. Rhonda had just put out another book, a children's book of the stories they had created, and sometimes had to be gone, even though she did her best to keep it to a minimum.

Rhonda's folks were at the party, having brought matching hats for the whole family, enough delicious food for an army and a pile of kid and adult DVDs to keep them all busy when they weren't leaving home much. Almost everyone who had been at their wedding was here for this occasion too, as well as the new friends she had made in her group. Everyone from the publishing house came too, and took Rhonda aside to let her know they were donating their sick time to Chloe so she wouldn't have to worry about money. Rhonda went into their bedroom alone and sobbed.

The whole bunch of them followed Chloe to the bathroom, crowding in the doorway to watch while Graham shaved Chloe's head. They sang songs from musicals, Motown, and 60's rock, several of them lining up like the Supremes and doing the dance to "Stop in the Name of Love." Chloe laughed so hard she almost peed in her pants. It was so stunning that they could have such a good time while preparing for chemo and hair loss. Chloe was glad that the few people who insisted on looking tragic and telling her what treatments she should try decided against attending, begging off with various transparent excuses.

It was a great night, but every time Chloe thought

she had gotten over her mother's absence, it plowed into her again. That night, as she lay in Rhonda's arms, she was surprised to hear herself say, "I want my mommy more than I ever have my whole life," and instead of taking that personally, as if she wasn't enough, Rhonda held her tighter and stroked her head.

"I know, my darling," she said, in a voice filled with love and sadness.

≥ll≥ll≥ll≥ll

The kids were off at the park with Emily when the mail came. Rhonda was writing in her writing room, now in the small shed they had built in the yard, and Chloe was sleeping off her second round of chemo.

Her group had warned her that she would feel very, very bad. They all knew the chemo she was on and they called it the soul crusher. She built up so much fear that she was stunned to be able just to sleep until she was better. The first time had gone by without anything worse than she had expected. This time, though, she was feeling truly sorry for herself. Why live? Why try? Not even her mother loved her.

When Rhonda finished writing for the day, she tiptoed into the room, bringing the mail to open as she sat on the bed, cradling the sleeping woman, her love. This had become their habit, getting a little time each day to be next to each other and checking in about how they were each doing. Right now, Chloe was just too out of it to check in. Rhonda moved slowly, getting as close to Chloe as she could, but not moving the bed and waking Chloe up.

She looked through the usual bills, requests, junk mail, nothing she had to deal with today. At the bottom, almost indistinguishable from the rest, was a hand-written envelope. She didn't recognize the handwriting, but it didn't look like bulk mail. The script was neat and beautiful, as if someone had spent a long time on the envelope. It was addressed to Chloe, but they had agreed that Rhonda would screen her mail. She had gotten some weird stuff from her siblings and her dad's wife since she had been sick and it wore her out to read the stuff. They were all trying to save her soul in one way or another, to reform her before she died.

Rhonda looked down at the envelope and was surprised to see that her hands were shaking. When she finally opened it and looked at the letter itself, she was too stunned to shake. She stared at the writing, not believing her own eyes.

The script was beautiful, like the writing on the envelope. She read with a knot in her stomach. She felt so protective of her beautiful love.

"Dear Chloe,

"How can I ever make up for what I've done? Maybe there is no way, but I'd like to try.

"I never realized how blind and brittle I had become. It wasn't until Del told me that you are sick that I became aware of the depth of my mistake. I know I haven't been good at apologizing in the past or taking responsibility for my own part of things, but I am trying my best to change.

"I've been seeing a therapist, if you can believe it, and she has been good at helping me to figure out what I need to do. I know you may never want me back in your life, but I have to try. I couldn't live with myself if I didn't let you know that this is all on me. You tried your best, and I didn't.

"I am happy to hear that you have love in your life and beautiful children. Only my blind behavior has kept me from knowing them. I know you don't need a pretty messed up mother when you have all that, but it would be a tremendous kindness to me to let me try to repair the damage I've done.

"Although I have no right to ask, please consider letting me know either way.

"I love you very much,

"Mom"

Chapter Eleven

Sally

Dinner night, Sal was as nervous as a teenager on a first date. She asked Randy to drive, picking her up in plenty of time to get there. Del had called Rhonda to get a time from them, since they hadn't mentioned one and Sal didn't want to mess up by intruding. Six o'clock.

Randy came a little early, dressed to the nines. Sal had never seen him dressed up, and he cleaned up pretty good. He had on a slim pair of slacks, dark grey, and a deep purple shirt. He had on his good watch and a kick ass pair of shoes. He'd gelled his hair and creamed his face. She noticed, for the first time, that he was a handsome guy. She also noticed that she managed to find that shocking, as if a gay man could not be handsome, an idea most of her younger straight friends would laugh at. The cut of his jaw was warm and inviting and still managed to be manly. She found herself thinking it was pretty surprising he was single.

"How you doing, girl?" he asked, almost seeming excited by this whole thing.

"I guess I'm hanging in," she said, despite the dull ache in the pit of her stomach.

"Hanging in?" he said, incredulous, "Your baby invited you to dinner! It's got to be better than that!"

"I'll let you do the excitement thing for me," she

said. "I'm too busy being nervous."

She had never been in Randy's car. It was a cute little sports car, really old, that he kept polished to a fine shine. It embarrassed her to think that all these years working with Randy, she had never asked him much about his life outside of Daily Grind. With a long ride ahead of them and needing a distraction, she thought she could remedy that now.

"So, Randy, dating anyone?" Even to her it sounded clumsy and forced, like an under rehearsed part in a bad play. It made him laugh.

"What do you want to know for? Planning on asking me out?" he said, taking the opportunity she'd given him for some teasing. "I don't swing that way, Mami." Although she knew he wasn't really calling her mom, the word pushed hard on her. No one had called her Mommy in a very long time.

"Okay. So I'm not very good at making small talk. I don't get much practice outside of work, and you know there's no time to get too curious. You're doing a big thing for me and I hardly know anything about you. C'mon, fill a girl in." She began to sound to herself like a person who rode in people's cars and made conversation. He didn't torture her any more.

"I was with Stan for ten years, but he left last year for someone else. It broke my heart, if you want to know the truth. But I'm starting to go out a little bit, nothing serious. I'm not ready for anything serious."

"Randy, did you know my ex's name is Stan?" Sal couldn't believe he'd gone through all that and he never showed it. She wanted him to know they had something in common.

"Yeah, I guess I did at one point. Two heels with the same name, huh? No more Stans, I guess." They both laughed hard and long.

Sal was grateful for the relief of laughing about it and thought, *I guess I'm pretty much over it, because laughing is coming sort of easy right now. What a relief.*

❧❧❧❧

They pulled up to the house and found a place to park, which wasn't all that easy. Cars lined the street and Sal suddenly wondered how many people were at this dinner. Her toes tingled with dread at facing a bunch of judging strangers. The only thing that got her through the gate to the back yard was her drive to see Chloe. She noticed in a distracted way that they lived on a beautiful street, lined with healthy, mature trees, and flowers peeking up between patches of moss laced through the gate leading to Chloe's house. Even the entrance seemed like magic to her.

Heading into the back yard and towards the house, which they could barely see walking through the gate in the redwood fence, was the most enchanting spot she could ever remember seeing. It was spring, and there were flowers everywhere there wasn't green. She could barely tell that a barbecue was steaming on a little patio area, with the top down, smelling delicious. She tried to recall if Chloe cooked when they were still talking, and she couldn't. Another thing about Chloe she had let slip out of the side of her brain. Then, suddenly, she remembered when Chloe was very small, four or five, and she would beg Sal to let her help with dinner. She would make her own suggestions too. "Let's put orange juice in with the chicken, Mommy. That would taste yummy." And, against all odds, it did. She felt the warmth of the memory washing over her, propelling her with a sense near excitement, towards the door of the cottage that contained her girl and her family.

Randy rang the bell for her, because her hand was shaking, and they waited, but not very long. The door opened to reveal a very beautiful black woman, about Chloe's age, with a towel over her shoulder – she must have come from the kitchen – and a smile on her face. She grabbed Sal's hand and it was impossible to resist the warm shake she gave her. "I am so very happy to meet you! I'm Rhonda, Chloe's wife."

"Nice to meet you," Sal managed, afraid that if she said more her voice would crack.

"Come right on in. This is our house."

"Girl, what are you doing here?" Sal hadn't noticed a man about Randy's age running up beside him.

"I didn't expect to know anyone!" Randy replied, grabbing his friend up in a last-all-day kind of hug.

"I'm Don," said the man, turning to give Sal his attention. He was tall and thin and looked like he spent all this time in a gym. He had on shorts, cut right above the knee, and his calf muscles stuck out from the bone in beautiful relief. His hair was cut short, with big blue eyes. He stood out in a crowd, for sure. "And you must be Sal. Edgar and Vince, come over here and meet Chloe's mom. This is Edgar, my friend, and his husband Vince. Husband, husband, I'm still getting used to the sound of that." Edgar was a gorgeous man, and Vince, although not as buff as his husband, was good looking too. Sal remembered a single friend of hers saying, "Why are all the cute ones gay?" and for the first time she got it.

"Well, Sal, you can't be all that bad with a friend

like Randy," Don said with familiarity.

Sal was stunned that he would refer so casually and directly to all the trouble with Chloe and her, but, somehow, it put her at ease. "Well, I'd say I'm trying to get better." And then she heard it, Chloe's laugh.

From the time she was very young, Chloe had the kind of laugh that caught everyone up in it. Whenever they were having a family fight, she'd make a joke and laugh and no one could stay mad for long. It came back to her now that when Stan left, she wondered whether one of the reasons might be that they had managed to make even Chloe stop laughing, that maybe he wanted her to have her joy back.

Sal realized she was pretty stunned that with everything going on, she was still laughing. How could she keep that joy going on, with cancer and chemo and kids and the way the world probably treated her and Rhonda? But there it was, that laugh, piercing through her fear and finding her heart.

"Hi, Mom," she said, as if it hadn't been ten years. "Come meet everyone."

The guests made an awfully large group, maybe fifteen people or so. Chloe took her mother's hand and led her around, and Sal was surprised they all acted friendly. Not one of them looked at Sal as if she were an enemy. She was embraced with hugs, kisses, told how glad they were that she had come, sit here, have a glass of wine. Red or white? Or maybe you need a whiskey right about now. Sal answered and nodded, taking a red wine, sitting in a big grey overstuffed chair, comfortable and inviting. She couldn't help thinking of Lonnie, the office she had spent so much time in lately. It was comfortable like this, like whoever bought the furniture really wanted folks to feel at home.

Chloe took a chair next to her, but chatted with her friends, giving Sal a chance to look at her without her looking at Sal. She still looked like the happy person Sal remembered, but no hair. This somehow gave her face a luminous quality, beaming full on with nothing to distract from the wide eyes, the pink lips. Sal missed her flame red hair. Now, she didn't even have eyelashes or brows. Her face stood alone, no distractions from her beauty. She had forgotten completely how somehow Stan and Sal's best physical qualities had blended in her and made her shine like a top.

"And the nurse said to me, 'how are you today' and I'm thinking, 'are you kidding me? It's beautiful weather, I have two amazing children who are home playing with my wife, and I'm here all day having poison dripped into my veins. Yeah, I'm just great!'"

It was startling to hear her daughter talking so off hand about this whole thing and even more startling when everyone in earshot broke into a hearty laugh as if something funny was happening. Sal was not at the place where she could see anything funny about chemotherapy and she must have let that show because, even though she hadn't been looking at her mom, it was clear that Chloe knew she was reacting.

"Mom, don't be concerned. I know cancer is no laughing matter, but I would rather laugh than cry. And it is kind of funny sometimes. I'm going to write a book modeled on Art Linkletter. You know, Kids Say the Darndest Things? Well, mine will be People Talking to People with Cancer Say the Darndest Things. Where shall I begin? Oh yeah, 'you'll be ok. You're strong' to which I reply, 'I'm writing a long list of the strong dead people I know.' Or 'make sure and keep a positive attitude' through their clenched teeth, to which I say, thank you Joanne Loulan, 'somehow cancer has not improved my attitude.'"

On that, Sal had to quietly disagree. She had honestly never seen Chloe so relaxed, so comfortable with herself, so engaged and talkative. She had been a little shy in large groups as a kid. But then, that change could have happened before the cancer. Maybe while she was getting over Sal's rejection? Whatever it was, she was enjoying this. That was sure a big surprise.

When the dinner was ready, they all went outside to eat at a long table. The light was just beginning to fade, and Rhonda turned on the strings of lanterns looping through the trees. As they neared the yard, Chloe said to Sal, "The lanterns were put up for our wedding, but we couldn't bear to take them down."

Sal managed a weak, "They're very pretty."

There were place cards at the table and Sal noticed with some disappointment that her name was not near Chloe's. She was sitting between Randy and a woman named Samantha. Sal had noticed her before because she was also without hair and enjoying the cancer jokes just as much as Chloe was enjoying telling them. She could almost have called her jolly, which seemed a very odd state for a sick person.

She seemed to notice Sal's discomfort and turned a little towards her, ready to coax her out of a truly self-conscious state.

"Well, I sure heard a little bit about you!" she started, and Sal was startled that she wasn't following the rules. They weren't going to talk about all that tonight.

"Can't imagine any of it was good," Sal replied, hoping that would end things.

"Well, I never heard anything until Chloe came

to our cancer support group with the letter you wrote her. That must have taken a lot. Of course, I'm dismal at apologies so it would definitely have taken a lot for me." She left the words hanging on the air, maybe waiting to see if Sal would say anything. To her own surprise, she did.

"Well, it may be my first apology ever and so, yeah, it was damned hard."

That made Samantha laugh, a big, hearty, full-on laugh that seemed to come from deep in her belly.

"I guess you picked a good time to start apologizing, didn't you? I think you should know, and no one else will tell you, that Chloe was mighty scared when she got it, but also really moved. No matter what happens, it meant a lot to her. I thought you should know that." She had leaned in close so that no one else could hear her breaking the rules of the night.

Sal felt the strongest urge to put her head on Sam's shoulder and have a good cry. The words were like massage oil on a sore muscle. "Thank you so much," was all she could manage.

♫ ♫ ♪ ♪

To her other side, Randy and Don were flirting so loudly that the whole table could hear. Sal wondered why she wasn't bothered. Being the homophobe she knew herself to be, she would have thought she'd have her nose in the air about it, but she was finding it kind of cute. It was clear to her that it wasn't the first time Don had thought of Randy in that way, but knowing what Randy had been through, she figured this was the first time he had taken it in. He was enjoying the attention, teasing back in equal measure. She was savoring it, the sexy sound of the flirt, the idea that Randy could find someone to love, and the attention it took off of her and her bad behavior.

"You two should get a room," she heard herself say, before she had a chance to censor herself, and the whole table laughed, with a warmth she had rarely felt in her life. These were good people, no matter what anyone wanted to say. They were giving better than they had gotten and that meant a lot to her. It began to seem much less important that they had sex with each other than that they were loving, accepting people. If she was being perfectly honest, she'd never thought sex was that important, period.

Out of the corner of her eye, she caught Rhonda smoothing the shirt on Chloe's shoulder, asking if she would like more water. Was she getting cold, did she want a sweater? *My girl is a lucky, lucky woman,* she heard in her head, then recognized the truth of it, even though to some she might be a pariah, and even though she had cancer. All these people loved her, just as she was, and she loved them. Sal felt the kind of envy that says, "I want that for myself!" She had given up on her own life, become stuck and bitter, refused to change even though it was obvious she needed to. In this one moment, she resolved to get a life she wanted to live. If Chloe could do it, why not her?

࿇ ࿇ ࿇ ࿇

After dinner, they went back inside, the chill of the Oakland spring outstripping their sweaters. No one sat down until Chloe had picked a chair, all of them wanting her to be comfortable, to have the first choice. She sank into the big grey chair, one of two, and Sal nearly ran for the one next to it, a straight back pulled in from their tiny dining room. She usually liked sinking into soft chairs, but she didn't care about her comfort right then.

"Chloe, I want to thank you from the bottom of my heart," she said, looking for any sign that she might be breaking the rules.

"Mom, you're welcome." She paused long enough to make Sal uncomfortable, but she could tell Chloe had more to say. "I think we have to take it slow, though, don't you?"

It was Sal's turn to consider her reply. Did she think they needed to take it slow? Part of her wanted to just sail past everything that had gone on and get on board with this new life. Another part was having a hard time catching up with all the new thoughts and feelings she was having. Still another part of her was impatient with Chloe having any feelings left from their time apart. But she knew that was just guilt.

"I want to go just as fast or slow as you're ready for. I made this mess and I know I've got to take the consequences. I'm ready to do my part, Chloe. You've been doing yours all along."

"Okay, Mom, we'll take it one step at a time. I've got a few other things going on, as you can see, so I just can't worry about your feelings right now, if that's okay."

It would have to be.

≈≈≈≈≈

"Thanks for taking me with you," Randy effused in the car. "That was the best party I've been to in longer than I can say."

"Glad you enjoyed it. And I could see that you

did! Did Don get your number?" Sal could tease a little too.

"No...but I got his." Randy replied, obviously proud of himself. "I've known him for forever, but I never saw how cute he is before."

"He wants to jump your bones," Sal said, astounded at the easy way she was stepping into this new world.

"Sal, I'm shocked! The way you talk!" He put his hand to his mouth, his eyes wide, feigning true shock and dismay. "You might be able to get used to us, huh?" he said, and punched her on the shoulder, reaching across the car.

"Hey, don't be punching me. You're driving!"

"All kidding aside, Sal, how was that for you?"

Sal had to think a while before she answered. How was that for her? A relief, more comfortable than she could ever have imagined. Impressive. Healing – god, how she had hated that word just a few months ago. Encouraging.

"Randy, that was one of the best nights of my life. The nicest group of people who have ever included me. And my daughter. She's a wonder, isn't she? And the way Rhonda takes care of her, I can't imagine being loved like that. Isn't it weird that they seem lucky, with all they're going through?" The words spilled out on top of each other, the most she had strung together outside of those hours with Lonnie for a long time.

"Whoa, girl, take your time!" Randy said, but the smile on his face said it all.

"Randy, can you tell me why they want to be so nice to me when I did the very thing that must bother them the most? Why would they want to welcome me after what I did to Chloe?"

"Well, Sal, I can only guess, but here goes. The rejection stuff we're all used to. Happens all the time. We're used to being disowned, beat up, yelled at on the street, and called sinners, heathens, dirty dykes, and faggots. You name it. What we're not used to is someone doing the work to change. What we're not used to is anyone, ever, admitting they've made a mistake about us, that we're kind of okay after all. That's worth paying attention to! The rest is just life as usual."

ᘓᘓᕟᕟ

Waiting to hear from Chloe again was pure torture. Sal spent lots of time trying to convince herself that it would be all right to call her instead, but she knew that would be wrong. They had left it that the ball was in Chloe's court and she should take the time she needed to figure out the next step. If Sal had been staring at a clock, time could not have gone slower.

Randy and she spent more time together outside of work now. She'd cook him a meal and he'd cook her one. Her favorite was his homemade pizza, with amazing things like goat cheese and roasted pepper strewn over the top, delicious in a surprising tickle your tongue way she never could have imagined. No big surprise to Sal, within days, he started going out with Don, and they would include her in their plans now and then. They were fun to be with, never making her feel like a third wheel. They both said they liked having a mom around, made them miss their own mothers a little less. But they also seemed to like Sal for Sal.

In the long hours she sat waiting by the phone, she would paint them little pictures. She painted some for Chloe too, and Rhonda, and their kids. She came as close to praying as she ever had. "Lord, I hope she lets me into her life. Please help her to forgive me." Even though she had used religion to justify her position with Chloe, she'd never been religious or spiritual enough for anyone to notice. Now she began to think that it might be a good idea to believe there was something at work that wasn't herself, because she'd done a pretty bad job on her own.

Lonnie was a big help, as always, listening, suggesting, guiding, but never pushing. Sal saw her less now, feeling stronger on her own, testing her wings. But she still valued having someone who cared about her to help her see what was going on.

The other thing that was slowly creeping in was that Chloe was not the only person in Sal's life she was on the outs with and she began to see that she had missed a lot of life, setting standards for herself and other people that none of them could reach. Even though it was hardest with her, Sal started with Del. She invited her over for dinner.

☙☙☙☙

When Del got to the door, Sal could tell she was suspicious. The thing about Del was that, whatever was going on, it showed in her face. Sal was always a lot more hidden. But Sal counted herself lucky that Del had really come. Sal had asked her not to come to Chloe's dinner party, because it would make her too nervous. She had said, "of course," but Sal could tell it smarted. Still, Del wasn't holding that against her.

Sal asked Randy, expert on wine that he was, for a recommendation. He said, "A good one is thirty, forty dollars. These are my favorites." Sal had never in her life spent that much on a bottle, but she bought his favorite without even thinking about it. She needed all the help she could get.

Sal offered Del a glass of wine, Pinot Noir like she liked. Del eased up a little. "Oh, I love that wine! How did you come across it?" That was an awfully kind way to say, "I know you know nothing about good wine so someone must have helped you."

"I've gotten pretty close to Randy at work and he's a big wine guy. It's his hobby. He told me what to buy, basically." Sal could have worried that admitting someone else had picked it would diminish her effort, but instead Del seemed flattered she'd gone to all the trouble.

"I've never heard you talk about Randy. Any sparks flying?" She said it playfully, like they used to talk when they were younger. Sal hadn't seen that side of her in a long time, and she was glad to know it was still there.

"Well, he's attractive, smart, funny, loyal, and honest. There's only one big problem." Del looked at Sal, her head turned a little to the side, wondering what could be wrong with such a perfect guy. "He's got a boyfriend." And they both broke up laughing, amused and surprised at the same time.

❧ ❧ ❧ ❧

Sal had made a better dinner for Adele than she'd made since she was first married and trying to impress Stan. She enjoyed the skewers of prawns, the fingerling potatoes, and the perfectly cooked asparagus, a dab of butter adding just enough saltiness. They kept the conversation light, what Del had been up to, how her kids were. Her husband's work. Her latest charity project as a fundraiser for PFLAG. Sal didn't ask what that stood for.

It was time for dessert, crème brûlée, Sal's best, with raspberries on top, before she felt ready to tackle what this night was about. She took a very deep breath, while Del was in her bathroom, to get ready. She almost chickened out, and then gave herself a little talking to. "Sal, you missed out on ten years of your kid's life and now she might die. Could anything that could happen tonight compare with that?" It shouldn't have been comforting, but it was. If she had faced that dinner party, with everyone thinking about what she did to Chloe, she could face her sister, alone in the tiny kitchen, the remnants of a good dinner still fresh on their tongues.

Del came back out looking like she might be thinking about leaving. Sal nipped that in the bud.

"Hey, sis, I'm not done with you yet." Sal poured a little more wine in her glass, giving her no choice but to sit down and drink it. She seemed almost happy to sit back down, as if she had been planning to leave on Sal's account.

"What's up, sis?" Del asked, and Sal remembered how, when they were little, she'd say that every time she came home. Sal tried to remember the last time Del greeted her that way. It must have been when Sal was in high school, just barely, and Del came home from college and said it just that way, and Sal had run into her arms. "I missed you!" she had said, overwhelmed by her own joy at seeing her big sister.

But their parents had made that visit a living hell, criticizing Del and demanding she do all the hard work around the house, and she had never come home on her breaks again. Sal felt abandoned and alone with them and she had to admit to herself that that might have been the point when she actually stepped away from her. In light of her new sense of justice, Sal remembered that Adele had asked her to visit many times, every time Sal would refuse, but she just kept asking. This was the first time Sal considered she might have abandoned Del too.

"Adele, I am doing a whole lot of work to improve my life. Well, myself really. I wanted to say a few things to you and it's hard, so don't interrupt."

"Sal, you don't have to—"

"Del, I told you not to interrupt! You are such a big sister sometimes. Just hear me out, okay?"

She was quiet after that, waiting for what Sal had to say. It seemed as if she physically backed away a little, creating a no-fly zone around herself. Sal could understand that.

"I thought my big problem was Chloe and our separation and her cancer. But I have come to see that I pretty much ditched my life and that affected lots of people. My friends, my other kids, my grandkids, nieces, nephews, everyone really. But right now, the most important person to mention is you."

Del looked startled, as if she was hearing something she had given up ever hearing. She looked a little sideways, as if looking Sal in the eye might lead to an attack that she wouldn't be able to defend herself from.

"There are some things I want to apologize for. I'm sorry that I've been so angry with you for having a good life. I could have been inspired or at least happy for you, but I just thought you were showing me up, as if you had a good life just to make me look bad. I'm sorry that you've done ninety percent of the reaching out, as if you owed it to me to carry on our relationship. I'm sorry for all the times I didn't answer the phone, or said no to invitations, especially the ones I got when you were away at college and I was still home. I thought you had escaped and left me to suffer with our parents, but really, you were just growing up. I'm sorry I was mad at you instead of them. I'm sorry for never recognizing that you are a good person."

By this point, they were both crying and Sal couldn't talk any more. But Del didn't say a word, just sat looking at her. It took quite some time for Sal to remember she'd told her not to interrupt.

"Okay, you can talk now," Sal said, and then laughed out loud.

"Thank you, oh my queen," she said, and Sal wasn't offended in the least.

"Sal, I love you so much. I guess you never knew how guilty I felt when I left home. I knew you'd be the target then, because I had diverted the attention so often to myself so you wouldn't get hurt. I thought I was failing at my job, big sister, so when you didn't visit, I figured I deserved it. That just turned into years of expecting to be on the outs with you. I thought it couldn't be fixed. I can't tell you what it feels like to have you back. Please, let's not get so far apart again." Then she got up from the stool and came over to Sal, wrapping her in a hug like the ones at Chloe's house. It felt so good.

"So here's what we're gonna do," she continued, "we're both gonna drop the guilt. Who needs it? And we're gonna spend time together; just the two of us, with our kids, with our kid's kids, hopefully Chloe and Rhonda and their two sometimes, we're just going to be a family and not worry about all that old crap.

I forgive you. And I forgive myself. And shit, I even forgive our parents. They're both dead, for Christ's sake, why waste time being mad at *them*?"

Sal could tell she meant it, and it felt like sun on a rainy day. This change in her life felt so sudden, but maybe it was as Lonnie had said. "You're sitting at the narrowest point of the hourglass, feeling the sands of time pass. It feels almost exactly the same as you're trying and trying, making what seem like grains of sand changes and then, one day, the last of the sand whooshes through and there you are, in a whole new world."

She had given Sal that image near the beginning, sometimes referring to it as they went along, and it never really connected. A nice idea that would never happen to Sal. Then, all of a sudden, she could see that she had reached the ground, the base, not up in the air any more. Time and gravity had brought her back to herself. She hoped she could learn to trust that life was really different, that this was not just an unexpectedly good day, but rather a permanent change in what she expected from living.

She didn't have to wait as long for Adele as she was waiting for Chloe. Del called her the next day to ask if she wanted to come over for a barbecue that weekend. Her kids were coming, did she want her to invite Sal's, no, don't bring anything, she wanted to do this. Sal said yes right away, happy to be asked.

※※※※

Sal hadn't been to Del's for at least a few years, but she remembered the way. She made her way up the hill, her little old Toyota just barely eking by, snaking her way to the top, to Del's beautiful house with the pool and the view of the entire bay. She noticed the beauty up here in a way she couldn't remember ever seeing. She opened the window of the car and smelled the eucalyptus and the damp spring dirt, fresh and clean.

The driveway to their house led to a circle in front where there were already at least six cars. These couldn't be hers and Frank's because they had a three-car garage and they always parked their cars out of the way when guests came. She recognized Chase's truck, an ancient Ford, and Grant's dilapidated Datsun, but she had never seen any of the other cars. She sat in the car and lingered, searching for the smile she wanted to bring in with her.

An image of Chloe looking up at Rhonda as she stood behind her flashed before her and the smile came naturally, a real one and not the put-on variety she'd been settling for. She lingered with the memory, even though she felt ready to go in now. It was a pleasure to sit alone in the car, enjoying a moment with the daughter she hadn't seen in a month now, and ten years before that. Such a long, and at the same time, short month. She closed her eyes and leaned back in the seat, savoring the sun through the window of the car and the California native garden it was parked in the middle of, poppies popping orange across the expanse.

She was startled after a few minutes by an insistent tap on the window. "Hey sis, what are you doing out here? We're all in the back yard!"

She smiled broad and free, happy to see Del and secretly flattered she had been looking out for her, saw her when she arrived. She got out of the car in a hurry, a little embarrassed at her hesitation. "Just taking a minute to feel happy I'm here, Del," she said as she caught her sister in a hug.

They walked through the entry of her Spanish style house, built in a "u" shape around a gorgeous courtyard, lavender and poppies and grasses crowding together with a waterfall plunging into a pool in the middle of it all. Sal noticed the excellent planning that, even on a cool Bay Area day, this was often a warm spot, protected from wind and positioned just right to receive the sun. Sal recalled vaguely that Del had designed this house herself, spending endless hours on every detail. She also remembered being asked for a painting to go into the house, which she'd never painted. She resolved to correct that as soon as she could.

Adele stopped in the entryway, grabbing her hand like a conspirator. "Sal, I have a big surprise for you. They're here!"

"Who?" Sal couldn't let herself think that maybe she was talking about Chloe and her family.

"I invited them but I didn't tell you because I didn't know if they would come, but they came. With the kids!"

And then Sal fell apart, right there in the entryway, sunny and inviting, with just a glass door between her and the people she wanted most in this world to see. She asked Del if they could go to her bedroom for a few minutes so she could collect herself.

"Of course," Del said, stepping back into the big sister part she had played in their early life.

But when they got there, Sal said, "Am I crazy? Why would I wait another minute to meet my grandchildren?" And they headed right back out.

Chapter Twelve

Chloe

When the invitation came from her Aunt Del, Chloe couldn't tell how she felt about it. She had been slowly getting ready to call her mother, to take the next step, but between cancer and the kids, the month had gone by incredibly fast.

This whole thing with cancer had taught her to enjoy her life more, not to rush, but also how to let things matter. Life seemed more important now, not to be squandered. So she hadn't been comfortable with all the time it was taking her to be ready to have her mother back in her life, but it was time she knew she needed to take. She didn't want to carry the past into this new thing, which she felt completely sure would ruin it for her. She wanted to bring excitement and joy into it, to be grateful for this new and unexpected pleasure. Still, she had to admit to Rhonda that she was having a hard time getting over all the things, big and little, her mother had not been there for.

Rhonda said, "Make a list. What did she miss?"

When she did, it was two pages, typed, single-spaced. She was a little surprised to see that the list went beyond the things she had missed in these last ten years. There was the time Sal was upset about something with her dad and didn't come to her play. Helena in Midsummer' Night's Dream. There was the time she was late for Chloe's graduation from high school, sneaking in at the last minute and standing at the back. There were times Chloe tried to tell her about the bullies at school or the bad teacher, and all Sal said was, "You can handle it. They're not worth getting upset over." She had a way of making Chloe feel she had failed if her feelings got hurt.

Chloe knew Sal had probably not turned into a different person. She wanted to accept that Sal was who she was, with her good points and bad points, just like anyone else. But if she hadn't been invited to the barbecue, she might have taken a little longer to get there. Once the invitation came, she knew she would say yes, even though it was rushing things a little. What could really be better? A family party where there were plenty of other people to talk to her mom if words failed her. A way for the kids to meet their grandmother without too much pressure. She accepted the invitation.

※.※※.※

The timing was fortunate. Not the week of her chemo and not the week when she and Rhonda were set to go to a workshop with Devin Paul, the guy whose books about dealing with illness had become like bibles to them.

They took him aside at lunch on Saturday, eager to tell him what was happening with Sal. Chloe described what had happened between them, and said she was afraid she wasn't going to be able to let her mother into her heart.

"Chloe, if you keep her out, the one who will be most hurt is you. She's already suffering from what she's done. You don't need to be in charge of her consequences. Can you remember what you used to love about your mother?"

Chloe's mind was flooded with pictures from the earliest times she could remember. Her mother singing to her before bed, or reading a book. Her mother covering her face with bubbles to make Chloe laugh in the tub, stay in the water just long enough to cover her with soap and rinse her off. The time in first grade when the teacher yelled at her and Sal came in the next day.

"You will not yell at my child."

She remembered, again, that Sal had changed when her marriage failed. That there had been a time before that when Sal had been warm and fun loving, almost kind. It helped her to imagine that Chloe's father had wounded Sal and she was just now beginning to repair. Chloe realized that she had blamed Sal for all the problems, but that was probably because they were closer than she was with her father. She absorbed for the first time that she had rarely heard from her father since she had been sick. She was so used to his failures that they hardly affected her.

Devin listened until they had told him everything. Then he put his hand gently on the center of Chloe's chest and said, "Do whatever you need to do to heal this beautiful heart."

❧ ❧ ❧ ❧

For the next few days, Chloe remembered to offer forgiveness to Sal whenever she came to mind. "I forgive you for all you've done to harm me, intentionally or unintentionally." At first, it was an exercise, but before long, it began to sink into that place that had been walled off since her mother stopped seeing her. She decided she needed to forgive herself too, for being a person Sal found hard to accept. It wasn't the kind of guilt thing she might have had years ago. She was just admitting that her choices affected her mother, challenged her in a place she had never wanted to change. In the end, she was grateful to both of them for coming to this point.

Rhonda had some work to do too, because Sal had hurt Chloe in a way Rhonda found hard to forgive. Her anger seemed to intensify as Chloe's diminished, and finally, she had to say something.

"Chloe, I have to admit I don't feel like letting your mom off the hook. What she did was terrible. I hate it. I don't know how to get over it."

"You're not letting her off the hook. The hook isn't yours to let her off of. She made her own hook, Rhonda, and she's trying to get down off of it. Can you see that? But thanks for being mad for me. It was pretty shitty, for sure. Thing is, what if I die? I don't want to leave it like this. Can you forgive her for me?"

That was why Rhonda loved her, as well as what she found completely frustrating. She really had to be her best self in this thing. Chloe would accept no less. Sometimes she just wanted to be not her best.

"I'm going to give it all I've got. For you, not for her. And I am going to have an eagle eye on our kids. They sure don't deserve any crap."

They shook on it. Agreed. Ready to go.

❧ ❧ ❧ ❧ ❧

Chloe's chemotherapy was getting harder. Her

white blood cell counts were getting low, and when she went for treatment, they almost didn't give her the chemo because those numbers were on the edge of not good enough. Even with all the drugs Chloe took to counteract the effects of the other drugs, she was literally sick and tired. This was to be her fourth of ten, and she worried she wouldn't make it through them all. She woke up the day after the treatment knowing she wouldn't be good for much that day.

Just last month, they had gotten Quin and Ari into a day care center around the corner. On good days, they walked the kids there together, were greeted by the staff, who had quickly grown to love them, and walked back home, Chloe resting in the yard and Rhonda writing at a little desk they had set up by the hammock Chloe liked to curl up in.

No matter how many times Chloe told Rhonda she was okay alone, Rhonda liked to stick close these days. Sometimes when Chloe was sleeping, Rhonda could hardly tell she was breathing and crept quietly up to her to see if her chest moved at all. Once, Chloe was so still she put a mirror under her nostrils, relieved when a faint steam appeared on the glass. They had worried like this when their children were newborns, not entirely trusting that they would survive babyhood. Chloe was seeming just that fragile.

Rhonda found herself writing articles about living next to cancer, blogs about the kids, taking notes for a novel about a couple facing cancer, unable to focus on the sort of novels she had always written. She was grateful that, with the success of her last two books, she didn't have to worry too much about their finances. April had assured her they wouldn't be cutting off Chloe's pay any time soon. They were getting close to having used all the sick time her coworkers had given, but April told them she could do the work of a week in half a day, so just do what she could.

On the good weeks, Chloe liked the familiar feeling of editing a book, using her slightly dulled brain to evaluate the strengths and weaknesses of the writing. They gave her all the small projects now, ones that needed less work or were shorter. It felt good that April still trusted her work, even on days she wasn't sure herself. But this was not going to be one of those days when she could sit at the desk, or even on the sofa, and work. This was a sleep day.

Even with the anti-nausea meds, she felt constantly as if she had a bad flu. That lasted a full week after each treatment. The cancer center had prepared her for unpredictability, but so far, each chemo had been almost entirely the same. This fourth time, though, she was tired as she could never remember being tired before. She could manage just a few hours of sitting with the kids, laughing at their playful mischief or singing, reading to them or playing peek-a-boo, before she went to lie down again. Sometimes she just lay down, right where she was, the sofa or the chair, and went out, asleep before she knew she was headed in that direction.

The kids seemed intent on keeping her awake by climbing on her, touching her face, and pulling her hair. She could respond enough to let them know she was okay, but then Rhonda would take over, gently guiding them to another activity. Deidre had long ago recognized they needed more help and their friends were in and out of the house all day, bringing dinner, a friend for Quinten and Arisa to play with, sprucing up the garden when Rhonda couldn't get to it.

The strangest thing, though, was that they were happy. There was so much laughter in the house. Chloe enjoyed hearing the voices of her friends as she drifted in and out of sleep. Chloe and Rhonda worked out their problems in front of whoever was there at the time, unembarrassed by whoever witnessed their everyday hassles. Chloe felt that she had nothing to protect, that she just couldn't afford the energy to worry about what anyone thought, and that was liberating, since she had always cared a little too much. Rhonda, who had always protected her privacy to a fault, let that drop completely. The vast majority of their friends couldn't wait to spend time with them, feeling somehow as if this uninhibited way of living was rubbing off on them.

There were a few exceptions. Mandy, an old friend of Rhonda's, was always very tragic when she came over. When they indulged in gallows humor, a new favorite in their household, she was truly scandalized and several times fled the room.

The day came when Chloe couldn't take it anymore. "Rhonda, it's wearing me out how sad she is. Doesn't she see we're not sad?"

The next time she came, they sat her down.

"Mandy, we want you to be able to hang out here, but we need you to take your fear and sadness somewhere else. That's not how we're usually feeling and it's bringing us down." Rhonda was speaking in her softest, most loving voice.

Mandy looked startled and then guilt swept over her face.

"You don't have anything to feel bad about, Mandy," Chloe said. "We know lots of people are feeling bad about this, but to us, it's just our life. We have to live, even though we have some challenges.

And really, in some ways, I'm happier than I've ever been. I don't worry about the future. I love my kids. I love my wife. If I were to die tomorrow, I will have had a pretty damned amazing time. These are the moments I have and I want to enjoy them."

Mandy's face changed, subtly but unmistakably. "I can do that. If I need to be sad, I'll go somewhere else and talk to someone else."

"You can talk to us. Just don't look tragic! There's no guillotine around here." Their laughter eased whatever tension had been there a moment before, and they hugged, Mandy hugging back with equal force. After that, when she came over, she brought cancer jokes she had found on the internet, or brought her guitar and sang little songs she had made up. The change was exhilarating.

Pam was a harder case. She came over with a new treatment she thought Chloe should try each and every time. She insisted that if Chloe meditated properly and got rid of all her old baggage, the cancer would run away scared.

"I have less baggage than anyone I know, Pam. I don't think baggage is why I have cancer."

After the third or fourth time they had this same conversation, almost word for word, they told Deidre they needed to change Pam's category. She could help, but she couldn't come in the house.

Chapter Thirteen

Sally

As Sal approached the French doors out into Adele's courtyard, she slowed down, taking a minute to absorb the scene stretching out before her. All of her children and grandchildren were there, with their families, Adele and all her family there too. The older kids were splashing in the pool, laughing at a high pitch and throwing a beach ball back and forth. Then she saw two little ones in the water with Rhonda, playing at the shallow end where the waterfall was. The older one was in a Puddle Jumper, the new brand of floating device that all the kids wanted right now. The little one was in a little floater seat, with her legs sticking out of the bottom, chubby and endlessly kicking. She thought to herself, *oh, of course, they aren't just white,* and she was secretly a little embarrassed that she'd pictured them as carbon copies of her own children. Right on the heels of that, she registered they must have removed all the pictures of the kids the night she came over. They hadn't wanted her to see them before they were willing to have her meet them.

Part of her wanted to stand here all day, drinking in their perfect little selves without interrupting the beauty of the scene in front of her. The other part could not wait to join them, to get in the water, to play and laugh with her family. Before she could decide, Adele opened the door and yelled out, "Look who I found!"

They walked out into the sun, ready to say hello, and Ralphy said, "Hi, Grandma," and splashed her full in the face with what seemed like buckets of water. Looking around, expecting to be chastised, he was the most surprised of all of them when she quickly reached down towards the water and splashed him right back. He laughed with the kind of glee she could just barely remember from the childhoods of his mother and her siblings. But before she knew what was happening, she was laughing too, pulling off her cover-up to jump, feet first, into the pool.

Chloe was resting on a chaise lounge, covered with a towel and laid across an appealing print cushion, looking beautiful but more fragile than the last time she'd seen her. Catching sight of Chloe in her peripheral vision, she felt a sudden alarm. She thought she had really considered the possibility of Chloe not making it through this but, in this moment, knew she hadn't. She had considered this all just a bad dream they would someday look back on, glad it was over. Suddenly, that seemed like a fantasy. This could kill her. Maybe it would kill her. For an instant, she could not catch her breath.

Then Rhonda and those beautiful babies swam over to her. "This is your grandma," Rhonda said, and they reached out for hugs, the way she imagined they did with their other grandmother.

⚜ ⚜ ⚜

Later, she would call this another one of the best days of her life. It wasn't only about those two adorable children, splashing and playing in the water, letting her scoop them up and swoosh them through the waterfall, giggling and happy. It wasn't just seeing everyone together, enjoying the din of the family life she had missed for so long. It wasn't even sitting next to Chloe and chatting about the music she had gone out to hear last night, leaving her tired today, or the little bit she was willing to say about how she was feeling. It wasn't the good food either, even though it was very, very good. She was enjoying feeling alive again.

⁂

Rhonda was sitting at one of the two tables, under the umbrella, sipping on a lemonade. As Sal walked that way, she almost lost her nerve, but now was no time to turn into a wimp. Rhonda greeted Sal as she sat down, leaving her feelings about sitting at the table together up to the imagination. Sal took one of the hundreds of deep breaths she had taken in the past six months and dove in.

"Adele tells me you're an author. What kinds of things do you write?"

"That's a good question these days," she said, looking suddenly amused. "I used to be a novelist. I was really pretty careful never to betray my own life in my books. I researched people I'd never met and then wrote books about them. Since all this, though, I don't seem to be able to write about anyone but myself and my family."

"Wow. That must be weird," Sal said, noncommittally.

"Well, some of my friends would say it's about time. They thought I wrote that way so no one would know I'm queer." Sal was surprised to hear the word, as if Rhonda didn't think it was an insult. And she was surprised it didn't offend her. "I guess I didn't want people to expect that, just because I'm gay, I only wanted to write about gay things. But since all this, I don't really care what anyone thinks."

"I kind of know what you mean about that. All of that worrying about what other people think just seems like a waste of time these days. I have to admit I still worry a little about what you and Chloe think."

"You do? That's a surprise," she said, not sarcastically but like it was really a surprise. "Do you want to know what I think?"

"I really do," Sal said, before she had time to reconsider.

"Well, first of all, I think you're brave. You faced up to a lot of people you hurt with what you did, and that takes courage. Us gay people have to be brave, in a way, or not live at all. You made a choice. So I admire that." She gave Sal a minute to absorb the compliment, but Sal knew Rhonda wasn't done. She kept quiet, wanting her to continue.

"I'm also pretty pissed, because I love your daughter and I've watched her go through a pile of pain over the years. She's very sensitive, I guess you know that, and it really undermined her. All the times something special happened, our wedding or getting pregnant or the awards she got for her editing, she always missed you. You were always missing. I wanted to tell her not to care, but if *my* mother were gone, I would never stop caring. I can't ask her to do something I wouldn't be capable of. So I'm a little cautious around you. I don't want to be, but I just have to be honest. I am watching out for her."

Sal couldn't keep looking at her. She turned to

stare at the sunlight on the water, all the kids out of it to turn their blue lips pink again. She took in Adele and Frank sitting by Chloe, her two kids on a towel falling asleep next to her. She tried to find the right words to say what she wanted to say.

"I understand that you can't just welcome me with open arms. I guess I'd want my children to be protected from harm, even from me. I know it's going to take time. I just hope we have enough." Rhonda looked at Sal for a long moment, sizing her up, but with more kindness than Sal felt, in that moment, that she deserved.

"Sal, I want to like you. In fact, I want to love you. Just keep showing up for her. Whether you ever love me or not, that will be enough."

꙳꙳꙳꙳

Sal didn't want that day to end. When Adele commented that it was getting dark, Sal ignored her implication and said, "I love your yard in this light."

By that time, Chloe and her family had gone home, worn out from it all. Sal's kids and her other grandkids were inside washing off before getting in their own cars.

"Can I stay a little longer?" Sal said to Del, wanting to linger with her sister.

"As long as you want," she said, sounding as if she really meant it.

"Del, I really appreciate what you did for me. I know I don't really deserve it."

"You're welcome, but you know I did it for myself too, right?"

"What do you mean?"

"I have never liked being at odds with you, Sal. I love you more than most other people I've ever known and I didn't know how to fix things up. Not to mention it wasn't easy being the middleman for you and Chloe and seeing all the pain between you. I am frankly relieved. I like things better this way."

❧❧❧❧

Sal couldn't wait to get to work the next day and tell Randy all about it. She could hardly bear it when she realized he wasn't working that day. She called him at lunch and asked him what he was up to that night. "Just hanging out with Don," he said. "Wanna come over?"

Randy and Don were quickly getting past the point where they had to be alone so much of the time, and Sal decided not to worry about whether they really wanted to be alone and he wasn't saying. He was a big boy. He could say it if he didn't want Sal over.

She had gotten awfully fond of Don, too, ready to tell him anything she would tell Randy, so now she had two people to catch up on the details of her swim party. The funny thing was that she hadn't noticed she'd never been to Randy's apartment. He'd come over to her house, they'd gone out, they had even invited her to parties their friends threw, usually in some gorgeous house in the hills. But never Randy's apartment.

It was in one of those Oakland neighborhoods that looked sketchy or posh from block to block. His block was somewhere in the middle. There were lots of apartments, but they were well kept and the houses interspersed were tidy. People cared about their yards and it was a time of year when things were blooming.

It was an old classic apartment building, mahogany woodwork and built in cupboards. When Sal admired the apartment, Randy surprised her by saying that he'd bought it when he was in a corporate job, about four years back.

"Why did you quit?" she asked, not able to imagine why he'd give all of that up.

"I guess to be trite, I wanted to follow my dreams," he answered.

"What are they?" she asked, wishing she'd asked what his dreams were a long time ago.

"I'm writing a book," he said and she imagined that with all his observing and how funny he was, it would be a damned good book.

"You should tell Chloe. She's an editor for a publishing company."

Chloe was more than Sal's gay daughter now. Sal's picture of her had expanded to include so many things about her, all the details of her full and rich life. Sal wanted to be a part of it all.

Chapter Fourteen

Chloe

Chloe wasn't well enough for chemo the next month. At first, she was scared and disappointed. She wanted to get this over and done with. But after she began to feel better, she decided to enjoy this time, without the chemicals, and make the best of it.

Without the hard knocks of treatment, a little of her old energy began to return. She walked the kids to school and worked more days. She saw her friends, just to see them, more often, instead of them simply doing things for her. Rhonda spent more time in the yard, and Chloe and the kids came out with her, the kids playing and Chloe sitting out with them.

Rhonda's state of mind moved in concert with Chloe's state of health, so she was better these days too. Now and then, she went out to do things she used to do, even if Chloe didn't want to go. She loved going to hear poetry, something Chloe had always been iffy about, and she gave herself that pleasure more often.

❧❧❧❧

It was one of those nights, when she was an hour from home, that Chloe texted her half way through. "Something is wrong," she said, and Rhonda ran out to the lobby, calling their number before she was out of the auditorium. "I'm so sorry to mess up your night!" Chloe was always concerned for her. "R, I don't feel right and I can't get anyone on the phone. Can you come home?"

"On my way," was all she said before she ran for the car, telling Chloe she'd get someone to come.

Deidre was away this weekend, she remembered after she dialed the number. She went down the list in her mind. Who was close? Without Rhonda's permission, Sal's face popped up in her head. Only five minutes away. Gotta try. She had to pull over to call, to look up the number. Sal was definitely not on speed dial.

"Sal? It's Rhonda."

"Rhonda, is something wrong?" That was the moment when Rhonda got it that Sal was for real. She had never heard so much concern.

"I hope not, but Chloe just called and said she's not feeling right and I'm an hour away. I wondered if you could go—"

Before she could finish the sentence, Sal broke in, "I'm on my way."

Rhonda texted Chloe. "Your mom's on the way. Hold on." Then she put the car in drive and began the way too long drive home.

❧ ❧ ❧ ❧

By the time Rhonda got there, Chloe was a little better, but they still thought she should be seen. Before they could ask Sal to stay with the kids, she said, "You go. Go right now. I'm on it."

One thing Chloe trusted she could count on her

mom to do was keep little kids safe. She had a heap of experience with that. Chloe was surprised to feel so secure leaving the house with her mother there, her kids asleep in their tiny beds, but there was no hesitation. The longing she had had, to have her mommy, suddenly felt possible, real almost. Rhonda packed her into the car, covering her with the flannel blanket they had brought with them, and she fell asleep, putting herself in Rhonda's, and her mother's, hands.

✄✄✄✄

The glare of the ER lights was different from the wing on which Chloe had given birth. It was harsher, and no one looked happy. They waited a long time to be seen, Rhonda taking her to the hard chair furthest from everyone else's germs. Rhonda went up to the triage desk every five minutes and asked to be put in a room. Couldn't they see how bad off she was? Through the door, they saw ambulances bringing the worst cases to the door past which they couldn't go. Rhonda felt terrified of Chloe being here with all the coughs and feverish dripping going on in the other chairs. By the time they were taken into a room, or rather a portion of a room divided by curtains, she was ready to scream.

Chloe was feeling too sick to worry. She sat with her head leaning against Rhonda's shoulder, feeling as if she could die right here. Some part of her thought, *well, if I die, it's been a good life. I've been loved and I even got back together with my mother.* She knew Rhonda wouldn't like to hear anything like that, so she didn't say a word. Besides, she felt too weak to waste her energy on talking.

When they were finally ready for her, the nurse

said, "Can you walk to the bed?"

She surprised herself when she heard herself say, quietly, "no." They brought a wheelchair and it seemed like a big effort just to get into the chair. By the bed, she asked if she could stay in the chair. The effort of getting onto the bed seemed too much.

"We'll lift you up there. Can you help me?" the nurse said to Rhonda, and they picked her up as if she were toothpicks, laying her carefully on the bed. She was so tired her bones hurt. It hurt to be moved, even though they were as careful as possible.

The nurse, whose nametag said Betsy, took her vitals. By now, she had had her vitals taken at least a thousand times. She was used to it. Old hat. This time, it took the last of her meager energy; even being touched too big an intrusion to tolerate. "No, no," she said weakly, but Betsy didn't hear or was used to going on anyway. After a torture of eternity, she was done.

"The doctor will be in as soon as possible."

As soon as possible. It could be a minute or tomorrow. Could they be more specific? Rhonda heard her heart beating fast in her own ear.

Rhonda was not much of a singer, but she had learned over the years that, when all else failed, Chloe responded to a song. First, she sang the lullabies that their children loved the most, "Dreamland" and "Circle Game," then moved on to "Power of Two." That was a leap off the cliff for her. Indigo Girls could really sing and the song always touched her so much it made her cry. But Chloe needed some comfort.

> *Now the parking lot is empty*
> *Everyone's gone someplace*
> *I pick you up and in the trunk I've packed*

A cooler and a two-day suitcase...

Chloe murmured, responding to the gentle voice in her ears. It was working. Rhonda could barely keep singing, crushed by the weight of her sweetheart's pain, and crushed by the unthinkable danger that the pain might stop forever.

To keep singing, she reviewed in her mind every weekend getaway she could remember. After they got in the car, they always played this song first. Heading down the coast to walk on the Carmel beach, watching the sun set over the sea, curled together under a blanket. Heading inland to the hot springs they loved, to soak in a tub and stare at the moon. Their honeymoon in Hawaii, when they each listened to the song in their ear buds on the plane, holding hands as they sat with the arm rest lifted between them. And now, traveling to this unknown territory, with it's strange and eerie landscapes.

You know the things that I am afraid of
I'm not afraid to tell...

Rhonda wondered when the friggin' doctor would show up, how long it would be, what the hell was wrong with these medical folks. She screamed in her mind, "People, she could die before you get here!" She felt desperate in a way she had not in her whole life. She had always been able to do something about anything. She could do nothing about this.

Adding up the total of a love that's true
Multiply life by the power of two

Just as she got to the last line, she saw the doctor turn the corner, heading for their little island in the E.R., the fixer headed for the problem. Rhonda thanked her vague concept of God that they didn't have to wait any longer. Chloe murmured in her sleep. She had not been able to stay awake for the end of the song or the doctor who came in now, ready to figure out what was wrong.

⚜ ⚜ ⚜ ⚜

Chloe hardly woke up while they took her blood pressure, her pulse, listened to her heart, and felt her cold feet for the second time. She stirred just a little when Betsy took blood. They hooked up monitors, which, regardless of the soothing words they said, looked dangerous to Rhonda. Surely only very sick people were attached to so many pieces of equipment, even in the emergency room. Chloe's nurse had only two patients to attend to, which also seemed alarming. What could be wrong that she needed so much attention? Rhonda took a deep breath. If she seemed scared, Chloe might pick up on it. When Chloe fluttered her eyes, maybe not completely awake, Rhonda had a smile for her every time.

The doctor was talking, but it was hard to concentrate on what he was saying. Rhonda glanced at his badge. She had not grasped his name. Dr. Rajeesh. He was asking her the questions because Chloe was too weak, or sleepy to answer.

"When was her last chemotherapy?"

"About a month ago. She couldn't have the last one because her counts were too low."

"How long has she been feeling so weak?"

"Seems to have gotten worse over the course of this week."

"I can tell you what I'm testing for now, or wait until I know something."

Rhonda appreciated the question, but for the first time since all this began, she wasn't sure she wanted to know. "Give me a minute," she said, and glanced down at Chloe, asleep again on the narrow gurney. "Okay, I want to know," she answered, before she could chicken out.

"I'm concerned about infection and I'm also concerned about thrombocytopenia. That's when the body, because of the way chemo works, stops producing enough platelets. We need to figure out which it is, but we have treatments to try either way. It's very good you came in, in any case." He smiled thinly and sauntered off to see the next patient. He'd been behind their curtain two minutes, tops, and Rhonda wished, for the first time in her life, that she had unlimited funds so she could hire a doctor to be with Chloe twenty-four hours a day. How had they missed that she was getting so sick?

The nurse after the shift change, Derrick, was a little more available. He came in and out frequently, and the third time he came in to look at the monitors, Rhonda spoke quickly, before he could hurry off again. "Can you tell me how much danger she's in, please?"

Derrick smiled, then pulled up a stool and gave Rhonda his full attention. "This is pretty common when people have a long run of chemo. I would guess, because of these splotches on her legs," and he showed them to her, "that her platelets are low. If I'm right, we'll admit her and give her a blood transfusion. That should perk her up. We deal with this stuff all the time." He touched Rhonda on the shoulder and let her know he'd be back as soon as the tests were back.

All alone sitting on the edge of Chloe's bed, Rhonda's take-charge personality finally kicked in. Okay, what did she need to take care of? For the first time since they had pulled into the emergency parking lot, she thought of her kids at home with their recently reunited grandma. She was surprised that she wasn't nervous, that she had confidence the kids would be well cared for. Still, this mending of the mile-high fence between Chloe and her mother had suddenly been leapt over. She hoped Chloe would be okay with that when she felt better. Rhonda reviewed how they had gotten here in her mind. She had to call the person who could get there the fastest. That was definitely Sally. Rhonda laughed to herself that all those years she and Chloe had lived together in their house, Sal had been so nearby. Chloe hadn't really talked about where her mom lived until they started seeing each other again.

When Derrick peeked in for a moment, Rhonda asked where the nearest phone-safe location was and he showed her to a waiting room down the hall. She needed to get some people going. She doubted they would be home tonight.

"Sal? It's Rhonda. Yeah, they're taking good care of her. They're thinking infection or low platelets. Did the kids wake up at all? No? That's good, I guess. Thanks for being there. Hey, I don't think we'll be back tonight. Do you want me to call Emily to get over there, or my par— Oh, you want to stay? Well, I'll set up relief for tomorrow, if that's okay." Long pause. "Well, Sal, I appreciate you're willing to stay indefinitely, I really do, but the kids don't know you that well. Okay, you can stay too, with whomever else I get to come over.

Okay, I'll check in later. Yeah, bye."

Before she could call anyone else, she sat for a few minutes in the striped, hard, waiting room chair, trying to absorb what had just happened. Chloe's mother had said, "I love you, Rhonda," right before they hung up.

⚘⚘⚘⚘

The day Chloe came home, the house was full. Sal was making a huge stew, the smell of beef and tomatoes filling the kitchen. Rhonda's parents were out cleaning up the garden and watering the plants, knowing it would upset Rhonda if anything died while she was busy at the hospital. Emily had set up her computer in the living room and worked while Quinten and Arisa removed each and every toy from the boxes and put them in a huge pile in the middle of the floor. Every now and then, one of them carried a book over to her, lifting their arms to be deposited on an adult's lap and read to.

Chloe still looked pale and drawn but came into the room with a big smile for the kids. Quinten ran to her, jumping up to be held, while Ari was still toddling over, only just having learned to walk. She carried them both to the couch and collapsed into it, covering them with kisses and hugs. Satisfied with the greeting, Quin climbed down and started his music box, showing Chloe his latest dance moves and bringing laughter to everyone around, Chloe included. Ari cuddled into her mother's arms, content to rest there. Rhonda brought a bottle and Ari cradled into her mother's arms, eyes fluttering, sucking the milk until, finally, she fell asleep. Sal gently picked her up and carried her to the crib, laying her down so quietly that she didn't stir.

An hour later, when Quin finally went down for his nap too, Chloe staggered into their bedroom, exhausted from the whole ordeal. They were told she would be leaving around ten, so she got up, got dressed, but by the time the doctor finally signed off on her discharge, it was one. Those three hours were some of the longest she could remember. Only Rhonda remembered the wait in the ER.

After Rhonda tucked her in, Sal came to the doorway, hesitant but unable to resist looking in on her daughter. She knew they hadn't repaired much yet, but she didn't feel like there was time to wait. She wanted to help as much as she could.

Not even aware Chloe saw her there, she suddenly heard a faint voice from the bed, "Mom, you can come in."

"Okay, Chloe, do you need anything?"

A slight shake left to right to left was the only answer. Sal came in and stood by the bed, unsure what she should do now that she was in the room. Chloe motioned her over, to the bed and then in, and then brought tears to Sal's eyes when she curled up on top of her mother and fell asleep.

Sal put her hand on her daughter's head, smooth as the babies' bottoms, not a hair to be found anywhere on it. She had a flash of Chloe's first few weeks of life, when they curled up just like this and napped together, recovering from birth. Sal remembered the delicious feeling of satisfaction she had then, when the whole world seemed to have improved because a new life had found its way to her. Even Stan was nicer right then, proud to be a father, if not a daddy. All things seemed possible to her at that moment and she wondered how she had lost her optimism.

When Rhonda peeked in fifteen minutes later, they were both asleep, Sal leaning against the pillows crowded around the headboard and Chloe splayed across her. Rhonda pulled the door to keep out the noise and shed her tears alone, happy for Chloe that her mother was back, sad for all the time they had lost.

* * *

Once Chloe had her energy back, she seemed eager to have some adventures. Often, she called up her mother on Sal's day off and asked if she wanted to go out. Sometimes Rhonda came along; sometimes she stayed home and worked.

Rhonda had put down her writing for longer than she ever had, but Chloe noticed she was becoming tense and unhappy. Finally, Chloe took her aside one day and said, "You better write something soon or I'm not going to recognize you." That was all the permission Rhonda needed. She still felt unhappy about missing any moment she could have with Chloe. But she had to admit that if she didn't do at least a little of the stuff that made her feel like herself, she couldn't really enjoy it much anyway. She made a little sign to put on the edge of her computer, "Put your own air mask on first," and she made a point of reading it each time she sat down to write, to answer emails, read a book, play a game of solitaire.

There were scores of people who wanted to take care of Chloe. She was so lovable that they sometimes had to lock the door to get some peace and quiet. Sometimes they needed the help and just threw the door open to whoever wanted to come in. The summer stretched into winter, almost indistinguishable except that the sunny days were further apart, the yard was more often cold and the living room more often full. Their friends and family learned to do everything at a low decibel so that when Chloe was asleep, they never woke her up. When she was awake but low on energy, large numbers of them would pile on the bed, watch TV, read books to her, or rub her back.

Chloe had told all of them to take care of Rhonda too. Rhonda got used to being offered a good meal, a cup of tea, a massage. In the beginning, she refused these love offerings; she knew they were for love, but she wasn't sure the love was for her. Then there was a long period where it seemed as if she was trying to talk them out of it. "Are you sure? Do you really have the time? I don't want to put you out." That began to wear thin. She didn't have the energy to take care of everyone else, and Chloe, and the kids. She resolved to say nothing but "thank you" whenever anything was offered to her or to the family. She rehearsed the many ways thank you could be said.

At first, it felt like an empty gesture, so inadequate to everything that was being done for them. She thought only of how strange it felt to say it. Over time, though, she began to notice how her friends and family reacted to being thanked. They seemed genuinely happy, gratified to be acknowledged. There was almost no gift that wasn't equaled by gratitude. What a revelation! Within a month, she stopped feeling as if she was running at a deficit. Her accounts were paid.

Now and then, thank you didn't seem to work so dependably. The first time was with Isabel, an old friend from a writer's group she'd been in years ago. She had insisted she wanted to help, just tell her what she could do, so they gave her Deidre's name.

She signed up to bring a dinner every week, and she brought it, dutifully, every Tuesday night. The second week, after she left, Chloe said to Rhonda, "I am not looking forward to this food. Last week, it just didn't taste right. I couldn't say anything exactly was wrong, but it wasn't right." Rhonda didn't go in for that woo woo stuff, but she knew what Chloe meant. Not right.

That was during the period when they were still hesitant to say things that might hurt people's feelings. They didn't say anything to Isabel. They threw out the leftovers every week, barely having made it through the meal. It was two months more of correctly cooked, wrong meals before they finally figured it out.

Isabel wasn't able to bring dinner that week but said she would come after working late and help out. By the time she came, they had all eaten and the kids were down for the night. All that was left was cleaning the kitchen, the dishes from the whole day piled in the sink. She walked into the kitchen with both of them sitting at the table and looked happier than they had seen her since she began bringing dinner. "I love doing the dishes," she declared, with true enthusiasm. "It's so much better than cooking."

Chloe and Rhonda looked at each other and almost broke out laughing. No wonder the food wasn't right.

"You are never allowed to cook for us again, but feel free to come over and do the dishes," Rhonda said, and Isabel thanked her, laughing and hugging them both before she headed out into the night.

"From now on, if something doesn't seem right, we change it!" said Chloe, and Rhonda nodded in agreement.

Chapter Fifteen

Sally

Each day Sal woke up and felt two things within the first few minutes. First would come the joy at being so close to her child again. And it was rubbing off on her other kids, too. They were coming around more, almost seemed to be enjoying time with her. They'd call out of the blue and invite her to dinner. They were visiting their sister more often, offering to take care of the kids or pick up meds from the pharmacy. Overall, they were circling closer to each other, with Chloe in the center and Sal one circle out. Was it Sal's imagination or were Chloe's sister and brothers beginning to think more about making something out of their lives? Grant finally finished graduate school and was looking for a job. Candice started to date again. Chase wasn't much better in the life accomplishment way but seemed to be smiling more and sometimes even told a story of something he had enjoyed or appreciated. And he didn't call in sick to his job as often.

Maybe the bigger change was in Sal. She had four healthy, good children, maybe not the most accomplished in the world, Chloe aside, but good people. She found herself caring very little about all the small disappointments that had dominated her thoughts about her kids just a few months ago.

She was spending most of her free time with her family and Chloe and Rhonda's great bunch of friends. About once a week, she would feel herself getting dizzy when she thought about the changes that had come into her life. At work, she talked to the customers like a friendly person. She noticed that sometimes the customers stepped out of line to wait for her and they would chat about their lives. Sal was really interested!

The only person who didn't seem surprised by the change in Sal was Lonnie. She was the same as always, steady and waiting to hear what she had to say.

"Lonnie, I haven't felt like this since maybe when I first met Stan."

"What was it like then, Sal?"

"Well, I was taking classes at the community college, Merritt was the one. It was up on a hill, and I loved the bus ride up there. We wound up the hill and there were hardly ever that many people on the bus. We would pass these houses and I imagined how happy people must be to live there. It always seemed sunnier to me up there, every house was a different color, and the yards were special, like the people who lived there really cared.

"I was planning on transferring to Cal, any Cal, after I finished the two years, so I was taking all the courses I needed for that, but I got to take an elective every semester, so I took an art class each time. And that's where I met Stan.

"He was taking watercolor because he was hoping for an easy 'A' but he was really bad at it. He asked me to look at his tiny, little painting a few weeks in and I had to hold myself back not to laugh. I've seen kid's art that was better than that. It looked a lot like stick figures.

"He said to me, 'What do you think?' and I said, 'I think you're gonna flunk.' At first, it seemed like he was going to get insulted, his face kind of scrunching up and turning a little red. But then he started laughing and said, 'Wow, an honest woman.' We hung out a lot after that, but I wanted to be with him so bad that I didn't stay so honest for long. I started trying to figure out who he wanted me to be and being that woman. That was probably the biggest thing that went wrong."

Sal paused, paying attention to Lonnie and how she was reacting to her life. Same as usual, she just looked like she was interested, as if Sal had her full attention. Then Lonnie surprised her and spoke.

"So, inside of you is a straightforward, honest woman who does not consider the costs of doing what she feels is right."

Lonnie had her there.

❧❧❦❦

Saturday morning the phone rang, early. That would have gotten on her nerves at one point, but now she bounded up, tripping over the shoes that she had kicked off before she went to bed. She didn't ever want to miss a call from Chloe or Rhonda if she could help it. She looked at the number on call waiting. Chloe's cell phone.

"Chloe, is everything okay?"

"Don't worry, Mom, I just want to ask you something."

Why had Sal been so evil to her? Why had it taken so long to come around? How could she live with this much regret? How did she expect Chloe ever to forgive her?

"We're going to Hawaii with Rhonda's family; her parents, Graham, the kids. We think we're going to go between the next treatment and the one after that and we wanted to know if you'd like to come along."

"Chloe, is it smart to travel? What if you get sick?"

She laughed, but just a little. "Mom, I'm already as sick as they come. Having a setback here or there, what's the difference? Missing out on every single thing I want to do in my life? That seems worse to me, for sure. I'm not going to have more time to see Hawaii if I wait. I think the beach would do us all good."

"In that case, you bet I want to go!"

⁂

Sal bought Chloe a sporty wheelchair. Her birthday was coming up, and none of them wanted her to waste her energy getting to the airplane or travelling around the island. The TSA guy was young, tall, and robust, friendly as they come. He wheeled her so fast they had to put Quin on the back of Ari's stroller to go fast enough to keep up.

"How long you been working here?" Sal asked, just to pass the time.

"Since I turned eighteen. My dad works here too." She had never imagined airport security could be a family business.

"It's pretty good pay and, mostly, I don't spend all my time working. Lately, though, a bunch of people have been out sick, so I've pulled a ton of extra shifts."

Rhonda and Sal caught each other's eyes. Neither of them had to tell the other what was on their minds. Chloe. Germs. Being pushed down that long hallway by an exposed person. Fear. Dread.

"And you? Have you had it?"

"No. I'm healthy as a horse. They all started getting sick a few weeks ago, so it's past the point I'd be coming down with it. Good news, I didn't get it. Bad news, I had to work for everyone while they coughed and hacked."

He had whisked them through security while they were talking, wheeling past the long lines of crying babies and business suits. She noticed there were a lot more women in business suits, their computer bags looking like hand bags, than the last time she flew. She counted in her head. Somewhere around twenty years.

✺✺✺✺

Stan and she had gone on what they were trying to call a second honeymoon, but even then, there was trouble. They farmed all the kids out various places and flew to Mexico to lay on a beach and eat food. They hadn't even gotten up in the air before they were fighting. Why didn't she bring more cash? Mexico, he'd never wanted to go there. What a lame place to pick. What was all this costing, anyway?

She didn't help the situation any either. She answered every question snappy, a little bit of a put down in each retort. You could have brought your own damn cash. Where were you when I was spending hours trying to figure it all out? Penny pinching cheap skate, cry me a river.

There was no one else in the three-seat row, so they got as far away from each other as they could. She snapped her book out of her bag and he pulled out his credit card and got plastered. Didn't even *need* the cash. Even though the flight was only a few hours long, he was hardly able to walk when they arrived. She sat him down and got the bags, rented a car, loaded the car and put him in it. When she looked back later, she figured that trip was the real end of things.

They were there a whole week. Went on forever. She thought, *it's almost a crime to have such a bad time there.* The little hotel, which was quaint and colorful, was on a cliff by Rosarito Beach. A little bar where they sold drinks in coconuts stood at the furthest point before a careless walker would fall right into the sea. They managed to sit there every night as the sun went down, taking an impossibly long time to dip below the horizon and splash vermilion light over the tide. If Sal hadn't been so busy hating Stan, she might have noticed that this was one of the most beautiful views she'd ever seen.

A few days in, Stan said, "Aren't I supposed to get some? This is a vacation, right?" He looked at her, accusation oozing from his pores.

"Oh, whatever!" she'd replied, but they did have sex when they got back to the room. She spent the whole time looking out the balcony door at the stars, distracting herself from what was going on. She had developed that strategy a long time ago, because this wasn't the first time she had given him sex just to shut him up. A few days of peace was worth enduring it. Usually, a little way through it, she felt something, but that time she'd felt absolutely nothing. She'd made a vow to herself she'd never, ever do that again.

It did shut him up though. The next few days he complained less. Wasn't pleasant, exactly, just less nasty. That's when she stopped hating him and began to pity him. She resolved to leave him when they got home, but it was another couple of years. She had not been a quick study.

ℛℛℛℛ

Clarence and Fay had rented a few cottages all in a row by a beautiful, calm beach on Kauai. Sal had tried to pay for her room, in Chloe and Rhonda's little three-bedroom cottage, but they had refused, told her this was their treat. She tried to hide her relief and thank them as if she didn't need the help, but she would have had to charge the trip. She ran close to the edge in the money department. She had even had to charge the new wheelchair.

Clarence and Fay were sharing a two-bedroom next door with Graham. They loved their two children with an obvious relish Sal had never felt about her own kids up until now. They wanted to hear what their kids had to say. They supported their ventures, trusting them to make decisions about what was best for them. Graham told her that when he decided to become an actor, they asked him how long he thought it would take to make it in LA. He told them he thought it would be about five years and they said, "Okay, you've got money for five years. Then we'll talk."

Clarence had made a fortune promoting hip hop and R&B artists all over the country and they knew almost everyone in the music business. They were getting some of the smaller artists together to give a concert to help Chloe, but they put it off a little to come to Hawaii.

All those musicians had known Rhonda since she was born, had carried her around back stage and let her sit at their drum sets or strum their guitars. Her first book had been a novel about living on the road, and it came easy to her, since she imagined as a child that she boarded the bus with the musicians and drove on to the next town. But only her father, Clarence, made those trips, coming back with endless stories collected to amuse the kids.

Sal was surprised to learn that none of the musicians had thought anything of Rhonda being gay. When she asked Rhonda about it, she told Sal she had been really scared to let everyone know, not just her parents but all these people she'd known all her life too. She put it off, but when she finally told everyone, most of them just said, "Geez, it's not a shock. Long as you're happy, honey." That was the end of it. There was not one of them, apparently, that didn't love Chloe. Easy to love, that one, they all agreed.

Sal's room in the cottage had a country style double bed with a quilt on it, extra blankets in the closet and down pillows covering the headboard. From the window to the side of the bed, she could see the ocean lapping on the shore if she kept the curtains open. If she stayed in bed late, she could watch Chloe laying on a beach chair under a rainbow-striped umbrella, watching the kids in the water with Rhonda. She almost liked this better than going out with them, to watch them when they didn't know she was there. Quinten had gotten big enough to run in the shallow water, giggling with delight when the tide got a little higher. Arisa preferred Rhonda's arms, and they went in far enough that Rhonda was up to her waist and Ari's toes got wet and cold when the waves came in.

Quin had learned to swim as a baby, but they put a life vest on him anyway, not trusting the surf. As the week went on, he got braver, diving in and coming up laughing with exquisite euphoria. They trained him never to go in alone, so when Rhonda got tired he sat with his sand toys next to Chloe, under the umbrella, and poured sand from one bucket to another as she dozed. Ari cuddled up to Chloe and napped the afternoon away, lulled by the sound of the surf. Rhonda wrote a little in the afternoon, inconveniently on deadline for her new book, a book of poems written to Chloe.

Sal had never spent so much time with Clarence and Fay, or Graham either. The first morning, she invited them over for breakfast. Pots and pans, plates, and cups stocked the little kitchen. They had stopped in town on their way and bought boxes and boxes of food, so they wouldn't have to leave their little paradise unless they wanted to. When Fay asked if she could help, Sal told her it was a one-person kitchen, which was true, but she also wanted to do something for *them* for a change. They had watched out for her daughter when she was too stubborn and depressed to do it, and it made her so grateful she wanted to give back. Breakfast for the rest of their lives wouldn't have been enough.

She made the coffee first, strong with half-and-half, and Fay sat at the kitchen nook table chatting with her while she whisked up the omelet and chopped the ingredients for custom made.

"I'm so glad you came with us," she said, absolutely genuine and warm.

"Me too. I can't tell you how lucky I feel to be here with Chloe and all of you. How could I have been missing out on this for so long?" As soon as she said it, she wished she could take it back. Why did she want to call attention to her shortcomings?

"Well, you're here now. Time to let yourself off the hook."

She enjoyed cooking the omelets, toasting Hawaiian bread, bacon on the side. They sat the kids at the table and took turns sitting with them until they finished. The rest of them ate in the living room, sitting in the big rocker, on sofas, on chairs. Graham was telling stories of the worst Hollywood moments in his career, making funny stories out of tense times.

"And then the director said, 'you're all fired. I'm recasting the whole damn play.' And we looked at each other like, is he for real? 'Cuz it was the day before opening! Needless to say, he hired us all back within the hour and after opening night he pulled us together for notes and said, 'this is the best cast I've ever worked with.' We couldn't help it; every one of us started laughing. Even *he* had to laugh at himself! Well, he would have if he'd been capable of laughter."

Sal dreaded the time when the trip would be over. Each day, Chloe was a little stronger, even swimming in the ocean and taking short walks down the beach. Sal would never forget the mornings, high tide, bright with sunshine glancing off the sand and the sea. She hadn't jogged in years, but she took little runs down the beach in her bare feet, Fay and Clarence joining her a few mornings, and she enjoyed the faint breeze on her face on the way out, her neck on the way back.

There were the times she sat next to Chloe and held her hand. They talked then, about their time apart. "I don't want you to feel guilty, Mom, that's just a waste of energy, but I want you to know how much it hurt. I missed you. I felt so rejected, injured, and alone. Now I just feel lucky that I got through it and I have a beautiful family, and you're back. Thanks for coming back, Mom." Then she looked at her, dewy eyes and open mouth, and Sal melted from top to bottom.

ॐॐॐॐ

The kids were napping, exhausted from a sunny day at the beach. Chloe was laying on the sofa, trying to read a book. Reading put her to sleep more often than not lately and it was one of the things she was saddest about in this whole thing.

Sal thought about her as a kid. When she was a kid, she learned to read early, spending endless hours with a book in front of her. It was one of many examples of how she used Sal's deficiencies to her advantage. Sal didn't have much patience with reading to the kids. They each got a book for bed and that was pretty much it. That was never enough for Chloe and she kept after her Aunt Adele until she got her to teach her to read. She was three.

She always wanted to read books above her level. By the time she was seven, she had graduated to chapter books and proudly carried one around most of the time. They had to keep a sharp eye on her, so she didn't read the most disturbing part of the newspaper. If they didn't catch it, she would be up all night with nightmares. Sal, of course, was the one up with her.

Her teachers were thrilled to have such an enthusiastic student. They never had to encourage her to read. She read whole books in a few days when the lesson plans called for two months of reading. No problem; she would just read them over again.

It hurt Sal to think of her not being able to read. When Adele had told her what Chloe was doing for a living, in spite of herself, she'd thought, *that's perfect for her.* So now, she wanted her to be able to have her books. She approached cautiously, still trying to hang back until she was invited, but when she got near the couch, where Chloe was laying with her hand over her eyes, Sal heard a weak voice rising up. "What is it, Mom?" she said, tired but patient.

"Do you want me to read to you?"

Chloe took her hand away and looked Sal in the eye, almost as if she was trying to figure her out. "Really?" she said after what seemed like a very long time.

"Really!"

Chloe was rereading her favorite books. Sal was afraid to ask her why. Did she think she might never get a chance to read them again? Was it like a last goodbye? Virginia Woolf, Willa Cather, George Elliot, and Sylvia Plath. Sal had never liked that kind of book. They were all too intellectual, too much hard work. But reading them to Chloe, she felt the beauty of the words, the language flowering on the page. She didn't need to understand the stories or the author's point. She just read word after word, keeping part of an eye on Chloe as she tasted the books.

They started with Mrs. Dalloway, Virginia Woolf's book. Decades ago, Sal had gotten maybe ten pages in on her own, before she gave up on it. What was Woolf talking about? But this time she read past her own resistance, suddenly noticing that the book was just a rich description of one day. Then she noticed that Sally Seton, Mrs. Dalloway's friend, was someone she wanted to be with. Sal had not gotten that far on her own way back when. Mrs. Dalloway's exquisite torture – she loved someone she couldn't be with – affected Sal deeply this time.

Sal would read until just after Chloe drifted off, breathing steady and quiet, then mark her place. She'd watch her while she slept, afraid to miss a moment. She slept maybe fifteen, maybe twenty minutes then drifted back into the room. Sal got good at noticing when she was coming around. Sal would focus on her finger, on the page where they'd left off, then start reading right there as soon as she returned from whatever world she had visited. Sal was not sure Chloe even knew she had slept and that was Sal's goal, that the story be continuous. She was hoping Chloe would want her to keep on reading to her when they got home.

⁂

The flight back was long. Chloe was not having a good day, and the kids reacted, crying and fussing two rows back from Sal. There was an empty seat next to her and she finally went and got Quin, strapping him in and drawing endless pictures on the edges of the airline magazine for his entertainment. They played peek-a-boo and I Spy until he finally rubbed his eyes, slumping over to her lap and drooling from the moment he fell sleep. Arisa cried a little longer then finally wore herself out and fell asleep too, two hours into the flight.

The flight attendant did all she could, bringing little flight wing pins and blankets and pillows, making faces and carrying the kids up and down the aisles. In the end, though, she had to move on, serving drinks to the tourists and the business guys, keeping all the passengers happy.

Sal gently eased herself out from under Quin and went to the bathroom, splashing water on her face and perking herself up. She hadn't really needed to go. She just needed to see Chloe's face. She was sleeping with Arisa spread across her chest, completely relaxed. They had the same sweet smile on their lips and Sal smiled too, in spite of herself. She had never in her life felt so much love. How had she gotten through her children's childhoods without feeling this? She couldn't understand what had been wrong with her that she had spent ten years without her precious child. She was relieved she had found her way out of it. She finally knew what gratitude felt like and she remembered that, early on, Lonnie had told her that gratitude was her favorite feeling but that it couldn't be rushed. She let Sal know she had that to look forward to. Suddenly she knew, beyond her own expectation, that gratitude was a real thing, a feeling beyond compare.

As she made her way back to her own seat, her mind drifted to her reasons for rejecting Chloe in the first place. Without strong religious objections, without any experience with gay people, how had she come to have such a strong bias? For the first time, she considered the answer not with guilt, but with curiosity and then, as if in return for finding some softness with herself, the memory came.

❧❧❧❧

She was maybe eight years old or so and her best friend, Denise, spent most of her time over at their house. Sal's parents weren't the good kind of parents who made cookies and took them to the movies, but they left them alone. Sal would close the door to her room and they were free to do whatever they wanted. At Denise's house, there was even more yelling and screaming and they might even haul off and slap them for some small offense. She loved coming over to Sal's.

One day, they were playing in Sal's room. The pink curtains let a soft light in. They decided to take all their clothes off and compare their bodies. What was the same? What was different? They were taking great care with their project and fantasizing about what it would be like to have someone interested in these very same bodies.

Instantaneously, Sal's mother flew through the door, wildly whacking at them, trying her best to make contact with their small bodies. Looking back on it, Sal could see her mother had been drunk or maybe had taken too many pills. They ran to the corners, trying to avoid her, but her words stung more than any slap could have. "You nasty girls. You are so disgusting. I can't stand to look at either of you. Denise, get out of here and never come back." They were never allowed to play with each other again, and Sal spent every night for a month crying herself to sleep.

Chapter Sixteen

Chloe

Life fell into a new pattern, as if it would go on like this forever. Chloe slept late, waking to her children running into the bedroom when Rhonda decided it was late enough. They jumped on her, most mornings covering her with kisses, now and then crying for her attention. Quinten had an uncanny ability to know when she was too sick to play and found his way into a cuddle at those times. On the better days, he pulled her hands until she got out of bed and found a book or a toy. It was usually his favorite, "Tails." He loved to turn the pages and touch the furry tails peeking out from behind the paper. Arisa didn't have the patience for the whole book, so she spent her time climbing up and down, waiting until the book was done and Chloe could pick her up and tickle her belly.

They had bought a new bed. It was Rhonda's idea, after the first treatment. "Girl, you need a super seductive place to do all this sleeping," she said, and Chloe laughed, looking forward to the comfort.

When the bed was delivered, the delivery guys took pity on them and set it up even though they hadn't paid for that, and she laid down on it, just the plain mattress with no sheets or blankets, her voice louder than usual. "I love you, you sweet mattress you!" Rhonda jumped on too, pulling Chloe into her arms and kissing her face.

So, the morning after the flight from Hawaii, Chloe was thanking God for a luxurious bed to spend the day in. She was tired in a bone aching way, spent most of the day dozing on and off, but resurrected a little by dinnertime. Quinten and Arisa were missing their mommy and both wanted to sit on her lap while they ate their dinner. She and Rhonda took turns shuttling them back and forth. By the end of dinner, there was more food on the floor and on both of them than in their children's mouths. Rhonda cleaned up while Chloe laid on the floor and watched her children play.

She was missing so much time with them, but the time they had together had become increasingly precious and amusing. Each new thing they learned, each chubby hand on her cheek, every giggle, and even the cries found their way to the depths of her soul, blending in an exquisite symphony of joy and melancholy. The terror of dying before they were grown gave way to a determination that they would have all of her they could have while she was here. It was the only thing she had the energy to be determined about.

Their friend Emily was over almost every day. That day, having missed them for the ten days the family had been away, she came early, taking the day off work just to see them.

Quinten ran into her arms as soon as he saw her, "Auntie Emmy, Auntie Emmy," bursting from his lips. When she had thoroughly kissed and hugged him, she made her way to Ari, sneaking up on her, crouching down like a cat, then plunging towards her at the last moment and scooping her up. The giggles could be heard from one end of the house to the other.

Chloe laid on the couch when she finally got up, watching her children enjoying their Emily. She felt appreciative in a way that reached down deep. The only thing wrong in her life was no one's fault, just damned bad luck. She really did have the best of the worst.

ঙ ঙ ঙ ঙ

"Mama C, why do you sleep so much?" Quinten was a big enough boy to have questions, to notice that Mama C slept a lot more than Mama R did. The questions always came out of nowhere, catching them off guard and unprepared, even when they had anticipated one of the kids would someday have questions to ask.

"Well, Quin, I have a sickness that makes people really tired and I have to rest so that I have enough energy to play with you when I'm awake." Quin didn't like baby talk or baby answers. He liked big words and grown-ups who gave him grown-up answers. He looked thoughtful for a minute.

"I used to nap two times a day and now I only nap in the afternoon. Is it like that?"

Chloe and Rhonda would never get used to the fact that their little boy, at three, could come up with such thoughtful questions.

"Well, Quin, a little bit. You napped that much when you were little because you needed to, and I need to now. But nobody knows if I will need to forever or not."

"My friend Max says his mommy is sleeping forever. Is that true? Will you ever sleep forever?"

"His mommy died. That's a little like sleeping

because if you're dead you can't talk to people or move a lot or play, but it's different too." *Don't ask how, not yet*, Chloe thought.

"What's the difference?"

He looked up at her with innocent but serious eyes. No letting her off the hook. He wanted real answers.

They had a stethoscope up in the closet from the time Rhonda was writing about a heart attack and wanted to hear, every day, how a heart sounded when it beat. Chloe got the stool and pulled the box down from the closet, being careful not to bring down the whole pile carefully balanced up there. She got it down and sat Quinten next to her on the sofa. She put the earpieces into her ears and the bell on his chest. Once she heard his heart, she moved the earpieces to his ears. She waited until he seemed to react.

"Did you hear that, Quinny?" she said, taking the earpieces out.

"Again, Mama," he said, and they spent the next fifteen minutes listening, resting, listening, resting.

"That's your heartbeat, Quin. Every person who is alive has one. But when we die, our heart doesn't beat any more and our body doesn't work anymore. It's not like sleep because when you are dead, you won't ever wake up again. We all die; it's the way life works."

"Oh," he said, and jumped off the couch, ready to go play, unconcerned and satisfied with the answer she had offered. Chloe thought to herself, *It's not children who have trouble with things, it's grown-ups.* She smiled, happy that she had been having a good day when Quin asked.

❧❧❧❧❧

About once every two weeks, Chloe made it into the office. They left it open and, if she woke and told Rhonda she was able to go, Rhonda dropped everything. At first, Chloe felt guilty taking Rhonda from her writing. She knew how much it meant to Rhonda to sit at her desk, putting words to paper, and she hesitated to take that away when Rhonda was losing so much already. Finally, she began to miss her work so much that she had to bring it up.

"Um, Rhonda, do you have a minute?" Rhonda looked suddenly very worried. "No, not like that. It's just, I want to be able to take April up on her offer to let me work when I can, but I never know when that will be and so, I don't know how to manage it."

"Baby, if you feel well enough to go to work, just let me know. No problem. I'll be happy to hear it."

"But then you can't do your work unless someone can come at the last minute."

"Chloe, I don't know if you've noticed, but my work is no longer in the front seat. It comes behind you and the kids. It has to fit in wherever it can. Don't worry about it."

Chloe had to trust her. That was the last she ever worried about asking.

The good thing was, they had a list of people that loved being with the kids and had weird schedules, so Deidre was often able to find someone. They had been managing it for several weeks before they stumbled over a new wrinkle.

～～～～

Chloe was at work, editing a chapter from a book

of essays about parenting. It was the perfect assignment for her because the chapters came in sporadically and there was no concrete deadline. Deidre had called their friend Audrey, who was more in the grandmother age group, retired, and often able to come at the last minute. She was in the family room watching the kids play when there was a knock on the door. She let Sal in the back. They had met several times now and Audrey knew Sal was free to come over whenever she liked.

They sat chatting while the kids played. Audrey, being older, seemed a little less comfortable talking about her life the way Rhonda and Chloe did. Even so, Sal was able to find out that Audrey had been with the same person for forty years, that they had only just recently had a wedding ceremony, and they now called each other "wife." The word didn't seem to slip off Audrey's tongue quite as freely as the younger people they knew, but it did seem to have more meaning.

Audrey talked about how she and Lacy, her wife, had both been very depressed as young people, feeling different, not knowing why, and then they got happier when they met. She said it was partly because they found someone to love and partly because it was the first time that they knew for sure that they were not the only person who felt that way. She laughed at herself, remembering how silly she had been back then.

When Rhonda came out of her writing room, they were still talking, even though the children had gone down for a nap and Audrey could have headed for home. They finished up the talk and after a cup of tea, Audrey took her leave, thanking Sally for listening and hoping they'd see each other soon. Everyone hugged goodbye.

"I don't want you to take this the wrong way,

Rhonda. I really like Audrey and I hope I see her again. But would you call me first when you need help?"

Rhonda was taken aback but managed to reply a little equivocally, "We can think about that."

"No, I mean it. I missed a lot of time and I love being with those kids. And I want to help you. Really. I know there are whole bunches of people in the same boat, but could they come when I have to work? Could I be first on the list when I don't have to work?"

"I'll talk it over with Chloe," she said, knowing it had to be Chloe's decision.

⚝⚝⚝⚝

"Your mom wants to be first on the call list, Chloe," Rhonda began, trying not to betray an opinion. "She came by today when Audrey was here and after Audrey left, she asked me. I said we'd talk it over."

It was hard to feel all the feelings Chloe was feeling at the same time. *My mother wants to be a part of our lives. She wants to make it right. I'm so pleased! And I'm so pissed! My mother thinks she can just come back after ten years and ask for things. My mother has no understanding of my life or the way that all these people have been my family, when she wouldn't give me the time of day. Then again, I do want my mom.* Then back to the start and all over again.

"I have to think about it, Rho. I'm finding it awfully hard just to take her back in and let go of all the past stuff. But this could be the end of my life. I don't want to leave with this stuff between us. I don't know if that means she gets to be first call on my childcare list, though. What do you think? I need help here."

Rhonda took her time to answer. Chloe had

learned over the years not to interrupt, but just to wait until the answer came. It was always better if she waited.

"Baby, I think she's your mother and you need to be really sure if you say no to her. I think we should hire your two therapists to meet with you guys and sort this thing out. I don't think anyone else will resent you if you want her called first. We need enough help that there's plenty to go around. If she hadn't done all that mess, she would have been the first call. Just make sure you don't want that."

As usual, Rhonda was right.

❦❦❦❦

They made a two-hour appointment and paid both their therapists for the time. Chloe wanted them to be on an even playing field. She wanted her mother to have whatever help she could to tell the truth, to hang on while they tried to talk it through. As she walked up to the door to the office, her mother's therapist's office, she felt the strongest urge to turn around. If she'd had no concerns about her possible life span, she would have put this off for another day. But she had resolved in herself not to put off important things. Don't leave things hanging. Don't take the chance. Devin's words rang in her ear. "There really is no time like the present." She put her hand on the knob and turned.

She was amazed that the office felt so much like Angie's office. It wasn't that the furniture was the same. Angie's office was mostly blue, with peach accents. This office, Lonnie's, was burgundy and heather. But both rooms invited a person to feel at home, comfortable. A person could literally feel the safety. Even so, Lonnie would still have to prove herself.

The waiting room gave way to a large office. She chose a cozy chair, not the couch. Her mom wasn't here yet, but she was afraid if she sat on the couch, they might end up on it together. She wanted some physical space around her while she said what she had to say.

Angie had taken a seat in a straight chair with embroidery on the seat cover. Chloe was sure she was happy to have a firm, upright chair, since she had let it slip once she had trouble with her back. They smiled at each other, Chloe's smile more forced than Angie's. "Hi, Chloe, proud of you for being here," she said, creating a touchstone to the deep comfort Chloe always felt in Angie's office.

Lonnie smiled too, as if she understood how hard this kind of thing might be. While they waited, the two therapists talked a little about how they would work together. It occurred to Chloe, for the first time, that they had never met. She and Sal had just depended on them to work together for a common purpose. In quick order, they decided both Chloe and Sal needed some time to be heard and that Sal should speak first. She had the amends to make, they said, and neither of them thought Chloe had any apologies outstanding.

Even though Lonnie was talking as if Chloe was the injured party, Chloe could tell this therapist had a high regard for Sal. Maybe even love. She was supporting Sal to come to terms with what she had done. Chloe began to imagine that maybe they could get through this and not just around it.

Sal was on time, to the minute, so Chloe should have expected the buzzer to ring, but she started out of her seat when the noise erupted right behind her. That intense impulse to flee hit her in the gut again, and she took a deep breath, overcoming the urge.

"Hi, Mom," she said as Sal walked in, her voice sounding high and weak, almost childlike.

"Hello, Chloe, thank you so much for doing this!"

Sal's eyes were teary, and Chloe thought she saw a shake in her hands. She had been so focused on her own dread of these two hours that she really hadn't considered it from Sal's point of view. What was it like to have cut off her own child and now to try to repair things? Chloe was unable to imagine anything Quinten or Arisa might do that would cause her to stop speaking to them. Murder? She would visit them in jail. Drugs? She'd get them some help. Bad relationship? She would try her best to support. She was angry, all of a sudden, in a way she hadn't been for years. Why now, when she was letting Sal back into her life?

Lonnie started them off. "Sal, would you like to begin?"

"How?"

"Well, I think it's important for you to let Chloe know what you've been thinking and where you're at. We need to know where we're starting so we can figure out the next steps. She needs to know more about why you got in touch, what's going on for you. And if there's anything you're sorry about, she might want to hear that too."

Sal shifted in her chair, unable to utter a word for the next few moments. They all sat quietly, waiting. Why didn't someone else say something? But no, they all looked at her. She was the one. She took a breath.

"Chloe, it's real hard to be here today. I have a whole bunch to be sorry about and I've never been that good at seeing my part in things." She caught Chloe eye to eye and could not read the expression. "I guess you know that. I guess I don't need to say it. So, I'm afraid I won't do this well enough and you won't want to go to the trouble, especially now when you're sick. That scares me the most, that I won't do it well enough to make this worth it to you."

Chloe opened her mouth, about to speak, but her therapist caught her eye and shook her head, ever so slightly, no. Chloe crossed her legs in the chair, burrowing into the back, wishing she could disappear into the next room.

"I was so mad when you told me you were a lesbian." Chloe started at the word. She had never heard her mother use it. "I truly thought you were doing it to punish me for something. I know that sounds silly, but I'd never known anyone who was gay, or at least I didn't *know* I did, and I really didn't get it.

"I'm completely responsible for the fact that I didn't try to get it. I thought if I rejected you, you'd change and do what I wanted. I know how bad that sounds. But that is pretty much the way I parented. Rejection as a method of learning. Until the gay thing, I'm sorry to say that worked pretty well on you." Tears were streaming down her cheeks by now, but Chloe didn't think they were the usual kind. These tears seemed to be saying, *what have I been thinking all my life?*

"Chloe, I am so, so sorry for not trying to understand. I don't think you did anything to me. I did something to you, really. I left you out in the cold, without a mother's love." Now Chloe was crying too. "I've read a lot of stuff this past six months and most people seem to think you don't choose to be gay, that you're born gay. But even if that wasn't true, isn't it your choice who you love? Why would rejection be my choice?

"So, I've been thinking that I was just absolutely, completely wrong about the whole thing. I can't blame my religion, because I really don't have one, for one thing, and for another, come to find out there's no agreement among all the different people who *do* have religions. So, I guess it was just me being pig-headed. What's new? You're probably not the only one of my kids to think so.

"I have missed so much on account of my wrong thinking. I missed you meeting someone to love. She's really special, Chloe, even I can see that. I missed your pregnancies and births. I didn't know those adorable children when they first came into this world. I missed knowing all your great friends and being a part of your life. I wish I had been there to call when you found out about the cancer. I wish I could have held you while you cried about it. I'm just hoping I don't have to miss any more. I'm so, so sorry, sweetheart."

Chloe could not speak, but her eyes were soft and watery. The dread was gone and, in its place, the beginning glimmer of hope. Chloe knew her mom. She could tell when Sal was working an angle. There was none of that now. Her mom had said her piece and sat quietly now, tense but somehow more relaxed at the same time.

Angie glanced at Lonnie, wordlessly deciding together which one would field the next step. Angie nodded, ready to talk.

"Sal, I want to acknowledge what it must have taken for you to say all that. I'm sure we all can tell you've done lots of work to get here. Whatever happens next, I want to tell you I admire that. It's not easy to admit you've made a mistake without blaming someone else, or making excuses, or taking it back in the next breath. You've done your part, for sure." She turned to Chloe. "Chloe, would you like to respond now? You know you have choices. You can accept the apology with no reservations. You can refuse the apology because you need to ask questions or know more. And you can accept the apology, but retain the right to keep your distance for a while. I also imagine you might have some things to say yourself."

Through all these years of remaining open to her own feelings about her mother, Chloe had learned to take her time. She had become less interested in whether this might be hard on other people. She felt a little pressure to respond to her mother quickly but was able to put that aside and focus on her own insides. She stared at the picture across from her, a print of the ocean she found especially soothing. She imagined herself plunging into the cool, welcoming water and riding the waves into the shore. She had often done just that at Drake Beach, even when it was cold, and found the feeling cleansing, delicious. She thought all of a sudden, *I haven't been well enough to do that in a long time* and felt a moment of mind numbing sadness. The loss of her health, of her security, of her promise of life hit her harder than it had in months. *Why now*, she thought, distracted by every other thing affecting her life. She struggled to get back to this room, with these three people, the couch, the chair, the ocean. One more plunge into an imaginary ocean, grasping the feeling she often had when coming out of the water.

Opening her eyes, she smiled at the two therapists and her mother, watching her with what she imagined was concern. Where should she begin? How to capture all that was happening inside of her? Which things needed to be said? Overwhelmed by questions, she began, accepting she might not say all of this well.

"Wow, it's really hard to pull apart all the things that are going on for me. Do I feel the way I do because I'm sick, might not have much time? Or Mom, is it because you're sitting here saying the words I longed to hear for so many years? I had to let go of hearing them to save my own life. It stung so bad that you didn't love me anymore." Sal opened her mouth, as if she was about to cut in, correct, try to change Chloe's mind. "I know that might not be how you would describe it, Mom, but it's how it felt to me. Because how could you still love me, how could you ever have loved me, and cut me off so completely and finally? I couldn't understand it any other way. At first, I thought maybe I just didn't deserve to be loved. I'm lucky that I had many, many friends, a therapist, and eventually Rhonda to reassure me that this was your problem, not mine. After I got through that, it just hurt.

"It hurt every time something important happened in my life. Every holiday. When I graduated. When I got a great job. Wedding, babies, every single thing. I'd wonder if anyone was telling you about me, or were you all just going on as if I didn't exist?

"I had a hard time when my sister and brothers hung out with you, or Aunt Adele. How could they act as if it was okay? I never asked them. I just tried to rise above.

"So now I'm having to change really fast. I'd take a lot longer if I thought I had the time. First things first, I do accept your apology. You've done your work to apologize to me, I know that, and I accept it. Completely. That being said, I'm still a little leery. My kids and Rhonda are the most important people to me and I don't want any of them to be hurt. I don't ever want the kids to get the idea there's something wrong with their parents. It helps that we've been spending some time with you and I haven't been concerned about anything you said. I just want you to know I get a little scared.

"You want to be called first if we need help, right?" Sal nodded. "Thing is, Mom, Quin and Ari know other people better than they know you. Emily, for instance, has been with them every week since they were born. And we don't usually make the calls. We call our friend Deidre and she gets someone. So, here's what I think. I think we need to work towards that. For now, I'm comfortable with you being on the list, if you continue to be diligent about being positive about our family with the kids. If you don't understand something, or you're concerned about something, whatever, you can ask Rhonda or me. We'll answer you, best we can. We just want you to love the kids, take good care of them, and play with them. When we need to be away from them, you'll be near the top. Honestly, Emily is number one at the moment. I'll ask if she'd be willing to have you come more often when she's there. And if she's not available, you'll be the next call. Can you live with that?"

"Chloe, thank you so much. That's more than I could ever have hoped!"

✦✦✦✦✦

Sal took care of the kids the night of the benefit Clarence had arranged to help Rhonda and Chloe's finances. Chloe and Rhonda stepped out the door dressed to the nines, both in gabardine suits of different deep shades, teal and magenta. Chloe wore an extraordinary print scarf in coordinating colors on her head, and Sal defied anyone to think there was anything wrong with her.

They were lucky. The benefit happened on a good day. Even though Chloe had just finished chemo, she woke up with some of the energy she used to have, spent the morning at the zoo with the kids and napped in the afternoon, waking up ready for a big evening.

Sal came in time for dinner, deep-dish pizza because it was Quin and Ari's favorite, and they sat talking and laughing as they ate together. It would have been hard for a stranger to tell that they hadn't known their grandma very long. They climbed up and down from her lap, asked her for kisses, and made funny little faces to make her laugh. She responded to them as if they were crown jewels in a queen's special collection, focusing her attention on them and enjoying the night.

When Chloe and Rhonda left for the benefit, the kids hardly seemed to notice. Sal was down on the floor with them, playing dead then bounding up suddenly. "Boo," she chirped, and they jumped, happily surprised. They stopped just long enough to kiss their moms, then back to the game. Before long, they were playing dead themselves, and shocking Sal with their sudden bounces.

By the time bath time rolled around, they were rubbing their eyes and looking for their stuffed animals. Sal barely got them washed, dried, and dressed before they each brought a book for her to read. They clearly expected a story and Sal wasn't surprised. Both their parents loved books with a passion. It was a one-book night, given the yawns and stretches coming from them, but Sal was sad about it. She was in no rush to tuck them into their little beds. She couldn't imagine anything better than their goodnight kisses and the way they reached up to pull her down to them, small hands wrapped around her neck.

"Night night Gramma," said Quin, and turned his head the other way, snuggling into the blankets for a good night's sleep.

***

Chloe and Rhonda came back from the night with miraculous stories to tell. The music was beautiful, with more musicians playing and singing than anyone expected. Everyone Clarence had ever worked with wanted to do it, and they had a hard time turning anyone away, so it was a long night. But each and every one roasted Rhonda and loved Chloe up, and many of them played together, giving the audience an unusual treat.

As the hours went on, Chloe felt more and more exhausted, but pushed herself through, not wanting to miss one minute. She could rest tomorrow. By the time they reached their front door, she was ready to lay down. She left it to Rhonda to tell Sal all about it, and Sal stayed to listen late into the night.

Chapter Seventeen

Sally

After the first time Chloe and Sal met with the therapists, Sal breathed a little easier. Looking at Chloe from across the room, she understood that the worst thing would not be to lose her, but to lose her without them ever having tried to work it out. She felt relief all over that they were working towards that.

The second session was rough, though. Both therapists encouraged Chloe to express her anger, and there was a load of it. She wasn't just mad about the gay thing, either. There was the time when Sal was depressed and stared at the purple cover on her bed for about two months. "Who did you think was taking care of the kids, Mom?" she asked, the accusation ringing in the room. Pretty justified, overall.

There was the time she forgot about Chloe's ballet recital and they didn't show up. This would have been Sal's job, keeping track of the schedule, not Stan's, so Sal carried the load of Chloe's disappointment. After that, Chloe always thought she had to keep track of her own stuff, and it made her kind of jumpy. Sal remembered the jumpy but didn't remember why. Chloe was angry that Sal didn't encourage her to pursue things she loved, and there were many. She reminded Sal of the time she said, in that harsh way she would, "Don't expect any money for college; we just don't have it. Eighteen, and you're on your own!" Sal thought to herself that one had worked out pretty well, but hearing it from Chloe's own mouth, she realized that although Chloe was the kind of person who always made the best from the worst, Sal had been that worst.

Overall, she spent forty-five out of fifty minutes of that session twisting the threads on the pillow, purple and tangerine colored, that always sat at the back of the chair she'd claimed as her own since the beginning with Lonnie. Lonnie had encouraged her to make eye contact with Chloe when they met, assuring her she'd hear what Chloe had to say better and Chloe would be more likely to feel heard too. She had gotten used to it with Lonnie, but it took an extreme act of will on her part to look at Chloe at all while she spoke. She wondered, as she stared at Chloe's wildly patterned scarf, covering her now bald head, whether looking in her direction would give the impression she was looking her in the eye. She doubted it. Then she thought, *since she's had a lifetime of me not looking right at her, she may not even notice.* After that, she looked her right in the eye, honestly trying to make up for all the years she nearly didn't notice her.

"Could you repeat that last thing?" She had drifted into her own regret, memories of all the worst moments in their relationship, and she hadn't heard what Chloe said. It was hard to believe she had done anything right as a mom, but she must have at least fed her, loved her enough that she grew into this amazing person. Anyway, even if she'd done it all wrong up to now, this was her second chance.

"Mom, I was saying how much I wanted your attention as a kid. You were my world. Dad wasn't even a part of the mix, really, and I wanted your love so bad. Even more than that, I wanted you to let me love you. I remember when I used to say, 'I love you, Mommy,' you would say stuff like, 'why would you want to love an old bag like me?' or you'd laugh and turn away. I would go in my room and cry. Then when I was about nine, I remember saying to myself, 'I don't need her anyway.' That was kind of the end for me. I kept it all to myself after that."

Glancing out the window, Sal noticed that the sky was gray. A tree just visible at the very corner of the window, popping out from behind the curtain, moved in the breeze. She sat quietly and almost didn't notice she was crying until her cheeks were soggy wet. It was a quiet crying, just the tears pouring down. Chloe kept talking, but her voice became softer as she went on.

"I never really succeeded in not loving or needing you, Mom. Even on my wedding day, I shed some tears because you weren't there. I have to take the chance on letting you back in my life, because my life is missing a piece without you. I've had to tell the truth to myself about that since you came back. I just can't turn you away. So, I'm going to have to try to forgive you, because I don't like being around someone so much when I'm mad at them. I gotta say I'm struggling a little. It would help to hear whether you've gone through anything on your end."

Chloe's usually open face was tight and guarded, which Sal guessed was no surprise considering the chance she was taking in giving her this chance. She cleared her throat, got ready to speak.

"Chloe, I used to believe I was supposed to make you turn out a certain way. If you weren't doing what I'd been told was the right thing, that would be my fault, make me look bad. I've been trying to remember who told me it was wrong to love someone of the same sex, but I don't know if anyone directly told me. It was just the whispers about my high school friend that someone caught kissing a girl. It was the pastors at church telling us what to do to avoid sin. Anything besides growing up, being a virgin, and marrying a man was wrong. Even though I've left church, I guess I kept some of the ideas without thinking about it. There was the one time my own mother thought I was doing something with a girl and leveled me to the ground with her ugly criticisms. I'm not saying this to excuse myself, but just to own that I was all wrong, for no real reason.

"Whenever you did something I didn't approve of, I thought it was my job to reject you, to teach you what you should do. That's kind of the way I was raised. It's not hard to see what's wrong with that now. Your sister and brothers are suffering for it too, but you got the worst. There's no excuse, I guess. I just didn't know.

"I've spent some hours trying to change my way of thinking. You'll have to tell me if I've done enough. I'm trying to use my own good sense now, and that tells me you have a beautiful life, a beautiful family. I'm sorry, Chloe, I really am."

After what seemed like hours of silence, Chloe began to speak again. "Mom, I forgive you. I'm not going to forget for a while, and you have to be willing to have me tell you when you step in the old mud hole. I don't expect you to change overnight, but I expect you to do your best. That okay with you?"

Without even giving her body permission to move, Sal found herself gliding across the room to take

Chloe in her arms. A little surprised, Chloe let her. Lonnie and Angie faded to the background, seemed to disappear. Sal closed her eyes, not wanting this moment to end, ever. Chloe was soft in her arms, no guard for this moment, letting herself fold into her mother. It reminded Sal of when she was a baby, such an affectionate little child, always raising her arms to be cuddled, climbing up next to Sal in the chair for a book, her red hair falling across her forehead.

⚶⚶⚶⚶

Chloe and Rhonda were as good as their word. The next Tuesday, the phone rang, and it was Emily.

"Hi, Sal, it's Emily. Want to come over? I'm hanging with the kids while Rhonda takes Chloe to her treatment."

Sal almost looked up to the God she'd been raised to believe in, to thank whatever that power is that she had the day off!

"Sure! Thanks Emily. I'll be right over." Although she'd had an open invitation to come over whenever, she had hesitated. With a supreme act of will, she still tried hard not to intrude on them or their friends. And she tried not to show her tears of relief now. She tried to sound casual. Then she thought, *wait, I'm not hiding anymore.*

"Emily, it makes me cry to be asked. I am so grateful to you for being willing to share your time with me."

"Sal, it's the kids! They need all of us. You know?"

"But I'm thanking you, Emily. You could so not want to do it."

"I had my moment, believe me. You convinced

me, Sal. I see you are really trying. That's all I need. So, if I give you a list, could you bring some salad stuff when you come?"

☙☙☙☙

Sal had been to their house so many times by now, but it looked different today. The cedar shingles looked warm and inviting, and the red door asked to be opened. The children and their parents had made tiles at the pottery studio and hung them next to the door, each with a name, Rhonda, Chloe, Quinten, and Arisa. Sal stopped to look at the stick figures on Quin and Ari's; Quin's with a head, body, arms, and legs, Ari's with a head, feet, and fingers. She got caught up in enjoying their little child view of being human. She might have stood there forever if she hadn't heard the children's laughter coming from an open window around the side of the house.

When she rang the bell, it took a long time for anyone to answer. That was no surprise. These were two active children, used to being given freedom and used to having lots of room to experiment. Emily would put answering the door a distant second to watching them finish the latest game or getting them settled with an educational video. Honestly, Sal was in no particular hurry. It was a sunny day, without the usual fog or rain common at this time of year, and the garden surrounding their little home was alive with flowers. Sal knew Rhonda was not getting out here as much as she liked, and that friends were helping her keep it up. For the first time in Sal's life, that looked like a pleasant activity, weeding out the flowerbeds, trimming the shrubs and trees, cleaning things up. She vowed to volunteer the next day off.

When Emily came to the door, she was covered in flour. She and the kids had been baking, and the kids had been unable to resist the temptation to blow some flour Emily's way. As always, she looked relaxed and content and Sal wondered idly how she did it. She motioned Sal in and led her to the kitchen.

Sal hadn't spent much time in this part of their house. The kitchen was very small but opened onto a part of the garden Sal often didn't remember existed. Through double French doors, which were open today, she could see a patio with container plants and surrounded by yet another green and flowering garden patch. Quin and Ari were on stools, mixing flour and who knew what else. Emily had been unconcerned, Sal imagined, that the glass bowls might hit the floor while she went to let Sal in. Sal would never have taken the chance and she felt almost guilty about that. The two kids were having the time of their lives, interested beyond measure in the results of their stirring. Little bits of dough found their way onto the counter, the seats, the floor, and no one was worried.

Sal joined in, getting her own bowl and pulling up a stool for herself.

"What are we making, Quinten?" He was going through a period when he insisted everyone call him by his full name. It had been Quinten Alexander for a time there, but he had dropped his middle name after a few days. He told everyone if people said the whole thing, he thought he was in trouble.

"Chocolate puffs," he said, in a knowing and important way.

"Can you tell me what to put in?" Sal asked, almost certain he'd need some help. But no, he began with a great sense of purpose.

"Gramma, first you has to put blow away white stuff." He handed her the flour and let her know when she had poured the right amount.

"Okay, now this white stuff." The baking powder. It seemed to Sal they were putting a whole lot of that in, but she was determined not to correct him.

"Um, I think we need a egg," he added.

They kept this up until Sal's bowl looked just like his, thick and chocolatey. She was finding it hard to believe he was only three. By the time they poured their batter into the muffin pans and got them into the oven, it was nearly dinnertime. But Emily wasn't the sort to make a mess and not clean up. She even insisted the kids help, which they seemed happy enough to do, even if they weren't entirely effective.

"Who wants macaroni and cheese?" Emily said when they were done. Sal waited for a box to come out, but instead, she pulled a beautiful homemade pan from the bottom of the oven. Sal hadn't noticed it, even when the baking went in the oven. She had brought the salad Emily suggested to go with it.

As they ate, Sal let Emily know she didn't think this stuff should be called mac and cheese. It was clearly mana from heaven! She had never tasted anything so good. The children agreed. Not long after they began eating, Chloe and Rhonda got home and joined in, laughing with the kids and hearing all the details about their baking adventure. Surprising herself, Sal added a detail here and there. She was rewarded with a smile on Chloe's face, not the kind of brilliant smile that came on the good days but the sort that said, "Even on a bad day, life is beautiful."

Sal knew she hated it when people talked about

how strong she was. "Like I have a choice," she'd say, and then laugh but not an, "I'm enjoying myself" laugh. Or they'd say, "You'll be ok. You're strong," and she'd say, "I know a heck of a lot of strong dead people." But at that moment, at the dinner table with her family, watching her enjoy everyone sitting there, laugh at their jokes, asking for more details, tasting the not very tasty puffs as soon as they cooled, even though she must be exhausted from her doctor day, Sal wanted to say, *I have never known anyone like you. The fact that you are my child astounds me. You have something I have never had. I admire you more than anyone I know.* And it was true. All of it.

࿐ ࿐ ࿐ ࿐

Sal was outside working in the garden the next Saturday. There were three of them, Rhonda's dad Clarence, Morgan, an old friend of Rhonda's, and Sal. They were old hands at this gardening stuff. Sal was beginning to feel like two hands full of thumbs and a bundle of nerves when Clarence turned to her and said, "I thought you said you never gardened before. You're doing great!"

She could not get over the way Rhonda's parents treated her like a long-lost friend. She had thought of their daughter as a pariah for years without even knowing her. They had reason to believe she truly was the enemy and they were never anything but kind. She wanted to ask him how he could be that way, but she didn't have the nerve.

"Thanks. I feel like I'm in a foreign country."

"Well, it doesn't show. That spot you've been working on looks real pretty, I'd say!"

Somehow, the compliment made the work easier. Sal wondered if a compliment from her would have the same effect on someone else. She resolved to try it the next time she thought someone was doing a good job at something. Then it occurred to her she could do that right now.

"I am in awe of your family, Clarence. How did you all get to be so, well, positive?"

He chuckled in a way he had, almost affectionately, and he said, simple as could be, "We just try to actually be Christians and not just go to church." Then he walked back to where he'd been working and tore at it again.

His words left an impression. Even though Sal had gone to church every Sunday for the first thirty or forty years of her life, she'd never once thought about the difference between going to church and acting like a Christian. What did a Christian act like?

She remembered a speaker she heard by accident once. It was at a fundraiser, but she went because the headliner was a musician she liked. She didn't even remember what they were raising money for, but it was sponsored by the Graduate Theological Union up by Cal Berkeley. The emcee walked up to the mic with this gigantic smile on her face and said something that came back to Sal now. "It's so wonderful to see you all out there, doing like Jesus Christ would have done and bringing the love!" Sal remembered feeling guilty at the time, because she hadn't come there to do that at all. She just wanted to hear some music cheap. But then the woman went on, "Even those of you who aren't feeling that way or didn't come for that, you belong here too. Someday you'll realize it!"

Maybe this was that day. It seemed weird that

Sal would be feeling lucky, feeling love, feeling almost happy with her daughter so sick, and thinking of all the time they'd lost. She wondered if she should feel guilty about that. She'd have to ask Lonnie. But life seemed so much better than it had a year ago. She was feeling optimistic and as if she could handle so much more than she ever thought. She had even bumped into Stan over at Chloe's house and didn't feel the need to run at full speed out of there. He was just a person, doing the best he could, and she couldn't even feel sorry anymore that he had left. She was glad to have moved on.

He seemed a little nervous at first, which Sal could understand, then he said, tentatively, "Well, Sal, how have you been?"

"Not bad, Stan, in fact pretty good," she said, and she practically got a smile out of him.

ล.ล.ฬ.ฬ.

"How about coming with us when we go to Devin's next workshop?" Chloe asked her mom, while they were lying on her bed the day after chemo. They had both dozed off as soon as Sal got to the house. The kids were both in nursery school now, and she arranged her schedule so she could be with Chloe after the treatment and Rhonda could write.

Chloe still tried to work some, but she couldn't work full time and the company couldn't afford to keep paying her full time, so things were a little tight, even with friends and Rhonda's parents and brother kicking in. There was another benefit in the works, many of their musician friends having offered to work again free, but that wouldn't be for months. Sal had been happy, and surprised herself feeling that way, when she learned Stan was helping out a little. She worried about their little family, trying to do all the things Chloe needed and not go bankrupt.

"Is someone going to help you guys pay for it?" Sal said, then regretted it. She had learned that Chloe and Rhonda knew how to take care of the business of their lives, no thanks to any training Sal had offered Chloe. Chloe did not need Sal's help.

"Don't worry about that, Mom. Devin and his wife Andi let us come without a fee and they want to offer it to you free too. They are so generous! I respect their work so much, and I just think it would be great to do it together."

"I'm there, sweetheart." Sal answered without a second thought, even though that kind of thing had always made her turn up her nose. She caught herself and changed "always" to "in the past." Lonnie had encouraged her not to write her past into her future. And what did she care anymore about those old opinions based on so little? Her child wanted to spend the weekend together. She really didn't care what they'd be doing.

❧ ❧ ❧ ❧

It was one of the biggest auditoriums Sal had ever seen. Instead of being filled with chairs, the floor was covered with rugs of every description. There were shag rugs, Persian looking carpets, plain beige rugs, print rugs. They formed a kaleidoscope of color. Sal imagined painting this room, the way the impressionists would have, swatches of print blending into each other and forming a patchwork quilt below the wainscoted walls and filigreed molding. She took a picture on her phone, having finally joined the cell phone club, planning on painting a picture of the room at the earliest opportunity.

Chloe had told her most of the people here would be sitting on meditation cushions and there were already a hundred or so set out in front of them. The people who had placed them just far enough apart to be comfortable were gathered in small groups around the room, greeting people they obviously knew or introducing themselves to strangers. The kind of shyness she felt as a child overcame her. Would anyone like her? Would she make any friends? What if she embarrassed herself? She felt the impulse, starting in her feet and landing in her belly, to run, that feeling of being pulled into an eddy in the middle of the lake.

Instead, after she went a little way down that path, she caught herself. The thought came to her, loud and persistent, *your daughter might be dying and you're afraid of a little embarrassment?* She almost laughed out loud, then realized that would be embarrassing. The joke was on her.

They had come separately, and Sal was early, trying to remove any chance of disappointing Chloe. She was determined to let her know with her actions how important this all was to her. It was ten minutes at least until she saw them walk through the door, hand in hand.

Rhonda had a rolled-up camping mat slung over her shoulder and both of their cushions. Chloe got very tired these days, so they had planned for her to lie down part of the time. Sal had brought a chair that sat on the floor, not sure she could manage to sit up without a chair back all weekend. She came over to them and gave them each a big hug, amazed, not for the first time, at the joy of seeing them.

In these weeks since the therapy with Chloe, they had all entered a new phase. Most of the discomfort had melted away, replaced by a feeling that was an awful lot like Sal's early fantasies of family life. When Stan and she had married, she expected things to feel this way, close, sweet, and pure. After the first few months of the marriage, that feeling vanished, replaced by a cloud of resentments and disappointments. But Chloe and Rhonda had what Sal had convinced herself before she knew them was a fairy tale, not possible in this world of meanness and suspicion.

ℒ ℒ ℒ ℒ

It wasn't that they never fought. Sal had even seen a few of those fights, but they didn't resemble how Stan and Sal had fought, or even how she'd fought with the kids when they were younger.

She remembered the first time she saw them disagreeing. They were all having dinner and Chloe had asked Sal to be there around five to help her cook the food. She still enjoyed cooking, but often had to take breaks and sit down, so when she cooked, and Rhonda was gone, they invited friends and family to come help.

Tonight was a good night. She seemed energetic and animated, telling Sal stories about the babies and stirring the pot. She was making a soup, almost a stew, with fish and vegetables and rice. Sal had always thought food that could be called healthy would taste bad, but after months in their home, she'd learned different. The smell of the fish and the spices hung over the room, a warm blanket, irresistible in its aromatic beauty. Sal was paying so much attention to what Chloe was doing, determined to learn enough to make it herself, that she hardly noticed Chloe's increasing tension. Something in the set of her jaw, in the quickness of her motions should have told Sal she was upset.

Ever since she was a kid, Chloe had been slow to anger. She would walk away before she would let anyone know they hurt her. Sal could sometimes tell she was upset when she wasn't upset with Sal, but she always missed the signs when it was Sal herself who had angered her. Once when she whispered, "Wow, Mom, that really hurt," so quiet Sal could hardly hear her, Sal retorted back, "Who could tell?" like an accusation. Chloe just went to her bedroom and closed the door, not coming out until it was time to leave for school the next morning.

Sal guessed it wasn't a total surprise she missed it this time, since she was rapturous just to be in Chloe's company. It took until she started yelling at the package of rice she was trying to open that Sal got it. "This thing won't open!" she said, louder than Sal usually heard her, pulling hard on the plastic packaging. "I'm so frustrated!"

She gave it a final pull and it opened all right, half the rice spilling on the floor. Chloe closed her eyes and put her hand on the counter, leaning over to collect herself. Sal was afraid to move. What was going on here?

"Mom, I've gotta go wash my face," she said, and only then did Sal notice a tear falling down that smooth cheek. Sal reviewed her behavior, looking for anything she might have done to set this off. For once, she couldn't think of anything. When Chloe came back, she went on cooking, as if nothing had happened. She had pulled herself together and seemed completely over it. Sal was just a little confused.

They finished cooking around six and fed the kids. "Let's wait for Rhonda and eat when she gets home," Chloe said, and that was fine with Sal. Dinners with the two of them had become one of Sal's biggest pleasures. They told jokes, talked about their day, sometimes talked about what had been hard, but always with warmth and love. Some days it felt like a salve on Sal's soul, breaking down the hard knots of hurt and pain she'd carried around with her for longer than she could remember. Sal was happy Chloe included her, even though they were done with the cooking. Sometimes she asked Sal to put the kids to bed and had time alone with Rhonda. But Sal could tell she really wanted her to stay.

Rhonda came in around 6:30, looking a little tense herself. Sal didn't think anything of it.

"Mom, I need to talk to Rhonda before we eat."

"Want me to go to the other room?" Sal didn't want to intrude.

"No, you can stay if you want. I was just letting you know."

She turned to Rhonda, across the table, with the delicious and waiting food between them.

"Rhonda, it's 6:30 and you said you'd be back at 5:30. I know you need your time, and that's fine, but not letting me know isn't okay with me. Please call when you're going to be longer than you told me."

Rhonda took a minute to figure out her response. Sal could see it was taking a real effort not to react and defend herself, and Sal watched how she waited to speak until she had figured it out.

"I know, Chloe. I apologize. You deserve to know

what's up with me unless I ask you for a no limit pass."
Sal knew Rhonda had gone on a writer's retreat a few
weeks ago, for just that kind of time to take care of
herself. "I got caught up, but that's not okay. I get it.
Glad you were here, Sal," she said, sending a shock of
surprise through Sal's body.

"Thank you. I forgive you. I love you." And that
was the end of it. Done. In the days of Stan and Sal,
that would have turned into three days of the silent
treatment or a knock down drag out fight. Or both.
It wasn't just how these two were dealing with cancer
that impressed Sal, it was everything about them.

While the kids played on the other side of the
kitchen arch, they ate, sharing what had been going on
for each of them, laughing at a friend who had called
after a long absence, admitting she didn't know what to
say. Chloe had told her to try "hello!" They all laughed
until it hurt over that one.

"People can be so dumb," Chloe said, and they all
agreed on that.

❧ ❧ ❧ ❧

Sal had thought very little about what this
weekend would be like. She knew the title of it, Living
Until You Die, but that didn't tell her much. She also
knew Chloe and Rhonda had been going to these things
since right after they found out Chloe had cancer. Sal's
last remaining friend from her life with Stan, Celeste,
said it was "real airy fairy," but Sal didn't know if she
should trust Celeste's opinion. She was a holdover from
the days of judgement. Sal was getting past that now.

Two chairs were placed carefully on the stage
in front of them. Plants surrounded the stage and an

artistic array of flowers sat on a table between the chairs with two glasses of water and a picture of someone who looked ancient and Eastern. The stage gave the impression that someone had tried out the objects in every possible arrangement and, at the end, said to themselves, "there, that's perfect." Chloe and Rhonda liked to sit near the front, which Sal would never have chosen on her own, but when they put down their bags and cushions, chairs and coats, and sat down, Sal liked being able to see the stage well. If she was going to check these people out, close was better.

Looking around the room, she could see that people were continuing to chat casually while they waited, but the room seemed incredibly quiet anyway. The talking was more a murmur than a roar, punctuated by an occasional shock of laughter. Although she was being secretive about it, she was checking out the people who were there already, as if she was visiting a foreign country and trying to figure out the language they spoke here. But she couldn't see anything so very different about these folks. And they didn't even have that much in common with each other. All Sal could detect was a certain calm, which seemed weird since they were all there to talk about death.

She watched without a word as person after person came over to greet her daughter and her wife. Each and every one seemed genuinely glad to see them and Sal, off to the side, enjoyed watching the hugs, kisses, glad to see you's.

Diligently, they introduced Sal to each one. "This is my mother, Sal," or "This is my mother-in-law, Sal," and she received from each a warm smile before they went on talking with Chloe and Rhonda. Sal swam in a sea of names, James, Erica, Deitrich, Evan. And then

Michael.

"I'm so glad to meet you, Sal. We have some things in common, from what I hear."

Sal was alarmed that this man knew something about her when she knew nothing about him. It felt like some sort of disadvantage in the game of acquaintances, but Michael soon put her at ease.

"My son is also living with cancer. He's here somewhere. I'll introduce you later. What a big thing to go through, huh?"

Sal doubted that this beautiful, sweet man had had to deal with repairing a broken relationship with his son. They were probably close all along and slid into dealing with cancer without a hitch. Sal watched him as he talked to Chloe and Rhonda. She could tell they liked him very much, the way they shared the real hard parts with him and listened to every word he had to say. Sal liked the easy way he had with a question, how he made it easy to tell him things. She liked the way he looked too, fit but not body builder fit, just like he liked to walk, run, do stuff. She was surprised to find herself drawn to him in a way she hadn't felt in a very long time. She had a strong urge to reach up and brush his greying hair off his forehead.

"Hawaii was the most beautiful place I've ever been," Sal heard herself saying, joining into a conversation about their vacation. "I loved watching those kids in the water. Better than an amusement park."

Michael seemed happy she'd decided to join the party, turning towards her whenever she said a word. She thought, *whoever he's with must feel pretty special*, and then felt her face redden just at the thought of that whoever. She hoped everyone thought it was a hot flash.

As the conversation wound down and the hall began to settle for the beginning of the workshop, he seemed hesitant to go. She saw him begin to speak two or three times. Finally, he managed, "How about meeting at lunch time? Gotta eat, right?"

She muttered a "sure, sounds nice" before he headed to the opposite end of the hall.

Immediately after he walked away, Sal began a circular conversation with herself about who he was and what his intentions might be. *He just wants to talk to someone with a sick kid,* she began, *but he must know lots of people like that. He kind of looked at me a certain way. But it's been so long, I might not be reading him right. What are the signals these days? He's cute, in an older guy way. I like the wave in that grey hair and the 'out in the sun' look on his face. What if I can't talk? God, why the hell do I feel like such a teenager? This is uncomfortable. Chloe and Rhonda know him. Would they approve? Would they think I'm good enough for him?*

Ditching her determination to hang onto their every word the people on stage might say, she missed the first hour of the workshop, drifting off into thoughts of this man, this Michael man. She hadn't considered a date, let alone a relationship, in a long time. Once burned, twice afraid, she'd been known to say, and it came as a shock that she knew she would say yes to him if that *was* what he was after. She also felt very sure that he wasn't a one date kind of guy. If they were to get involved, she had better mean it!

♫ ♫ ♫ ♫

Michael and Sal grabbed the lunch boxes they

had preordered and walked out into a perfect Oakland day. Across the street from the hall was Lake Merritt. Sal remembered bringing her kids here when they were little to feed the numerous ducks, crowding around them when they saw the bread in their little hands. She couldn't remember if she'd been back since.

Chloe and Rhonda had caught the action earlier, so they were not surprised when she took off for lunch without them. Chloe smiled in a way that seemed much older than her thirty-two years and said, "Have a good lunch, Mom." Rhonda smiled too, not feeling any need to add to that.

Michael and Sal waited for the cars to whiz by, treating the road around the lake like a freeway, but Sal wasn't impatient. She heard herself thinking that she could be happy nearly anywhere with this man, even waiting for traffic. She got a dry feeling in her throat, shocked by the outpouring in her heart for a perfect stranger.

"How about sitting on this wall here?" he asked, guiding them to a spot with the best possible view of the boats on the water. There were sailboats, rowboats, boats that you paddled, and a gondola. He caught her looking at the gondola with, perhaps, a bit of longing in her eyes.

"Have you ever had a ride?" he asked, casually and with a keen interest at the same time.

"No. I didn't even know they had those on the lake," she answered, pretending to herself that the longing look in her eyes had nothing to do with the man sitting next to her.

"Let's do it sometime. It's a pile of fun. They even sing to you."

She caught herself about to say, "It's a date," and

said, "Sounds nice" instead. She felt as if the world was suddenly moving like the eye of a twister and she had been caught up in the motion. She remembered hearing a guy talk about really being caught in one and how, once he was in the center, it felt quiet and calm. That's the way it felt right then. If she had not had lunch in one hand and a bag in the other, she would have reached out for his hand. Had she ever felt so free with another person? She wasn't concerned about what he thought of her, if she was doing what he wanted, if he thought she was pretty. She was just there, herself, ready to see what happened.

She opened the box and spent a moment looking at the contents. She would have made fun of this kind of lunch a few years ago. There was a couscous salad, some fruit, a lettuce wrap, a kombucha drink. All she could see were the magnificent colors and the careful way someone had nestled each item into the cardboard box, so that no one item would be bruised. When she tasted the salad, it turned out to be delicious beyond what she could have imagined. Lemon, cilantro, and very fresh tomato. And a year ago, she wouldn't have had a clue what was in there. She said a silent thank you to her daughter for feeding her so well.

"What do you think of it?" he said.

"Delicious!" she said, sensing that he was somehow invested in the answer.

"It's from my restaurant. Just down the block."

"You have a restaurant?"

"Yeah, it's called Fresh Delish."

"It sure is," she managed to say, then added a smile that was, she hoped, more convincing. He smiled back, and she felt that smile through and through.

Later she would try to remember whether

they even talked about him sitting with them for the afternoon, his son across the room with some friends. There he was, right next to her, for hours. She had to talk sternly to herself. *Listen to what Devin is saying. You're here for a reason, Sal.*

After the first meditation of the afternoon, something Devin called Loving Kindness for our Pain, she managed to put the explosion going on inside her to one side. She was fully concentrating for the next part, Embracing Your True Heart, which honestly seemed to fit in with what was going on with her. Chloe had played Sal some of her meditation tapes and Sal had told her, "That body awareness thing, I don't think I could ever get the hang of that." Now it came naturally, just because her body was so alive. Every inch of it was talking to her. *You're alive, you're alive,* and she was answering, *I guess I am.*

❧❧❧❧

Sal stayed at Chloe's that night so they could drive together for the second day. The pain of parting from Michael was almost physical. She was stunned that someone she'd just met could have such an impact on her. She would usually have kept it close to the vest, but she didn't seem able to keep her feelings to herself.

"Tell me all about that man!" she said, the moment the kids were in bed.

They burst out laughing and Chloe said, "Wow, Mom, I've never seen you like this my whole life!"

"That's because I never have been," she said, and they spent the rest of the evening talking about Michael, the thunderbolt crashing across her sky.

Rhonda took the lead, which was a little unusual.

"He's a great guy. He had a rough life when he was young, and he dealt with it by studying philosophy and psychology. He says he wanted to understand himself but ended up understanding a lot more about just about everyone else. He has two kids, both grown, and his son, who is the older, has brain cancer, in remission, I think. He comes to the workshops sometimes, but Michael comes whether he does or doesn't."

"How is he as a dad? Good as it seems like he'd be?"

"Very affectionate and loving. They seem real close."

"Why isn't he with the mom?"

"She left him for a woman, I think. But it was a long time ago. No hard feelings, either. They've been taking care of their son when he needs it and they've become really close in a friend way. I asked him once how he could be so sweet to her and he said, 'It's not her fault. She didn't know herself. Just one of those things. It's part of why I try to keep up with myself.'"

She continued, "We got close the first time we were at a workshop together. He was serving the food at lunch and we asked about it. He said, 'Love to feed people!' He shared at the mic during a part of the day on grief and I went up to him afterwards and said how much it touched me. We just kept talking after that. I think you can trust him, Sal."

Okay, she wanted their blessing. Trust was not her strong suit, but she guessed she trusted them. If he was okay with them, he was okay, period. It was less than a year since Chloe had come back into Sal's life, but she couldn't think of any people she trusted more than the two of them. She smiled to think of it.

It was a long night waiting to go back to the

workshop the next day. Sal's dreams were crazy. She was in a cave with Michael and Chloe was painted, like a hieroglyph, on the stone above them. He said, "I will never leave you," and Sal said, "I know."

She woke up in a sweat, not sure she was ready for whatever was going to come of that day. But nothing could have kept her from finding him, keeping her eye on the huge mahogany door, opened and waiting for the arrival of that one person.

He saw her right away, his broad smile lighting up the room. He didn't run, but it seemed as if he did, approaching their corner of the room as if he was flying. Behind him was a younger version of himself, his son. She knew that before he reached them. His son looked almost exactly as he must have looked at thirty, fit and athletic, a handsome face and those blue, blue eyes.

"I made Josh sit with us today. I told him there was someone he had to meet," he said, making it clear he was talking about Sal. Rhonda and Chloe hugged Josh warmly, engaged immediately in a conversation about the depths of their lives.

"No hair, must still be doing that chemo stuff," he said, rubbing the top of Chloe's head.

"Yours is growing back!" she said, pulling it to make sure it was real. The awkward moment passed, and he turned to Sal.

"My dad tells me he hopes I like you, cuz you might be hanging around some."

He was as engaging as Michael, pulling Sal into a hug that said, 'if my dad likes you, you're ok with me.'

It was strange that she felt no surprise Michael had said those things. If she was honest, she couldn't see it going any other way than him and her together.

It's not that she had all that much confidence, she just knew.

"I was a fool to leave you last night," Michael said, pulling Sal into his arms, "What a miserable ten hours!"

They all clumped together on the carpet, a pile of humans. Michael and Sal put their heads on the meditation pillows they had brought, lining up next to each other with their hands folded across their own laps. She enjoyed the anticipation of time with him, someday, with no one else around. It felt delicious and achy to imagine it. She flashed back to when she had first gotten involved with Stan, but the only memories she had kept were of a party and his saying, "Hey, girl, you wanna dance?" He had owned her right away, possessive and all in charge.

With Michael, she felt a sense of acceptance, that even if what she wanted wasn't what he wanted, he'd find a way to work with it. She imagined him being *for* her in a way maybe no one her whole life had been. And she didn't doubt herself when it came to him. The absence of doubt left a vast expanse inside of her waiting to be filled with something entirely new. Not only Michael, but also a new way of being her.

֍ ֍ ֍ ֍

"I think I love you," he said, way too soon.

"I think I love you too," she responded, her hand resting on his cheek after their first kiss.

When Stan and Sal fell for each other, she made him wait a long time to hear those words. To be fair to herself, he made Sal wait longer. They'd been hedging their bets, not wanting to be the first one, but Sal blinked first.

"I love you, you creep," Sal had said to Stan, hoping the insult would save her if the feelings weren't returned. He just snorted in that way he had and turned over to go to sleep. He never had much left after sex.

The next week he said, "We may as well tie the knot," and she didn't say yes or no, but a month later, they stood in her sister's back yard and said forever. Obviously not with complete knowledge of what forever meant.

ৠৠৠৠ

She could not compare this thing with Michael to Stan in any way. There was such a respect in every move he made, everything he said. He would take a moment to find the right words, laying his hand on her waist to let her know he was right there with her while he felt his way to the truth.

The first few times they spent the night together, they went to Sal's place. He seemed as nervous as she was, shaking before he reached out to touch her. He seemed more interested in looking in her eyes than anything else, and that was new too.

"I'm in no hurry, just so you know," he said, and she believed him.

"I kind of am," she said, and they both laughed as if they'd never laughed before. They still didn't rush. He discovered her body inch by inch, and she discovered his. By the time they were having sex, in the traditional sense, it flowed from their affection in a seamless unfolding. It was all love. It was all regard. There was really no difference between their talking and their lovemaking.

The third time they stayed together, he called her and said, "I think it's time you saw my place."

"Do you live alone? I don't want to be interrupted." By this time, Sal would say anything to him. She'd never known she could be this bold.

"Josh stays with me from time to time but he's in Brazil right now with some indigenous healer. Don't worry; you have me to yourself."

Michael lived east of High Street on a tiny little block she'd never been on before. Before she moved to Berkeley, she had stayed north of Park where there was less crime, less drugs, less chance for a stray bullet to hit someone. But his place was a small house on a quiet street, all the yards well-tended, all the houses tidy. She drove up and parked in the driveway, as he'd suggested, and felt the warm air on the back of her neck. Since meeting Michael, her body had come alive, every nerve ending calling for attention. As eager as she was to see him, she took her time, noticing the grasses, lavender, princess plants, and potato bushes planted close together, creating a snug medley of color.

He must have been looking out the window, waiting for her, because three-quarters of her way up the driveway, he bounded out the door.

"Sal, you're at my house!" he exclaimed, and she couldn't help imagining what he must have been like as a boy, all enthusiasm and delight. He had already cautioned her about thinking she knew what he was like when he was younger. He said people he'd grown up with passed him on the street without recognizing him, that's how different he was. Walking into this house, she was drawn first to a ledge of pictures in the entry.

"Which ones are you?" Sal asked, wanting to

throw an anchor into the life he'd had before her.

"This one, this one, this one. And I'm in some of the group shots too."

The child and man in the shots didn't seem completely different from this present-day Michael, but she could see why people missed it was him. In all these portraits of the past, his face had an innocent, almost naive look she didn't find in it now. It had given way to a wise man look, not old yet but beyond uncertainty.

"You were a cutie," she offered, and he laughed that full laugh he had.

"Thanks, Sal. Glad you like the past me."

"I'm ready for a tour," she said, feeling a little awkward standing in the hall. As if he suddenly woke up to the situation, he answered quickly, with just a little embarrassment.

"What a terrible host I am!" He sounded as if he had left her in the garage for the day. "Come right this way, madam."

When she smiled, the moment passed, and he set out to guide her through this tiny cottage and share each corner with her. He had opened up all the walls and made the living room, dining room, and kitchen into an open, flowing space. He'd told her before that when he moved into the house, the kitchen was hardly usable. He got a great price on the place because of its need for help. Now, the kitchen was bright, airy, and updated. Sal envied the shiny appliances and cheery cabinets, but not in a jealous way, just a 'this is so cool' way. Michael had avoided making this beautiful kitchen feel too modern for the house by leaving some of the shelves open, with different colored dishes stacked on top of them. The few cabinets he had installed had frosted glass doors, the contents barely visible from the island, which stood, substantial and inviting, in the middle of the kitchen area.

She could imagine cuddling on the roomy, deep red, overstuffed couch that dominated the living room area. It was the only colorful item except for the pillows, solid colors too, like the plates. The dining area held a vintage table with six chairs, all different, that she could imagine dinner conversations around.

All in all, the front of the house looked as if he had taken a great deal of time and care, but at the same time, it looked relaxed. She could picture him reading books, making a plate of food, having company, all in a quiet but somehow also spirited way. In short, the house seemed to be a lot like its occupant.

They made their way down a hall and he opened the door to a bathroom he had also updated, with a deep claw tub and a two-person shower. The colors in it were less vivid than the front of the house, but nicely tiled and painted. The color in this room was the towels, deep, plush, and voluptuous.

At the very back were two bedrooms across from each other. One of them was decked out as an office, but she could somehow tell the sofa could be made into a bed. She walked into the room, looking at the books on his shelves and the computer, open and waiting to be typed on.

There was one room left. His bedroom. Part of her was running to the door and the other was unable to move. He took her hand and pulled her along, overcoming her sudden case of nerves.

"I've been waiting since the moment I met you to share this room with you." Right through the door, she could see a queen bed, covered with quilts and pillows, its wood frame conjuring up an old farmhouse. There was nothing in the room to disturb this impression. The few pictures were of happy times with his children at various ages. The books on the nightstand were novels she'd never read. She silently vowed to give them a try, just to see what world he was visiting before he drifted off to sleep. It hadn't taken long for him to tell her that when they weren't together, he fell asleep that way.

Here, in his own territory, he took charge. When he had led her to the bed, he pulled the covers down and invited her, with a slight motion, to sit. He sat next to her and unbuttoned his shirt, then hers, taking time with each button. She expected the lovemaking to start, but instead he took a long, deep look at her. Not just the beginning of nakedness, but all of her. Then he started to talk.

"Sal, I don't know where you're at, but I want to tell you where I'm at."

She hadn't heard 'where you're at' in years. "Okay," was all she said.

"You're it for me. I know what I know. I'm here for you and I don't ever want to not be here for you. I'd run to marry you today, if it wouldn't freak out everyone we know. That's where I'm at, can't change it. But I know you might not feel like that. I hate the thought, but it's only right if it's right for both of us. So, I'll be here for as long as it takes for you to decide…" He couldn't continue. Sal thought she saw tears coming to the corners of his warm, liquid eyes.

"How do you not know that I feel the same?"

They didn't need to say any more. The deal was sealed. Michael and Sal for as long as they were given, by powers greater than themselves.

Chapter Eighteen

Chloe

The months of chemo were continuing to take their toll on Chloe. She slept most afternoons, trying to gather all her energy for dinner with the kids, baths, and story time. Sometimes what she felt was a little like those times way back that she now called depression, but the difference was that in her mind, she was happy. Her body was another story.

It seemed forever ago that her mother had come back into her life. Now that Sal was happy with Michael and healed with Chloe, she seemed like a completely different person. Chloe was still occasionally angry with the person Sal had been, but her current mother was everything she ever could have asked for. She was grateful that this tragedy of her life had been removed.

Rhonda had been a little cautious with Sal at first, but not so much that anyone knew but Chloe. There was a certain tilt of her head, a quiet reserve that became pronounced when she was guarded, and it took some time for that to dissipate. In a way, Chloe was grateful for it, because it meant she wanted the best for Chloe, didn't want anything to hurt her.

Chloe could tell that things opened up a little in Hawaii. Sal was a big part of it. She listened for how they wanted things, and not just Chloe, Rhonda too. She followed their lead with the kids and waited to be asked to help, thanking them, over and over again, for taking her along. Halfway through the week, Sal and Rhonda took to playing Scrabble together, evenly matched and fighting over whether words were really words. Chloe could hear them during her nap, playful disagreement washing over her like warm water.

Rhonda's hesitation amped up a little when they came home, but not for long. Now, six months later, Sal and Rhonda were almost as close as a mother and daughter. Sal had fit herself into the corners of their family, finding unoccupied crevices to take up. She had developed a knack for stopping just short of intrusion, a talent Chloe had never witnessed in her before. When she asked how Sal had suddenly learned boundaries – which popped out unexpectedly, playfully, then gave Chloe a start when she heard her own directness – Sal said, "A little therapy goes quite a way when you're paying attention, and when you have so much to learn."

Sal came over for dinner almost every time she had the night off. And it wasn't long before Michael joined her, crawling around the floor with the kids and making his famous soup when the weather was cold. Some nights, especially chemo nights, Chloe stayed in bed, allowing a kiss from her mother to send her to the land of dreams. When she was feeling better, she sat at the table, or even cooked now and then. Her laughter filled the room, bathing her family in its warm light. Her mother surprised her by asking questions about what she was feeling and thinking, curious about Chloe's deepest pains and joys.

"How do you stay so calm with everything that's going on – kids and wife and cancer and all these people in and out of your house every other minute?" Sal asked her one day.

"I guess I just got sick of feeling sad and scared. I'm still here. That's a real success. And besides, I have to die sometime. I just eventually came to the point where it was more important to *live* at least, no matter when I die. But I had to feel panicked for a while before I could feel like that."

"Wow, it would be good if we all could live like that," Sal said.

✺ ✺ ✺ ✺

Chloe thought about what her mom had said a few days later. Sal and Michael had come over the night before for a really good dinner. Rhonda had made their favorite quinoa thing and Sal told them she was shocked that it tasted so good. The kids put on a little show for them all, being two and three now and able to do such things, and the crowd was delighted. Quin was the director, telling his sister what to do. "Now walk across like you're a queen ready to meet her subjects." "Subjects" sounded so serious coming out of his little three year old mouth and they all laughed a loving laugh, which almost startled his sister into paralysis. But when he said, "Ari, don't stop, keep walking," she came to and took her scepter, just a stick with feathers on the top, and proceeded to the far corner, where her subjects, every stuffed animal in the house, awaited her pronouncement. She couldn't remember the line, and Quin ran across to remind her.

"Dear subjects, I grant you food for a year, a house for each family, and lots of ice cream!"

When it was all over, Quin and Arisa bowed as low as they could and came up shouting "ta da" at the top of their lungs.

Chloe watched Michael, his face showing his obvious enchantment with the whole thing. She was so happy her mother had found someone who could really love her and wondered how long it would be before he sealed the deal.

≈≈≈≈

The next day the phone rang early, right after the kids had left for pre-school, startling Chloe out of her sleepy morning reverie.

"Hi, Chloe, it's Mom."

"Wow, you're calling early. Is everything okay? I mean, besides the obvious."

"Everything is more than fine. I wanted you to be the first to know. Michael and I went up in the hills to watch the moon last night, you know it was full, and well, when he got me up there he went down on one knee and proposed! Imagine that!"

"My God, you said yes, right?"

"Several times in rapid succession, believe me. Ring and everything! I'm kind of beside myself, if you want to know the truth."

"Well, me too. When's the engagement party, Mom? How about having it here?"

"You should check with your wife, don't you think?"

Chloe liked the way "wife" rolled off Sal's tongue as if she had approved all along. Her judgement was so far in the past that Chloe could hardly remember the devastation of her rejection.

"I'm pretty sure I know what she'll say, Mom. She loves you both. I'm so excited! I have no reservations about him and I was hoping you'd end up feeling the same. Being married to the right person is heaven, you know. Well, even if I am kind of in hell in another way."

"Well, if Rhonda's for it, I'd love to have a little engagement get together at your place. Can't think of anything better."

ﾞﾞﾞﾞﾞ

The winter afternoon felt almost like spring. The party had been planned for inside, in case it rained, but all the guests spilled out into the yard, light sweaters enough to warm them.

It was the first time Chloe had all her family together ever, both the family she grew up with and her in-laws. Her siblings came, each one hesitating just a moment before saying yes. Her sister brought her kids, who climbed and swung on the new play structure at the far side of the yard, their high voices and laughter floating over to the patio. Rhonda's family was there, passing out icy mojitos, rum and no rum, topped with mint and lime. Michael's family was there too, his son, daughter, and his ex-wife, proving she really had become a friend. It was the first time the future in-laws had met each other, the awkward silences evaporating within the first few minutes.

Chloe and Rhonda's friend, Mel, who played such beautiful music at their wedding, came with her guitar and sang in the background. Even though the music was quiet, the whole party stopped talking intermittently, listening instead to the clear, bright quality of her voice and the wonder of the words.

She sang all her own music, inspired by her life and the lives of everyone around her. Sal had a favorite, "In this Moment, Here and Now,"

I love you in this moment now
Promising I will never go
Pledging to love, deeply and true
Until time itself parts me from you

Chloe and Rhonda sat at the table with Sal and Michael, listening together. The younger couple thought about the possibility that that parting could be so much sooner than they wanted, and the older couple thought about how short their time together might be, starting so late. But underneath these fears, regrets, was a piercing gratitude that they had each other, that in this moment, right now, they loved and were loved. That love extended, just for the moment, to everyone around them, their friends, their family, their children. Nothing Chloe could imagine could improve this day. There was nothing missing or inadequate, nothing she needed. She thought, *no matter what happens, I have had something so few people have in this life. I am so, so lucky.*

She looked over at her mother, who seemed to her like a different person from the mother who had raised her, critical, unhappy, and harsh. They caught each other's eyes, and the open smiles were sincere, loving, accepting, welcoming.

❧ ❧ ❧ ❧

Chloe was getting gradually sicker, so slowly that anyone who saw her every day hardly noticed. Her naps in the afternoon became longer. She came less often to sit at the dinner table, hold the kids, laugh at their jokes, and watch them play. She and Rhonda more often lay on the bed together, holding hands, drifting in and out of sleep. Even when she finished her chemo, things did not improve.

Rhonda had had a hard time adjusting to their new slow pace at first. She was a fast mover, always busy and managing three to one hundred projects at once. But sometime in the last few months, she noticed that there was too much time that Chloe was alone in their room, no one to hold her or comfort her. Rhonda wrote early in the morning, before anyone was awake, but mostly just notes for the someday she began to imagine, when Chloe might be gone, and she would write to heal herself, as she always had.

Their blog went viral, read by hundreds of people. There were the lesbians, gay men, bisexual and transgender people who read it because they were talking about their life together. There were the people with cancer who read it because Chloe and Rhonda were talking about their life together. Some people read it because they were fans of Rhonda's books, or they had worked with Chloe on their own books.

But more and more, Rhonda made the entries for both of them. She would secretly tape their conversations and add Chloe's comments from the things she said. Chloe was grateful, since she was often too tired to put pen to paper. Now and then, though, she would say, "I think I'll put that one in, Rhonda," and then open the computer she rarely touched and update the blog.

Early in the summer, she made her last entry.

"I don't think I'll be writing this blog any longer. The cancer is eating my energy like a Venus fly trap. When I have a good hour – it is no longer about good days – I spend time with my family, especially my kids, and then go back to bed. But I want to say how much it has meant to me knowing that you kept up with how I was doing. I have felt you all there, just out of my line of vision, caring about what I'm going through.

"Rhonda will keep writing, and please don't stop commenting. She'll share those comments with me when I'm up to it. Meantime, life is a big surprise. I would have thought being up against a killer disease I'd be depressed, panicked, in a bad way. Instead, I feel two things. Love and gratitude. What a life!"

❧ ❧ ❧ ❧

"I sit here watching my wife sleep. Her bare head lays on the pillow, creating a hollow to hold her close. None of her body shows. She is nestled in the blankets, shivering anyway. Her mouth, just slightly open, has a drop of liquid streaming down her cheek to form a dark area right below those impossibly pink lips.

"How can I consider losing her? What would life be without her? How will I go on? Devin says I don't need to know that now. Just continue, day after day. No need to be ready, to prepare. I will never show her this entry. How can I tell her I'm so afraid? The children laugh in the kitchen, and the door muffles their voices. I have the best worst life I know."

The blog had become Rhonda's place. She said the things there she wanted to keep to herself, or at least didn't want to share with Chloe. It was hard to adjust to the need to deal with some of it on her own. They had always helped each other. Since they first met, she had never felt alone with anything.

She knew that one of these days, she would have to say something about her fear. Chloe would know something was wrong whenever she was alert enough for long enough to switch on her radar. But she had been so sick lately that Rhonda had chosen to spend the few times she was awake enjoying family life and playing together. There was the day Chloe was suddenly full of energy after a nap and they piled in the car to spend the sunset hours at the nearest beach. There was Quin's best friend's birthday party, which they almost thought they would have to miss but somehow managed to get to. There was the night Quin and Ari stayed overnight at Sal's house with her and Michael, and Rhonda ordered in, candlelight and all, for an early birthday dinner, months before either of their birthdays. They both knew Chloe might not be here by then, and almost surely wouldn't be up for a party. They kissed by the gentle light and Chloe surprised Rhonda by gently pulling her to the bedroom, making love as she had before cancer, sweet and slow and long.

Rhonda shocked herself with the things she was doing in the long hours when Chloe slept, and the kids were at school. Except for the blog, she gave up any real writing, continuing to take notes but not much more. She read mystery novels by the dozens, somehow getting used to the idea of death by reading books organized around it. Sometimes she imagined how she would change the house after Chloe died, the only things she could imagine about that unimaginable possibility. *I'll put the dresser in the opposite corner. I won't have those papers on the desk in the bedroom; they'll go in the office. I think I'll take the kids to that other preschool over the hill. The kids that go there seem happy.*

At first, she felt vaguely disloyal, picturing a time when Chloe would be gone. She worked up the nerve to mention it to Deidre, whose only comment was, "You're trying to imagine how your life will continue, even though you don't believe it now. I remember that." She was so grateful to Deidre, because from that day on, she figured she must be normal, that she wasn't the only one thinking these things as their dearest ones gradually died. Dying. The word increased in proportion from week to week. In moments of clarity, Rhonda knew that Chloe's death was approaching. Afraid to ask herself when, a quiet voice in her mind whispered, *three months. No more.* No attempt to shut it off had any impact.

❧ ❧ ❧ ❧

It was April when Chloe stopped getting out of bed more than a few times a week. A visit to her doctor just confirmed what they had known for a while. Despite the torture of her treatment, her cancer continued to grow. She continued to get sicker. It had come upon them so gradually that they hardly realized that they began to live their lives in that twelve by twelve room, their bedroom. The shock was that they were still living. There was no loss of contact, connection, joy, life.

About a month before Chloe finally admitted she was on her way to death, she pulled Rhonda into their bedroom one day when Sal was out in the kitchen with the kids.

"Rhonda, I'm fading out. I want one more trip. One more time with the kids, with you, and my mom. Please don't make it far away!"

Rhonda asked Sally to help figure it out. They settled on the Russian River. It was close and they found a little house with a pool where they could enjoy the weather without moving from the place. When they arrived, the owner had left flowers on the table, and plenty of spices and staples for them to cook for themselves. Sal had learned quite a bit watching Rhonda and Chloe cook, and she fed them the whole weekend with sumptuous, healthy meals, which the kids, in particular, gorged on.

Rhonda bought a huge inflatable boat. Chloe somehow managed to get in it and then spent the day floating in the pool, Quin and Ari occasionally swimming over to her and climbing in. While they napped, she floated on the water, Moses in the basket, so still that Rhonda checked on her every few minutes to make sure she hadn't slipped away.

They had planned to drive down to the river, but it was easier just to stay at the house and enjoy the quiet warmth of the sun and the water. Rhonda knew that this, finally, was the last. There would be no more memories for her or the kids of bright weekends and chill spring mornings. She drank in the moments with Chloe, as if she could fill every corner with Chloe, enough to fill her for a lifetime.

Quin and Ari were happy that weekend, unaware that it was a goodbye weekend. They squealed and ran, Rhonda and Chloe watching Sal chase them down, "I'm gonna *get* you," echoing through the yard. Rhonda had to smile at the way they loved their grandmother, as if she had been there from the first moment. Blissfully unaware of all the adult trouble, they reveled in her, her in them. Surprising herself, Rhonda thanked whatever power was greater than herself that they had gotten Sal back. Her kids would have her parents, her brother, and Sal, not to mention Chloe's siblings, who all seemed to have emerged out of the woodwork once Chloe and Sal were good again. Life was terrible, but beautiful too.

❧❧❧❧❧

Chloe teared up often, too short on energy to really cry, but unable to stop the leak. When they came back from the weekend, she slept for the better part of two days, surrounded by the pillows and leaving just a corner for Rhonda when she finally collapsed, kids asleep, dishes clean, lights out.

Chloe's pain was increasing, but she wasn't ready to tell anyone. She knew that once she really took enough meds to dull it, she might be a little faded. She had been able, up to this point, to take small amounts and put the pain she still had in a padlocked cage somewhere near her, but not with her. It was an animal in the corner, ready to pounce but, until this point, miraculously still.

After that weekend, though, the beast sprang from its corner, unleashed and vicious. Rhonda finally woke up, about a week later, to Chloe moaning in her sleep, a noise like nothing Rhonda had ever heard.

The next day she told Chloe they had to call hospice. "It's time," she said.

Chloe cried for real this time, racking sobs she couldn't control. She was heartbroken to leave her beautiful life and everyone in it. She nodded, then added, "You all only have to let go of me. I have to let go of every single person I love."

"Oh, baby," Rhonda cooed, holding her closer than it seemed possible, but careful not to hold too tight and bring that look of pain to her face. "I can't know, but it must be so terrible. But we both know things can't go on like this forever." They finished talking, then made the call.

It surprised them all when the hospice folks made a difference with the pain and Chloe was still herself. They had to keep the visitors down, which wasn't easy once word got out that this might be it. But it was a tranquil and happy household, full of love and laughter and fun.

She couldn't get to the bathroom by herself, but her sharp mind and wit still came in handy. "Rhonda, if I start peeing in the bed you have my permission to scold. And put me in diapers!"

"That would not be stylin'," Rhonda replied. They had fun inventing diaper outfits for Vogue magazine, "the latest in death wear." The people who had been around through this whole thing laughed uncontrollably. The ones who had stayed away and were just coming to say goodbye squirmed and usually made a quick exit. Fine with Chloe and Rhonda.

Rhonda gave up writing altogether, but by some miracle, her novel continued to do very well, thanks to a ton of reviews on Amazon. She wondered what angel had produced all those five-star recommendations. "Best novel I've read in years." "Don't miss it." On and on. It felt right that the book that had brought them together was sustaining them now.

The blog was a comfort, a way to use words to remember everything that happened. But even that was occasional, once a week or so was the best she could manage.

"Chloe sleeps most of the time now. I creep in through the door, careful not to wake her. Even with the blackout curtains, a ribbon of light streams across the bed, lights her shoulder under the blanket. I lay down, almost sleeping too, and we are transported to a different universe. She stirs and glances towards me, the smile gracing me with love. Then she's out again, resting for some big event that will likely never come now. Just resting to prepare herself for the hard work of dying."

April read the blog religiously and printed out each entry, planning to ask to publish the whole thing as a book after...April couldn't say it. But she knew the day was coming. She visited regularly, surprised that it was a pleasure to be with them, especially Chloe. If anything, Chloe made April laugh more, feel better. She always left with a smile on her face. Sometime in the twenty-four hours after a visit, the tears would come, when she felt the steady ache of what was about to come for all of them

Once, April said to Chloe and Rhonda, a little too forcefully, "I don't know how you do it. You are so strong! I couldn't do what you're doing." They both laughed for what seemed like an hour, calming themselves down then catching each other's eyes and breaking up again. "What, it's not funny! What's so *funny*?"

"Oh, sorry, April," Chloe declared, finally catching her breath. "It's just that we think it's so very amusing that people think we're doing something special. Geez, we just don't have any choice. If you really think you can't do it, better kill yourself before you get old or sick!"

April wouldn't have been able to tell anyone why that was comic, but she laughed harder and longer than she had in months, maybe since before her employee, her friend, this person she had come to love so much, had gotten the diagnosis.

Chapter Nineteen

Sally

Sal woke up Sunday morning with a lot on her mind. She turned to the side and slid out of the bed, wanting Michael to sleep as long as he wanted. The first few months together, any stirs from one woke the other, but they had settled into a comfortable coziness, so he murmured and let her arm slide out from under his.

It was one of those warm winter days. She left her slippers, the ones that lived at Michael's, under the bed frame and tiptoed to the kitchen, setting water on to boil and staring out the window through the back door. Michael's garden, almost as wonderful as Rhonda and Chloe's, met her sleepy eyes with its beautiful colors and heathery grasses.

It was one of those times when moments in her life crowded through the lens of her mind, demanding a mention in the top ten. The whole long drama of her failed marriage, the rift between Chloe and her, the good moments when the kids were young, meeting Michael, therapy. Nothing was in order and she swirled through it all, feeling it in the pit of her stomach and having no opinion on what it all meant.

She couldn't have said how long all of that lasted, maybe a half-hour, but could have been half the morning. She startled when she felt a hand on her shoulder, so far away she didn't know, at first, who it was.

"You're a million miles away," Michael said, warm and loving.

"I was. Now I'm right here." She smiled softly, reassuring him that they had no problem he didn't know about. "I want to talk about something."

"Okay," he said, with just a bit of a question mark at the end.

"I know we planned the wedding for summer, plenty of time to plan. But…" Sal took a long pause, hoping this wouldn't disappoint him. He just listened, still as a stone. "Michael, I'm afraid Chloe won't be here that long. I'm having a hard time waiting. I missed her wedding and I just don't want her to miss mine."

The look of relief that spread across his face brought air into the room, light into the corners.

"Oh, Sal, why didn't I think of it myself? God, I'm sorry I missed that! I would marry you in a pair of overalls and have peanut butter sandwiches instead of wedding cake. We can get this going in a hurry! When do you want to get married, my love?" She got up, walked around the table, sat on his lap, and gave him a really good kiss, which she could tell he appreciated.

꿏꿏꿏

Chloe teared up when Sal told her they were moving the wedding up. They were all on the bed, Chloe, Rhonda, the kids, eating dinner and watching Sesame Street.

Chloe wasn't eating much these days, but she loved for her family to share mealtime with her. She let the kids put small bites in her mouth, expectantly waiting for the smile that always came, progressively weaker as her body failed.

Today was a better day, and she was sitting up against a big slanted pillow with a bunch of extra pillows wedged in around her. For some reason, if she was supported all around, the pain was less. Some days she laid on her side, quiet but absorbed in the chatter of her wife and children, and all the other people who filled the corners of their little house. Other days, like today, she threw herself into the chatter and laughter, the jokes and reports, giving it every ounce of energy she had. Rhonda complained from time to time about how hard it was to get to her wife, and how careful she had to be once she did, so she didn't worsen anything. Sal knew there was nothing Rhonda hated worse than seeing Chloe's pain, except somehow contributing to it. Of course, Chloe always just said, "No big deal and no way around it."

Anyway, since it was a pretty good day, it seemed like a good day to share their new plan. Michael and Sal had decided Sal should tell them without him, because if they had any hesitation it would be more likely to show without him there. They were focused on giving him the message that he was part of the family. They were nearly always positive about everything when he was around. With Sal, the trust had built enough that Sal knew when they were having a hard time. In fact, she had become a listening ear for Rhonda, in particular. She'd stay after everyone else was asleep and listen to Rhonda, her fear, her love. She felt the honor of it.

"Hey, big news here," Sal started, taking a light tone and putting a happy look on her face. All four of them turned to her, full attention, waiting for whatever this was.

"Michael and I have decided we can't wait to tie the knot. We want to move the wedding up. Do you think Dani would be okay with it?" Their front neighbor had offered to host the occasion, just as she did for Chloe and Rhonda, and they had accepted, knowing how much it meant to her to be able to do things for Chloe and Rhonda's family. She was getting a little bit feeble and couldn't do the heavy lifting anymore.

"Wow, Mom, are you pregnant?" Chloe began with mischief in her eye. The kids looked confused, but the rest of them laughed until their stomachs hurt. "That's really exciting. I was so worried I wouldn't be there!"

One thing about Sal's amazing daughter was that she didn't beat around the bush. Whatever was happening with her was right out front. She looked at Sal with a kind of gaze Sal was coming to expect in her life. Chloe and her family, Michael, Michael's family, even some of the friends they had, all looked at Sal with the eyes of love. There was really no other way to put it.

Rhonda called Dani, who said yes without thinking. Despite the joke about peanut butter, Michael's employees had already agreed to handle the food and the service. His restaurant was almost like a family, everyone pitching in when something was important to any one of them. Sal knew the food would be "off the hook," as the younger folks said.

"A week from Saturday, if that's okay with you. And...Do you think you could marry us? You know more about how to really be married than anyone else we could think of. Plus, you're both good with words and I, for one, tend to need help in that department!"

With no hesitation, Rhonda answered for both of them, a habit she was getting into to save Chloe from putting out too much. "We would be so honored." They laughed, they cried, they hugged and, by the time she left that night, they had settled nearly every detail.

❧ ❧ ❧ ❧ ❧

Rhonda stood before the crowd, with a journal in front of her. They had asked her to pick the readings and to talk about marriage, with Chloe adding whatever she wanted. Rhonda and Chloe were both dressed in purple, Chloe in a wispy see-through fabric with deep blue underneath, Rhonda in purple denim and a splashy shirt in deep, saturated colors. It was clear to Sal they looked far more beautiful than she and Michael did, but when she mentioned that to Michael later, he said, "I don't know about me, but you were the most beautiful one in the yard."

After the hundred or so people settled in to their seats, Rhonda opened the book and began to speak.

"Chloe and I are happy to welcome you to this most beautiful occasion. We can't think of anything better than being asked to help two people we care about so much join their lives together. Beverly Clark offers some words that Chloe and I have lived by through everything life has brought us. It goes like this.

"'We need a witness to our lives. There are a billion people on the planet. I mean, what does any one life really mean? But in a marriage, you're promising to care about everything. The good things, the bad things, the terrible things, the mundane things, all of it, all of the time, every day. You're saying 'Your life will not go unnoticed because I will notice it. Your life will not go un-witnessed because I will be your witness.'"

She looked over at Chloe, reached for her hand,

and for long enough to mean something, they regarded each other. Even though Sal was eager to marry Michael, she could have watched them watch each other indefinitely. She thanked them in her mind for restoring her belief in love, in forever, in loyalty and good intention, in a thousand beautiful qualities that she had given up on ever finding.

Sal pulled herself back to the moment, taking a deep breath to drink in the beauty all around her. She looked at Michael, who was looking at her. She imagined he'd been regarding her that way the whole time she was focused on them. He smiled, pleased that he had captured her eye at just that moment.

Rhonda continued, holding Chloe's gaze.

"When you have found a love like I have with Chloe, you want everyone you love to have a love as sweet. When you know it's possible, you ache for anyone who hasn't had it. So, when Sal and Michael found it, we celebrated. Their love is strong and sure, the kind that grows you, that distills you, that makes you your best.

"It's like Rumi says, 'In your light, I learn how to love. In your beauty, how to make poems. You dance inside my chest where no one sees you, but sometimes I do, and that sight becomes this art.'" She paused again, drinking in Sal's daughter as if she wanted to fill up every corner of herself. Then she turned to Michael and Sal, seated before them and holding each other close. Chloe turned too and began to speak.

"You have committed to each other and now place yourselves in the hands of this community who will love and treasure your relationship throughout this life. Are you prepared to fulfill the promises you have brought with you today?" They both nodded, leaning in with everyone there to hear the words she said so softly.

"Sal, do you take Michael as your partner in this life, to walk with and help, to challenge and support, steadfastly and with your whole self?"

"Yes." Sal could feel how complete that promise was, that nothing could break it.

"Michael, do you take Sal as your partner in this life, to walk with and help, to challenge and support, steadfastly and with your whole self?"

"You know I do," he said, grinning from ear to ear. Sal thought how much like a boy he looked when he was happy.

Chloe continued. "Do you have more you'd like to say to each other?"

They did.

"Sal, when I met you, I became a new man, but remarkably, everyone still recognizes me. You have reached a place in my soul that I hardly knew I had, where I am wholly for you. And the thing is, it is completely clear to me that that means I have to be the best Michael. I can't forget myself or leave stuff messed up. I have to do whatever work I have so I can be your best Michael. And it's all a big relief, as if someone let me out of jail. I love you, Sal. I really do."

Sal was crying by now, full out, as she never did in front of other people, but it felt good, right in line with what was happening.

"Michael, I didn't believe I would have a good love in my life. I had given up on it, actually, and I wasn't even looking. Then you arrived in my life like a complete remodel, readjusting everything, changing me, waking me up. And I have to give myself credit that I was trying to wake up already, but then you turned on the light. I am yours, through and through. And I am so grateful."

Then Chloe and Rhonda pulled out their rings and helped them exchange them. When Michael and Sal's were done, Chloe and Rhonda spoke in unison.

"By the power of our love, we bless your love and call you married and whole. You may kiss each other."

There had never been a kiss like that.

❧ ❧ ❧ ❧

Michael and Sal decided to wait on a honeymoon. Neither one of them wanted to be away from Chloe that long. They traded proposals about how to celebrate until they came up with something in the short term.

"One day trip to the beach."

"Or an overnight at Inverness."

"Or three days in Big Sur."

"A four-day weekend driving up the coast."

"Sold."

They made sure there was no need for them in the next few days and that the restaurant was covered. Michael had a new manager who seemed trustworthy, but he designated a spy who was very reliable. He'd wanted to hire her when the manager left, but she didn't want the headache.

They left when they woke up, which they had thought would be midmorning but came along with the sun, around six a.m. Sal laughed at herself remembering when she was allergic to six a.m. The light along Highway One was just beginning to bathe the hills, glinting off of the rocks and grasses. Even with all that was happening with Chloe, it was hard to imagine being happier. Michael drove the speed limit, telling Sal he didn't want to hurry, connected his phone to the radio, and played old jazz, Sarah Vaughn and Cleo Laine to start with. She had never liked that music because it seemed too romantic. Now she couldn't imagine how she could have felt that way.

They stopped early at a little bed and breakfast with a vacancy sign, hidden among the ice plants and grasses. The room had a jacuzzi and a view over a cliff. They could leave the curtains open and no one would ever see them. They took each other's clothes off and settled into the warm water, but didn't last more than five minutes before, without words, they stepped out, pulled the plush towels around them, and headed for the big, four-poster, inviting bed. The view lost its appeal.

꧁꧂꧁꧂

It was the quickest four days they had ever experienced. Part of Sal wanted this to be her life forever, but some other part of her was feeling the umbilical cord tugging at her, pulling her back to Chloe.

"You're ready to go home now, huh, babe?" Michael said, without disappointment or resentment.

"I wish it could go on forever, but that will have to be later," she said, stunned that she had no worry that he would be angry, or even disappointed. She knew, with every cell of her being, that Michael wanted the best for her, wanted her to have what she needed. That didn't mean he was just a milk toast. If something didn't sit right with him, he'd keep working until they came to a solution they could both live with. There was still a part of her that didn't believe in that, that thought it was one or the other, but Michael would not let her cheap out on herself or him either. So, a little earlier than they had planned, they u-turned and headed back down the coast. She knew that she didn't have to worry about him resenting it. He wouldn't be doing it under those conditions.

When they got back to Oakland, they headed straight for Chloe and Rhonda's. Neither of them had a good feeling. Sal wished later that they'd been wrong.

❧❧❧❧

The calm in the house was not normal. All the lights were on, so they knew the family hadn't just turned in early. The kids were asleep, yes, but there were at least ten people in the living room, just sitting quietly, waiting for something. Michael and Sal didn't want to know what.

Emily got up and came over to them, gave Sal the kind of hug meant to offer comfort. "She's in and out," she said, in a voice so low Sal wasn't sure she had heard her after she spoke.

Sal turned around, running to the bedroom, and just as she peeked in, heard Quin crying down the hall. She changed direction, opened his door, talking as she walked towards his little bed.

"What's the trouble, little Quin?" she said, hoping her words formed a coo in his ears.

"I had a bad dream, Gramma. Mommy was flying away from us, really high, and she said don't worry, but when I woke up I was really worried."

Sal took him in her arms, holding him closer to her chest than she had ever held her own children. He surrendered to her arms, whimpering a little but taking the comfort. Within minutes, he was back to sleep.

An even stranger calm covered the scene in Chloe and Rhonda's room. At first, Sal thought Rhonda was reading one of Devin's books, until she realized that Rhonda was really singing it. Chloe was drifting in and out, stirring when the music rose, almost coming to now and then.

By three in the morning, they all found corners to sleep in, or try to. They knew that the moments they might have with Chloe on this earth were numbered. They thought it might be that night. But when morning came and they all pulled out of sleep, they heard her breath, shallow but unmistakable, still, even.

The children woke up needing a lot of attention, agitated by not being able to rouse their mother and confused by the crowd that was not going to leave until something changed, one way or the other. Sal wasn't going to leave Chloe's room unless Rhonda specifically asked, and she wasn't asking. She was in a secret world with Chloe, but she didn't need anyone to leave, just leave her to comfort her true love. She sang, cooed, talked, and whispered. Sal had never seen anyone give themselves so completely to another human being. She realized that real love was not just love you could live with but love you could die with. When she thought about Michael, out in the living room, she knew she had that now.

In the afternoon, Chloe came out of wherever she was, and saw her mother sitting at the end of the bed. "Hi, Mom," she said, the same smile she had had as a child spreading across her face. "Good honeymoon? Lots of loving?" Sal must have started to cry without knowing it because Chloe reached towards her and Sal scooted over to catch her hand.

"I'm sorry we didn't have longer, Mom. But I'm glad we had what we had. I love you and I don't want you ever to give yourself a hard time for anything. It was the only way it could be. Thank you for coming back. I don't want to go." And she drifted off again.

The next few days, she wasn't with them much in the usual sense, but at the same time, the whole house seemed filled with her. Rhonda stayed with her all the time now and the rest of them came in and out. The day after Michael and Sal came back, Clarence, Fay, and Graham came. They stayed in the front house with Dani, but they really just parked their suitcases there. They didn't even want to be those twenty feet away from the family and that was pretty much the way everyone felt.

Quin and Ari stopped coming in the room, didn't sleep well, cried out at night, but during the day they seemed to enjoy all the people. Sal imagined they thought all their people were there to play with them, and as painful as it was, Sal left Chloe's room now and then to read a book, solve a puzzle, dance to their music. They managed to delight in their grandmother still, the stubborn drive of being children winning out over any difficulty.

There was more quiet hanging around during a deathwatch than Sal ever would have thought. They talked about small things, told jokes, laughed. Yes, now and then they were sad, but honestly not much more than usual, at least where Sal was concerned. And there was a strange beauty all around. Sal thought about how few people on this earth got to die with this much love around them, how few people loved each other as much as they all loved each other. Chloe had done this, brought them all together to walk her out of this life. Sal felt strangely lucky.

She mentioned it one day to Emily. Her face cleared of the worry for a moment before she said, "That is so true." Then she gave Sal one of her very best hugs, which went right through Sal. She was grateful for that.

❧❧❧❧

The hospice nurse everyone liked the best was the only one they ever asked for predictions. About the third day Chloe was mostly out, Rhonda asked how long this would be. Sal was glad she did, because it was hers to ask but everyone wanted to know. Maddy, the nurse, took a minute to look at Chloe's chart, where a rotating squad of monitors neatly wrote every blood pressure number, every medication to keep her out of pain, every waking and going back out.

"If it was someone else, I'd say before tomorrow," Maddy began, looking a little puzzled, "But since Chloe already outlasted my prediction in my own head by several days, I can't really tell you."

She told them what usually happens, blood pressure wise, extremities getting cold, all the physical manifestations of this kind of death. She told them young people last longer and mothers of young children, in her very subjective experience, fought the hardest. It was hard to let your body go when you left a child without a parent. Sal looked at Rhonda with concern and gratitude that Maddy hadn't said "without a mother." They would have a mother, but they would not have Chloe.

That night, her breathing changed, what Maddy had called "death rattle." Sal could never have imagined what it sounded like, a rhythmic cement mixer but louder. They had moved one of their overstuffed chairs into the room, so someone, usually Sal these days, could sit in the room and get Rhonda anything she needed. She was determined not to leave Chloe except to shower now and then or check in with the kids and they had been asleep for hours.

Chloe's even, labored breath lulled Sal, once she was used to it, and she drifted off. It could have been an hour or a day when Rhonda touched her shoulder. "Sal, I think she's going."

Sal peeked out the door and caught someone's eye out in the living room and everyone in the house crammed into the room. Sal didn't know so many people could fit in such a small space, but it didn't feel crowded. Chloe's breath stopped now and then and they all strained to hear. Was this the last one? Was she gone? But each time, another breath came.

They didn't know how long it would be. But they knew what to do in the meantime. They sang her lullabies and love songs, rounds and hymns. When each song was over, someone started another one. They spilled into each other, washing the room in their melody and harmony. Whether the singer was a pro or didn't usually sing a note, each voice was perfect in itself. Chloe was slipping out, evenly and peacefully, without tension.

Then without warning, both children cried out in their sleep, louder than Sal was used to hearing them. Their voices broke into the room and commanded all the attention. And Chloe, who had seemed so near death a moment ago, went back to even breathing, loud and even. Her body warmed up as if a furnace had been lit under the bed. She was not going now, while her children wailed in the other room. Emily ran out to soothe them and the piercing cries stopped. Chloe was not going to die tonight.

᠊᠊᠊᠊

The morning found them littered over the floors of the house, exhausted and spent. Chloe didn't wake up anymore and Maddy said this was a deep coma. They kept the singing up on and off, for Chloe but also for Rhonda who hadn't really slept in days. She did a good share of the singing herself, with a voice Sal had never heard from her before. She put a tune to everything she said now, and Sal would have sworn that Chloe heard her.

Rhonda was generous with Sal, letting her stay in the room and sometimes even inviting her to climb into the bed next to her beautiful child. There was a calm over the house today even though it was still filled with so many people. Graham went out and got food enough to feed the crowd for the day, then took the kids to the park down the block, leaving strict instructions to call if anything changed.

Chloe showed no change that day, but the rattle could be heard all over the house, steady and deafening. Rhonda, who had not left the room in longer than anyone could remember, was finally convinced that a shower would soothe her, and began to take her clothes off, unconscious of whether she was alone or in a crowd.

She padded to the bathroom, leaving Sal in charge of Chloe for just the moment. Feeling the responsibility, she watched Chloe's breath with all her attention. She even sang to her, no longer self-conscious about her singing or anything else.

It wasn't a minute before her breath started changing. It faded out a time or two, then started up before even a minute had passed. Sal ran to the door and called Rhonda. She couldn't hear the shower and Sal knew she hadn't gotten in yet. Rhonda ran back to the room, wrapped in a big purple towel. Back on the bed, she took Chloe's hand and murmured, "It's okay, my sweet love. It's okay to go."

The room had filled with all the people Chloe loved, all the people who loved her. Graham had returned with Quin and Ari, who ran into the room, no longer afraid, and hopped onto the bed with their mothers, rubbing Chloe's head and arms, sitting next to Rhonda.

Chloe's breath stopped once, then twice, longer. They all waited for it to return and it was a long time before it did. Then one big sigh out and quiet. She was gone.

"Mama R." Quin broke the sacred silence in the room. "I see birdies!" He was pointing to the ceiling, wonder filling his expression. He called them birds, but everyone imagined they were angels.

EPILOGUE

The weeks after Chloe died passed in a blur. Sal helped Rhonda plan the memorial, and it was the most beautiful thing she had ever been part of, except her marriage to Michael. There was music, of course, and dancing, and crowds of people who were sad, yes, but also happy to celebrate Sal's little girl.

Chloe had touched the people around her in a way Sal had never experienced before. She told Michael that without her Chloe, she could never have let herself love him. "I will thank Chloe for the rest of my life," he said, holding both of Sal's hands and looking deep into her soul.

Sal even spoke at the memorial, Rhonda insisting that her voice needed to be included. "My daughter was the best person I've ever known. She loved when others hated. She knew who she was and didn't apologize for it. She did her work and lived her life in a way that was consistent with her goodness. The only thing she hated was injustice. And I will miss her for as long as I live."

Rhonda spoke too, of course. "Chloe was the love of my life. I will know what it is to be loved for the rest of my life because she loved me. I can't be anything but grateful."

The music was laced through it all. Most of the people who sang at the fundraiser sang again, some of them working up new material just for her.

Sometimes an angel comes to earth
Just with her love, she shows you what you're
worth
Never forget what she gave you, my friend
Never doubt she's behind you to the end.

The reception afterwards was a real party. Sal expected to cry all day, but was strangely light and happy. She looked from person to person, grateful for all they had given her. There was no tragedy here, just an inevitable, too early, failure of the body. Everyone would pass this way, but how many people would gather so much love and care around them? Sal had never seen any group of people, including any church she'd ever been to, that knew how to care for each other like this group did. Sal knew she would grieve long and hard. She would never be the same, but she would be sad, mad, and grateful for a start and she would give herself all the time she needed.

She called Devin to tell him Chloe was gone. He listened to every detail of the last few weeks, asking questions to hear more, his voice more downcast than she'd ever heard it. He told Sal that he had loved Chloe too and that he wasn't liking this death thing. Then he said something Sal would remember as long as she was able to remember anything.

"You know a good death when everyone around that person is healed."

Acknowledgments

There is no way to thank everyone who had a hand in this book. It has taken a lifetime to be the person who wrote it, supported by the people who have stood behind me. Nevertheless, I must try!

To my friends who have taught me so much about love:

To Denah Joseph, who has been such a true friend and supporter and always has a fresh way to look at things. Thank you for your support through the hard stuff.

To the hundred or so people who, during the long illness of my first wife, cared for us so lovingly when we needed so much. You are always in my heart.

To Stephen and Ondrea Levine, who helped me to face up to death and sit with whatever was going on in me. Thank you for everything you gave me.

To Richard Olney who expanded my world beyond the boundaries of time and space. Thank you for helping me to see beyond this imperfect world.

To Erving Poster, who knows when to push and when to sit quietly. Thank you for the transformations you shepherded.

To the people in my Training Group who have offered me love and honesty no matter what. Thank you for your continuous presence.

To all those I've worked with:

To the many clients who taught me so much about being where we are and inviting where we're going. Thanks for the inspiration.

To the many people who have participated in support groups I've led, who shared their lives, their hearts, their fears and triumphs, as long as they could. It's an honor.

To everyone at Sapphire books, especially Christine Svendsen and Kaycee Hawn who read the book with care and attention and understood the story I was trying to tell. Thanks for guiding the process so well.

To Sheryl Traum, Alex Austin and Wendy Levy, who helped me navigate an unfamiliar world.

To every guest that has come on my radio show, Good Grief, and their constant reinforcement that it is not what happens to us, but how we respond to it, that really counts. It is a supreme honor to share your stories.

To my family, for whom there could never be adequate thanks:

To my parents, who quickly realized that the only way forward was acceptance. They toiled tirelessly within the American Baptist Church, where they both worked, to bring understanding and peace and to educate their colleagues. Their living room saw many tearful conversations as other parents grappled with the sexuality of their children. They accepted and loved every person I brought into their lives, reaching beyond their experiences, and lack of experience, to be true Christians, living in love and acceptance.

To my children, Caitlin, Kelley and Amber, who opened up the heart of the matter. I won't try to imagine my life without you.

To Joanne, who taught me that nothing is too bad to bear or too good to be true.

And, of course, to my wife Deb, who makes everything possible.

About the Author

Cheryl Espinosa-Jones has spent a lifetime exploring human loss, revelation and transformation. When she was training to practice psychotherapy her first wife lived with and died of cancer. That experience more than any other taught her that human beings are capable of astonishing epiphanies and inspiring grace. Cheryl's radio show, *Good Grief,* tells the stories of people who have changed their lives through confronting loss. Along with an occasional blog, Cheryl has written articles for Open to Hope, a website dedicated to inspiring grievers. She has also been a contributor to two books, *Journey to the End* and *Who Will Take Care of Me When I Die*. Her first novel, An Ocean Between Them, came out of a belief that fiction is the perfect vehicle for telling the truth.

www.weatheringgrief.com

Good Grief radio: https://www.voiceamerica.com/show/2264/good-grief

Facebook:https://www.facebook.com/CherylJonesMS/

Twitter: @CherylJonesMFT

LinkedIn: http:/www.linkedin.com/in/canspringbefar/

Google+: Cheryl Jones MS

Instagram: http:/www.instagram.com/canspringbefar

46563457R00168

Made in the USA
Lexington, KY
28 July 2019